I0695277

Lying Still

—by—

Marilee Zdenek

2023
SUNGOLD EDITIONS
SANTA BARBARA, CALIFORNIA

Also by Marilee Zdenek

FICTION

Lying Still

NON-FICTION

*The Right-Brain Experience: An Intimate Program
to Free the Powers of Your Imagination*

*Inventing the Future: Advances in Imagery
That Can Change Your Life*

MEMOIR

Between Fires

Splinters in My Pride

God is a Verb!

BOOK AND THEATER PRODUCTIONS

Someone Special

Catch the New Wind

God is a Verb! and *Catch the New Wind*
written in collaboration with Marge Champion

In memory of my two husbands,
Leonard S. Picker and Albert N. Zdenek, MD.
I will always love them both.

PART ONE

CHAPTER 1

WEST LOS ANGELES

They came with their sirens and their cameras and their incessant questions. Their prying hands fumbled through drawers. They marked things and measured.

Leah Vasseau sat across the room from the body of her sister that lay covered at the bottom of the stairs. "Please don't. Please…don't take her picture." Her voice was soft. Vulnerable.

They didn't answer; perhaps they never heard. Their voices blended into a single drone. The only word Leah remembered was *murder*.

Asking permission of strangers to use her sister's bathroom, Leah forced herself to walk past the body of Nicole, the last of her family. She was careful not to walk too close. The police made sure of that.

Leah held tightly onto the wooden rail as she went upstairs. What had happened here? Had Nicole tripped and fallen? Was she unable to catch the railing? Why would they even use the word *murder*?

Leah could hear the voice of the cab driver repeating the story, as if he hadn't told it to others twice before.

"I picked her up at the airport around noon and brought her straight here. She was so happy and full of stories about her sister and how good it was that they could finally live together again. She came from Switzerland and her sister was studying medicine at UCLA. And like I said, I carried her bags to the door and turned to leave, but I heard her scream so I came back in and she just kept screaming. Then…oh, God…I'll never forget the sound of those screams."

The privacy of the bathroom was a relief from the sights and sounds of the police. Leah washed her face with cold water, letting it drain down her neck onto her dress, not caring. She needed time to think her own thoughts, to escape from the intrusiveness of their questions. She needed to sit down now, in a quiet place—*was this really happening?* She wondered. Maybe she would wake up the morning and all of this would have been a terrible nightmare. How could it possibly be true?

Aware of a numbness throughout her body, she slowly slid down the wall onto the yellow vinyl floor, locking her knees beneath her chin. She huddled there, rocking slightly, thinking of her sister.

A stack of books lay on one end of the bathroom vanity. Leah saw the spine of a green leather journal placed second from the top. She recognized it immediately. For years, she had watched Nicole write in that same refillable journal, the leather cover stained with wear. Leah reached over to hold it, running her hands across the cover. Inside would be the names of friends, the places Nicole had gone, shadows of the last months of her life. Leah had promised her sister she would never read her journal. It was perhaps the most intimate thing that Nicole had owned.

There was a loose sheet of notebook paper sticking out between pages. Even without opening the journal, she could read what was written on the top of the paper: Paul Tabor, then a phone number. Who was Paul Tabor? On the other side of the note, there was a poem. Leah opened the journal to the page the note seemed to be marking. *September 5, 1975.* Today. This book had been in her sister's hands *today.*

Scrawled across the date was the note, "Call Paul Tabor." And again, the phone number. The handwriting on the paper wasn't neat like Nicole's usually was. The pen strokes were heavy. It was hard to believe that they had been written by her sister.

A rapping on the bathroom door interrupted her thoughts. "Hey, you all right in there?"

"I'm all right," she said, as if that were true. As if this were a nightmare that would pass.

"Miss Vassaux, Detective McKenzie is waiting for you."

"Yes, I'm coming," she said, making an effort to sound more centered than she felt. Quickly Leah folded the note and returned the journal to the stack.

Then she hesitated. If she left Nicole's journal there, those men would read it. She picked it up again, taking the single sheet of paper from its pages. Folding the note twice more, as if to lock the words more tightly into a secret place, she slipped the paper into the zippered compartment of the inside of her purse. Leah could practically feel her sister's energy through the pages of her journal. Nicole would have wanted her to take it. She was a very private person when she was alive. She certainly wouldn't want the police to have it. Leah imagined Nicole's personal thoughts and made a quick decision.

Again, there was a knock on the door. "One moment, *s'il vous plait!*" Leah said. She tried to fit the journal into her handbag. She turned it at angles, pushing and twisting. The purse was too full. She emptied its contents onto the vanity, then pushed the journal into the empty bag, covering it with her passport and billfold, keys to Nicole's apartment, a few receipts, and a small brush. She went out to face them.

Detective McKenzie quickly began with his questions. "So, can you think of the names of anyone your sister was close to?" What a harsh voice he had.

"No…no one."

"Was she dating anyone?"

"I don't know."

"She must have mentioned some names to you. Can't you think of anyone?"

"No. No one."

He continued with the insistent tone to his voice, but Leah just sat there, shaking her head slowly from side to side.

She's a strange one, Detective McKenzie thought. He could understand the ones who cried. But this one? Her voice was little more than a whisper. It got on his nerves. It seemed more natural to cry.

McKenzie saw that she seemed to be shutting down and tried to bring her back. "Miss Vassaux, I need you to pay attention to what I'm asking. I know this is hard, but I don't think you're really hearing me. You must know something about your sister's life. Anything about who she hung out with, where she worked, anything to get us started. In a murder case, we don't have the luxury of taking our time. No matter how difficult this is for you."

The word *murder* felt like a slap. She forced herself to look at the officer. "How can you say it was murder? Maybe she tripped or something."

He could tell she didn't believe that. Or maybe she did.

"Well, Miss Vassaux, someone covered her body with that quilt, right?"

Leah struggled for an answer. "Maybe someone was with her when she fell but was afraid to stay. Maybe a friend didn't want to leave her like that and covered her out of respect. It could have been an accident, and someone just couldn't face having to explain it."

Detective McKenzie was silent for a moment. "Who do you think might have made that choice?"

"I don't know. I don't know anyone in this whole country other than my sister. I'm also trying to make sense of this."

There was a long pause, then he sighed. He would come back to that later.

"Look, I know how hard this is, but I'm going to ask you a few more questions and I want you to tell me everything that you remember. When is the last time you saw your sister?"

"She came to spend Christmas with me in Geneva two years ago." Leah sighed deeply, remembering. "Then we went skiing in St. Moritz."

"She must have talked with you about her life here in LA, about friends she had, or someone she dated."

"Nicole was very self-contained."

He gave a guttural sigh. "Okay, take yourself back to that point in time. In St. Moritz. There must have been a time when you had a glass of wine or something fancy to drink at the ski lodge and you talked about…something…you didn't just sit there, saying nothing. What did you talk about?"

Another policeman called out from the yard, looking in through the open kitchen door. "This looks like the easiest way out."

"Yes," Leah said in a whisper so soft he almost missed it. "Someone went out that way."

"What did you say?" His voice was hard.

"When I came in, I think I saw someone there."

"Well, why didn't you say so before?"

"I don't know." She cowered beneath the voice that swung at her. "I shouldn't have said that. I'm not sure."

"You think! You're not sure?" He tried to sound more patient than he felt, but without success.

"No, I'm not sure. I just thought I saw someone running."

"Well, what did they look like? This person you think you saw?"

"I don't know! I just thought I saw someone through the window in the kitchen door and then I saw my mother's comforter on the floor. Nicole never left things on the floor. Then I realized someone was covered beneath it and I saw Nicole's arm. I saw our mother's gold bracelet. All I could think was *that is my sister*. Maybe no one was outside the window. It was like a flash from an old dream."

The questions continued and she retreated from them to a place within herself, withdrawing as if she were an observer of the events. Almost as if it were someone else's sister who lay at the foot of the stairs, dead.

Leah heard her own voice, toneless and dry. "I didn't see anyone. I don't know why I said that; I'm just upset. I'm sure I didn't see anyone at all."

Before Leah had arrived at Nicole's apartment, Mark Favre had been in the living room making sure there were no signs he had ever been there. Carefully he had wiped his fingerprints off the stair railings, believing he had all the time in the world. Nicole never had visitors. He had looked upstairs and down, checking for notes by the phone, making sure no shadow of his presence could be found that would incriminate him.

If the police did find his name in Nicole's apartment, or he missed a fingerprint, Mark would claim that he met her not long ago, that he had been in her apartment the night before, at her request. They were casual friends, he would say; she hadn't been feeling well. She was upset but she wanted to talk. For an hour or so he had sat with her while she rested in her bedroom. Nothing more. If he could make himself believe the story was plausible, the police would believe it too. He had to make them believe it. His life depended on it.

Mark finished in the living room and started toward the kitchen. That's when he heard someone at the front door. Someone had a key! He ran out the back door, then heard someone calling into the silence: "Nicole, *es-tu là? Je suis ici…*" and then in English, "Nicole are you there?"

Then he heard the screams. The sound of her agony followed him down the walkway to the street. It was like a bomb exploding inside of him. It felt like his own scream, coming from someone else. There was a terrified child sound to it.

He needed to run, but forced himself to slow down, to walk confidently. A man running calls attention. Mark moved toward his car, his legs aching to run. He tried to appear casual. He brushed imaginary dirt off his coat sleeve. He was sure no one saw him, but just in case…If anyone was watching they would have seen a man obviously in no hurry, well dressed, medium height, medium build, mid-thirties. There was nothing distinctive about him that they could see from a distance. They couldn't see the sweat on his body, or the trembling of his hands as his car keys fell to the street. He picked them up slowly, as if there was no rush. Then he climbed into his shiny new Porsche 911 and slowly, oh so slowly, Mark drove down the tree-lined street.

He fought against panic. His thoughts were racing. *Who else had a key to Nicole's apartment? Who was the woman who screamed?*

His only thought had been to get away from Westwood, to become part of the LA traffic that pushed its way out of the city like a slow-motion wave that would carry him along. Turning onto Beverly Glen, he headed through the canyon toward Mulholland Drive, then waited to pull around the cars, longing to feel the Porsche untethered. The traffic held him tight, as onward-coming cars forced him to keep his place. Mark knew he wasn't being followed, but his emotions still told him to run. His hands were slippery against the wheel, his breathing was heavy. Again and again, he looked in the rearview mirror.

Turning left on Mulholland Drive, Mark followed the winding road to where the pavement ended and the road turned into a trail. He drove a few yards more, pulled off onto the dirt and stopped. Then he put his head in his hands and forced himself to take slow deep breaths. He was alone on the mountain.

Mark knew he should have called the police from Nicole's apartment. But what would he have said? Would they have believed him if he said it wasn't murder? Only a terrible accident? Remembering the intensity of his anger, such a short time ago, he could still hear the bitterness in Nicole's voice and the threatening tone of his own. They stood on the upstairs landing. He saw himself move toward her, his rage pushing against her. She backed away from him, forgetting her proximity to the stairs, stepping into space. She fell backward, screaming, flailing, landing at the base of the stairs like a broken doll tossed by an angry child.

Mark knew it wasn't only his rage that had pushed against her, but his hands as well. She had tried to grab his arm, but he pulled away. He saw her body twisted, and her eyes wide open, staring at him. Mark relived the moment he took the coverlet from the end of the sofa and laid it over Nicole's body. One arm was curved above her head, her hand exposed as if she had moved it in her sleep. He left it there. He wanted her out of his life—but he hadn't planned to kill her. What if he had called the police and told them…told them what? Even his presence in her apartment was incriminating. He could imagine them around him, bombarding him with questions and accusations, then locking him into a small, dark cell. Caging him like an animal. Mark Favre would never let that happen.

From the mountain, he looked out across the vastness of the San Fernando Valley, house after house after house spread out for miles. A dog was barking. Rain clouds formed. Five vultures circled.

Then there was the sound of a helicopter. It grew louder as it hovered above the car.

Mark's hands shook as he gripped the steering wheel. The helicopter circled the car once and then again. How could they possibly have found him? Mark tried to think of what he would say, and then the helicopter veered to the right. The pilot had no interest in him.

With the relief that came, an idea struck him. He felt foolish for wasting his time reliving a situation that could not be changed. He looked at his watch, turned his car around, and drove to his bank. If he hurried, he could still make it before they closed. But not too fast, not fast enough to draw the attention of a traffic cop.

Just as he pulled his car up to the door of the bank, one of the clerks was beginning to lock the doors. It was a Friday afternoon, and they would shut things down for the weekend.

Mark called out to him as he closed the car door. "Hey there, give me just a minute inside, will you? I have to get something out of my deposit box. It's an emergency."

"Not a problem. Glad I can help."

Once inside the bank, Mark went straight to the vault. He signed in and handed his key to a beautiful young woman, without even noticing her. She smiled and slipped his key into the slot and inserted the bank's key next to it. She turned her back to give Mark some privacy.

Mark pulled the metal drawer out of the cabinet and saw his passport next to his wife's, right on top of a mound of legal papers. Mark put both passports in his pocket and then removed a large envelope with a stack of hundred-dollar bills inside.

He began to relax, and perspiration dried on his body. Tomorrow he would move most of his cash into his account in Geneva. The one he had planned to close when he left. It would come in handy now.

Now all he had to do was go home to Jayne and act as if nothing had happened. He had plenty of options. He was young and could start over. It didn't have to be in Europe. Maybe he could go to Bali, or South America. His brain was spinning. There were no limits.

Then a devastating fact struck him like a brick to the head. He could hardly get his breath.

If he hadn't covered Nicole's body with that blanket, her death would have looked like an accident.

CHAPTER 2

WEST LOS ANGELES & MALIBU

It was evening by the time the police finally left. Leah took the smaller of her two suitcases, called a cab, and signed the register at the Camille Hotel. Someone gave her the key to room 103, said the usual pleasantries, and offered to help her with her suitcase. She shook her head. "No. I can do this."

"Your room is on the first floor, and we just planted a tiny garden outside your French door. You might want to take your breakfast there in the morning." For a moment Leah was puzzled. A garden on the first floor? Then she remembered that in America the first floor is at ground level. Nicole had told her that. In Europe the first floor was always one flight above the ground. Leah remembered that, of course. She wasn't thinking clearly.

Inside her room, she was relieved that she didn't have to talk to anyone. She had never traveled outside of Europe. Never traveled anywhere alone. Now there was no one to call. Alone in the room, she opened her purse and pulled Nicole's journal through the opening. Leah held it for a moment, allowing memories to return, pushing them away again. It wasn't that she didn't want to read the journal. It was just that she couldn't. Not yet. Leah carefully put it under her pillow and forced her thoughts away from it. Everything in her orderly Swiss background urged her to unpack and try to get her world in order. But she couldn't.

There were only two items that she needed from her suitcase. She removed a small, framed drawing, wrapped securely in cardboard, paper, and twine. Slowly she untied the cord, unfolded the wrapping, and put the drawing on the dresser. Two children sharing secrets on a wide rocking chair. Leah, intense and confiding. Nicole, just listening.

Then, her own journal. It was the same size and style as Nicole's, but Leah's was the dark red color of the pinot noir grapes that grow in the hills above Lake Geneva. It was a gift from Nicole. Memories of that day returned, but Leah set her guard against them; she would not think of them now. She put her journal on the nightstand by the bed. Lying back against the pillows, Leah thought of all the wishful things she had written on yesterday's page. And she thought of today's empty page beside it. She considered leaving it blank, setting it apart from all the other pages by the words that would not be written there.

Nicole had told her that it doesn't rain in Los Angeles in the early fall, at least not most years. But here it came: storm clouds gathered in the night and the dark lining tore to let the rain spill slowly and steadily upon the city. Leah lay there, her eyes dry and burning, staring into the darkness, listening to the sound of the rain. Turning on the light, she reached for her own journal. Something, anything, had to be written on this day; she could not bear the void. The dark pen moved silently across the page.

There are no words. There are no thoughts.
Only the feeling of emptiness and death

tears that will not come
and sighs that come like dry heaves when the vomiting is done.
I am falling in the darkness of an empty pit. Alone.

Leah closed the book and turned off the light. She was still wearing the same dress she had on when she left Switzerland. It didn't matter. She had to sleep. She would try not to think of her sister, not to wonder who covered her with the quilt, not to wonder if the person she thought she saw running away was real, or just a memory from another time and place. She tried to sleep, but images of her sister lying dead on the floor invaded every thought. Exhaustion made her body ache. On the plane to Los Angeles, she had been too excited to sleep. Now she couldn't stop thinking about Nicole. She had watched the policeman remove her mother's gold and amethyst bracelet, the one that Nicole always wore. He had put it on the table before they took her body away. There had been no private time to grieve, to sit with her body, to weep, to whisper as if Nicole could hear.

There would be an autopsy. Is that where Nicole was now? Lying naked on some cold metal slab? Leah couldn't bear the thought of that. She lay on the bed in the darkness, curled like a child in fetal position. Rocking silently, like she used to do when she was little. Listening to the silence.

She imagined what might have been different if she had come to California even one day sooner. She stared into the darkness of the room seeking comfort that never came. Her hands closed around Nicole's bracelet, their mother's bracelet, now hers. Did the police even know she had taken it? Perhaps no one had noticed.

All Saturday and Sunday, Leah stayed in her room while the rain fell. She never dressed. She ate the continental breakfast that was delivered to her door and the Swiss chocolates she had brought for Nicole; but she had no other desire for food. There was only one phrase that slipped into her grief: Call Paul Tabor. She would make an appointment to see him. When she dialed the number that was in her sister's handwriting, she reached a doctor's exchange. The office was closed. It was Sunday. How could it still be Sunday? Leah hung up quickly, thinking, *On Monday I will call Paul Tabor*. It became a mantra that she clung to through the night. *I will call Paul Tabor on Monday*. It was the only thing that kept her from screaming.

Dr. Paul Tabor was thinking about Europe. Two of his patients had canceled their afternoon appointments. One because he had the flu, and the other because he was trying to avoid talking about an incident he had brought up in his last session. A new patient would be taking the second of the two spots, but for now, Paul was lost in thought studying the map of Switzerland that was sprawled across his desk. He imagined only pleasant surprises for him there, no unsolved problems needing attention. He thought of his wife, Stephanie, who would be seeing the Alps for the first time next week. After Paul's conference, they could go wherever the wind blew them for a few days.

Taking a yellow marker from the drawer, he studied the map and circled a few places he wanted to go after his conference in Lausanne was over. He stretched back in his chair, his long legs reaching forward, his arms locked behind his head. The chair groaned as he leaned back. It occurred to him that the chair was getting noisier with age and the burgundy-colored fabric on the arms was badly worn.

Maybe Stephanie was right; the office might be getting a bit shabby. He looked around, trying to be objective, trying to see it with fresh eyes. Was it really getting as bad as she said? He had grown so comfortable with the signs of age. The brown carpet with the deep pile had held up well over the years. A good investment, he decided. But the sofa and chairs had found their own way of slouching since they were moved into his office some years ago. The wood pieces were better looking with wear. The old barrister's desk had been his first desk and had taken just about all his savings at the time. The ancient Mayan urns came much later and were transformed into the base of lamps, without altering their composition. They were not identically matched; even functioning as a pair, each one retained its own uniqueness. Colorful lithographs hung on the dark-paneled walls, collected over the years from various places and styles.

Paul remembered the first time Stephanie had asked to see his office. She kept talking about the space being an extension of himself, a physical expression of his attitudes. Tradition and the break with tradition were represented, she said. The old and the new coexisted.

His eyes softened when he thought of her that day, analyzing his office, picking up the symbols he had never considered when he had just put together some things that he liked.

Stephanie read something into all of it. Even the wooden tissue box on the coffee table. "If I am ever in trouble, I sure would like to come to you," she had said then. And he remembered wanting her to come to him at that moment, to come into his arms and into his life and all he said at the time was, "I don't think you're likely to need me," and then added softly, "not professionally anyway."

The office wasn't in such bad shape. He felt comfortable with the way it looked. *Why did aging have to be such a negative sign anyway? The sofa could go without re-covering for another season or two*, he thought. It might be a good metaphor for the acceptance of aging that some of his patients were struggling with.

Maybe Stephanie just wanted to put something of herself in his office. This room represented a side of him that she didn't know much about—the part of him that worked and heard confidences here. It was the only part of his life in which she had no place, except for the interior design.

He decided to ask her to find a new graphic for the wall. That might be something she would enjoy looking for in Lausanne or the nearby villages. She kept talking about a certain Swiss graphic artist; she had even mentioned picking up some of his work for her gallery.

Paul heard the outer office door open and then close softly. He folded the map and laid the papers on the table by his desk. The woman didn't seem to hear him walk into the waiting room. She was sitting in the chair nearest the door, her eyes closed, her legs pressed together.

"Miss Vassaux?" Paul asked.

She looked up at him, forcing her thoughts into the present. Her hair fell softly to her shoulders, a dark frame for a pale, delicate face. She stared at him without speaking. "Hello," he said. "I'm Dr. Tabor." He reached out to her, and she put her hand into his. Her fingers were cold to his touch.

He watched her struggling for control. Whatever was going on inside her was hitting hard.

"Let's go into my office," he said. She nodded and walked in front of him into his therapy room. She chose a chair that flanked the sofa, settling herself into the cushion. Her body was rigid; she looked down at her hands. She looked more like a child than a woman.

Paul took a pad and pen from his desk. "Leah, I can see something is causing you a great deal of pain."

He let the silence rest between them, letting her come in her own way to the subject. "My sister…" She finally said, "My sister was a friend of yours. Or a patient. I need to talk to you about her."

Paul hadn't expected that. "I never discuss my patients with anyone. Whatever is told to me is confidential."

"My sister was Nicole Vassaux, I know she had to be a patient or a friend."

"I don't recognize the name."

"I've heard that psychiatrists do that; they deny they even know a patient. Please tell me, Dr. Tabor, I have to know. This is terribly important to me. Did you know her? Was Nicole your patient?"

Paul looked into the deep brown of her eyes and saw her reaching out, pleading. He wanted to help. "Why do you think I knew your sister?"

"I found her journal and your name was written on a sheet of paper I found tucked inside of it." She looked at him with the most intense expression, evaluating his reaction as she said, "Nicole died last Friday."

Paul absorbed the weight of her words. He was silent a moment, then leaned forward in his chair. "I am so sorry, Leah. Tell me what happened."

"Dr. Tabor, I need for you to be honest with me. Please, did you know her?"

"I don't know anyone named Nicole." Paul watched her confusion and focused on what she was feeling, rather than the reason she said she came. Gently he asked, "You were very close to your sister, weren't you?"

It wasn't words that answered him, rather a desperate almost mocking sound. A sudden outburst of breath, nonverbal, expressive. The sound was of anger, and more. He was reading tone, emotion, and body language. All of it told the story. And then she spoke in crisp, sharp sentences, in a voice that blocked the emotion of her words. "I just came here from Switzerland to surprise her. To live with her. She wanted that too. I came to Los Angeles and when I arrived from the airport, I found my sister—I found my sister on the floor. She was dead." She was trying to lay the facts before him, leaving her pain out of the tone. But her control broke down and she wept.

Paul instinctively moved toward her, but she turned away from him, hiding her face while deep, agonized sobs wracked her body. Leaning into the far side of her chair, she dug her fingers into the cushion. Paul went with her into the pain. He wanted to comfort her. Wished he could touch her hand. He offered her some tissues from a wooden box. She took them without touching him. Finally, in exhaustion, she quieted and looked at him. "I'm sorry," she said. Still leaning close to her, his voice was comforting.

"Sorry for what, Leah?"

She had no answer for him. Paul watched her reach the traumatic moment and retreat from it. She hesitated. Trying again. She let the words carry the factual content, ignoring the agony that was implicit in her words.

"I have a key to her apartment. I always have that. But when I arrived…" Her tears were spent but her body shuddered when she spoke of her sister. Paul was aware that she was handling the feelings without his help; he let her work through it by herself, staying close.

"The police came. They went through her things." Her voice hardened. Resentment pushed against the words and her voice broke. "She was such a private person. They asked me questions I couldn't answer…. I didn't know what to say to them!"

Paul hoped she would tell him without his asking, but he saw that she would avoid it if she could. "Leah…how did she die?"

The sigh was heavy, an old woman sound. "I don't know. The police seemed to think she was murdered. But they don't really know. They think someone pushed her down the stairs. I think someone cared enough about her to cover her body and that doesn't sound like a murderer to me. Her neck…was broken. She was lying under our mother's coverlet. The one that was always on our bed when we were young."

The silence lingered and she looked at Paul as if for direction.

"Where is your mother now?" he asked. "Is she still in Switzerland?"

Even before she spoke the words, Paul could see her retreat behind the well-rehearsed answer. The public answer, that denied all feeling beneath the words. "My mother died when I was five years old, Dr. Tabor. My sister was my only relative." She paused and her voice softened. "She took care of me, always let me visit her during school vacations. She was ten years older than me, but she was like my mother."

Paul noticed that she didn't mention her father.

"Boarding schools are very cold places to spend your childhood," she said. "Nicole did the best she could to help. She always sent me a key to her apartment when she moved so I could show it to my friends and tell them that was my new home. No one ever wanted to call the boarding school home."

"Leah…what will you do now?"

"What will I do? I don't know what I will do. I will survive. I always have. I can't go back to Switzerland because there is nothing to go back to. My financial guardian has transferred my inheritance to a bank in Los Angeles…in Westwood, near the university. If I live frugally, I will have enough to live on."

"Do you have friends here? Someone you could stay with for a while."

"I don't know anyone here. My plan was to live with my sister, like we always wanted to do. We talked about it, but we hadn't set a date. I flew here to surprise her. I suppose I should notify someone, but she never mentioned any friends.

"There is one thing I want to do. I have heard about a woman, Estelle Harmon, who teaches acting. I would like to take some classes from her. After that…I don't know."

"You barely have an accent, so I assume you lived in the States at some point."

Leah almost smiled. "No. I'm told that I have a good ear. Considering that Lausanne is only a few hours to the borders of France, Italy, and Germany, it is important to know several languages. It is a requirement for graduation from the boarding school I attended."

"That's impressive," Paul said.

"Not really. It's normal there." Just for that moment, her voice lifted, then flattened again.

Paul changed the subject. "What are you going to do now? Today?"

"I don't know yet. I'm staying at The Camille Hotel in Westwood. It's not far from UCLA. It's where my sister stayed when she moved to Los Angeles. But that's just until the police finish with their investigation. Then maybe I'll move Nicole's things out to another place. I haven't thought it through. I just know what I can't do. I can't go back to Switzerland. I must put the pieces together here."

Her hand covered her face for a moment and then pushed her hair aside, revealing a heavy frown. Something else was surfacing and Paul saw it. "Dr. Tabor, there is one more thing I need to tell you." Ambivalence forced another hesitation.

"It's hard for you to talk about this," he said.

"Yes. And it's hard to trust anyone right now." A heavy sigh. Then with a sudden impulsive determination to tell him: "I told this to the police and then was sorry I mentioned it. When I walked into Nicole's apartment, in that first moment that the door was open, I thought I saw someone outside in the back. I thought it was a man. But the image was so fleeting, I can't be sure."

Leah squinted into space as if trying to look at the scene more clearly. "I can almost see him, but it's like a cloud is between us. I don't know if I really saw the man who killed Nicole or if I just imagined it. I was so upset. When my mother died…" She stopped abruptly. And he saw the fear.

"You what, Leah?"

"Pardon?"

"You said something about when your mother died."

"No, it was nothing. I'm sorry, I'm not thinking clearly now."

"You were thinking very clearly up until you said that. Then there was something you almost said and wanted to say, and maybe didn't want to say, as well. Can you go back to that thought and try again?"

"No! I mean…no. I don't think I remember what I started to say. The important thing is if I can remember whether I really saw that man at Nicole's. That's what I want to remember. I feel like I am losing my mind!"

"You are not losing your mind. You've been through a devastating experience and when people are under terrible stress, they often feel confused. It will take some time to unravel all this."

When she talked about the man outside Nicole's window, she had interrupted her own thought and said, "When my mother died…" It was a clear association. A man outside the window had something to do with her mother's death. But how could the two losses be connected? There were years between them. They were continents apart.

Leah quickly changed the subject. "I told you that in Nicole's journal there was a piece of paper with your name and phone number. Actually that wasn't all. On one side of the folded paper was a poem. Then on Friday's page she wrote, 'Call Paul Tabor today.' And, again, your phone number." Leah reached into her purse as she said this, and she pulled out the single piece of paper, then handed it to Paul. The poem was in Nicole's handwriting.

I should thank you.
Finally, after all this time,
you have killed the last remnant of my love
which lay like the smallest of hummingbirds,
wounded and vulnerable on the ground.
I should thank you
for stamping the last vestige of breath from it.
What a tiresome bird it was, my love,
stealing every crumb of joy
in the final days.
I should thank you for the condescending
mockery you made of my love, for
you have freed me from it. Finally.
Now, if only I can extricate myself from your shadow.

"That doesn't sound like Nicole," Leah said. "I can't imagine that she wrote it. Maybe she only copied it from something else…"

"Whether she wrote it or copied it, it tells us the same thing. Something in it spoke to her feelings of rejection and anger. In either case, Nicole was feeling that someone she loved really let her down."

"I can't believe that she wouldn't have told me if she was in love with someone."

"You said she was a very private person."

"But why would she have told me I could come here and live with her, if she planned to be married? Maybe she just said that to make me feel good. Maybe she never expected me to come. I wanted it to be a surprise."

"The poem doesn't say anything about marriage, Leah. Did you show this to the police?"

"No."

"I think you should give it to them right away. And, Leah, you said there was a journal…"

"I haven't read it. I tried to on Saturday. Sunday, too, but I couldn't do it. I don't want the investigators to see that. Not unless I find something in there that would really help them."

"Can you make that evaluation? There might be something in it that wouldn't seem important to you, but it might provide a clue to experts. The poem and the journal could be critical in solving this case."

"I hadn't thought of that. Well, if you think I should, I'll do it…I'll turn it over to Detective McKenzie."

Paul thought she was surprisingly quick to let a stranger guide her. With her dark brown eyes and delicate features, she reminded him of a fawn. She appeared so fragile. He also knew it wouldn't be long before he had a meeting with the police. They would be anxious to know the answer to one specific question—why was his name written on that poem?

He wondered that too.

"Leah, when the police have the poem and the journal, they will come to talk with me, as they should. So, anything you tell me, I will have to reveal, if they ask."

"Yes, of course," Leah said. "Or to anybody else you think should know. I don't care; there are no secrets here. Just help them find the person who did this to my sister. Will you help me through this, Dr. Tabor? Could I come and see you again, as a patient?"

"Under normal circumstances, I would gladly be your doctor. But, Leah, my name is in your sister's journal. My phone number is on her poem. I don't know why it's there or what the police will make of it. For me to be your psychiatrist would be most unwise. And certainly unethical."

"You mean you won't help me?"

"I didn't say that. There are many ways I can help you. You didn't come here looking for a psychiatrist. You came to find something—anything—that might help catch the person who killed your sister. You came to me looking for information, not therapy.

"You don't have any support system and I'm offering you just that. I can just be your friend. There is never a charge for friendship.

"We shouldn't meet here; this is where I see patients. But I will gladly meet with you in another location and be supportive. There might be some connection Nicole mentioned to you a long time ago and you've forgotten. Sometime those memories will return, when you're talking about them in a safe place with someone who is listening, not interrogating."

Leah looked wary. "Why are you doing this?"

"Because I am somehow involved in this tragedy, though I can't imagine how. And because you are alone in a foreign land with a broken heart and not a confidant in sight.

"You shouldn't go through this time alone. Unfortunately, I'm leaving town a week from Friday, and I'll be gone a couple of weeks. I need your assurance that you'll take the name of my colleague, who is a fine psychiatrist. He will be taking my calls, and you can see him if you want to talk with someone. You might want to meet him and decide if therapy is a good decision for you, given the circumstances."

"Are you bargaining with me?" she asked, with almost a smile.

"Let's say I'm just being responsible."

"All right, how could I say no to that?"

"There's a café a block from here that has a table outdoors, in the back." Paul wrote the name, Sam's Café, on a piece of paper. "I'll reserve the space. Is two o'clock Wednesday afternoon good for you?"

She nodded.

"Is there a phone number where I can reach you?" Paul said.

Leah gave him a card she took from the hotel and sighed deeply. She wasn't entirely alone now.

As he was driving home to Malibu, Paul kept thinking about Leah and the journal and wondered what else was written in that book.

Nicole could have gotten his name as a referral from a patient; maybe she was considering asking him for professional help. That seemed the most likely reason his name was there. He hoped the police were inclined to look at it that way. In any case, they would probably want him to account for where he was when Nicole was killed. Leah hadn't mentioned what time she died.

Paul relaxed despite the traffic and his apprehensions. The roads were washed clean by the rain. Somewhere along the line he had learned not to fight battles that couldn't be won. He listened to Laurindo Almeida playing classical guitar, then he opened the windows and heard the surf blending with the sounds of the music.

Paul crossed traffic and pulled off to a narrow drive that led to a contemporary house, lush with bougainvillea.

He pulled into the garage where a collection of camping and skiing gear shared wall space with the overflow from their small but spectacular home.

His practice had bought him the house, and he tried to leave his patients' problems at the office. At least that was his intention.

When he walked into the house, he stood for a moment, watching the ocean through the two-story glass windows that faced seaward. It was a spectacular location for this open floor plan, and it felt much larger than it actually was. The young architect who had built it early in his career had gone on to make quite a name for himself. This house continued to shine as his first love, as unique as his own genius. Now, he built spectacular hotels and office buildings that people traveled miles to see. Sometimes when magazine writers asked him which job had been his favorite, he mentioned this small retreat on the private beach in Malibu.

Paul managed to leave his stress at the door. A satisfying yawn was a tradition as he stepped into the house. The wall on the right side of the room housed a wide-mouthed fireplace where bookcases stretched upward for the full two-story height of the house. It was complete with a rolling ladder and thousands of books, most of them read and treasured by Paul or Stephanie.

There was a small powder room downstairs and a spacious bathroom on the upper level. Paul climbed the spiral staircase to the bedroom, which was cantilevered over the living room. Beyond was a spectacular expanse of ocean. The house was a romantic retreat, perfect for two people. No doors separated the bedroom that seemed to float above the lower level. It was an artist's dream. The master bath did have a door, which the architect had shipped from Paris and was only one of the antique accoutrements that married the ancient with the contemporary.

Changing into his swimsuit, leaving his clothes crumpled on the bed, Paul started for the beach. The cool stone floor felt good against his bare feet before he moved out onto the warm sand. There were a few hours of sunlight left and the surf was up. He swam hard, using the sea for his gym, working his body against the tide. He was lean and supple, brown year-round from the sun. At forty-seven, his hair was just beginning to gray. Floating in the sea, he absorbed the feelings of the moment, tuning in consciously to the feel of the saltwater on his body, cool and restless against him. Over the shore, a bright red kite danced its way across the sky, with its long tail floating after it, a fantasy bird in flight. Seagulls screeched at it and moved on. Paul breathed in the ocean smells, tasted the salt on his lips. For an hour or more, he relaxed in the water, letting his tension wash away in the sea. Then with long, powerful strokes, he moved along with the tide, catching a wave and riding it to the shore.

The water dripped from him as he walked the short distance from the shoreline to the house. Taking the towel from the doorknob, he dried his feet and went upstairs to the bathroom. He slung his gritty trunks onto the brass hook and stepped into the shower. The water ran until the last grains of sand worked free and floated down the drain.

Reaching to turn off the water, he saw Stephanie through the steam and the lightly frosted glass. She moved toward him, dropping her clothes piece by piece, like so much surplus, discarded. Playfully she teased him before she opened the shower door and moved toward him. They greeted each other with words that rolled from his tongue to hers and back again. He covered her with soap and massaged the lilac-scented suds across the smooth arch of her back, over her breasts and into the tiny pocket slits beneath them.

"You find the nicest places to say hello," she said, and already the sound of her voice had that husky longing that he only heard when she wanted more. In the shower, eight water jets of varying pressures shot from faucets at different angles against their bodies. The tallest one wet her hair and sent a halo spray of mist into the air. Two more touched the gentle curve of her hips. Others were staggered around the sides of the tiled walls, with the last one shooting its warm spray from the base of the wall to reach the hidden softness between her thighs.

The first time she showered there, she said, "I feel like I'm in a rainstorm that got confused and doesn't know which way to go."

"No confusion, lady, just soft, warm, raindrop tongues, kissing everywhere at once."

Suddenly she pulled away from him and was out the door, calling after herself, "Someday! Someday, Paul Tabor, you're going to slip doing that and we're going to fall and break our butts, or something worse, and then how will we explain that!"

"To whom?" He followed her, twisting the water faucet as he moved, drying off as he entered the bedroom. Together they slipped between cool sheets.

He caressed her with words of love as she moved her breasts against his lips. His tongue followed in fluttering movements. Then her whispered longings, heavy as musk: "I want to give you every pleasure I know how to give…feel the fullness of you… taste the sweetness of you…love you…" Phrases faded into silence and back again. His lips brushed the softness of her belly, then sought the taste of honey, warm and scented with love, that waited for his tongue. They moved together in a smooth, unbroken rhythm. Passion caught them like an ocean wave that twisted and turned them, rocked and pushed them, until they rolled at last to their own breaking point.

For a long time, they lay there, not moving, resting in their own intimacy, needing time to feel the completion of their oneness, then time to separate identities and become two people again, before he withdrew.

Later that Monday evening, fog crawled along the edges of the shore, moving slowly toward the houses in the sand. Paul closed the glass doors against it.

"Paul, where did you put Jayne's gift?" Stephanie asked. "I'd better get it wrapped before they get here."

Paul took the small bronze sculpture from his drawer, turning it over carefully.

"You really think she'll like this?"

"How could she not like it?"

"I think the piece is great. But…you know Jayne. After so much birthday jewelry from her ol' dad over the years, will she be open to something different?"

Stephanie walked over and clasped her hands behind his neck. "Now listen, my friend, you're setting yourself up again. You always do that with her."

"Hey, I'm the shrink around here—how come you're so perceptive?"

"Perceptive nothing! I've just picked up a few things from you over the years. She's your Achilles heel and that's been going on for a long time. For longer than we've been married, I'm sure."

"Yeah. I just want her to like it."

You want her to like you, Stephanie thought, but knew when to keep her mouth shut.

"The woman who sculpted that piece is one of the finest new talents I've shown in the gallery. She's brilliant, sensitive, and if Jayne doesn't like it, she can hold on to it for a few years and, after I get through promoting the artist, she can sell it for a nice bundle."

"You're getting bristly. What's wrong?" Paul said.

"I don't know. I guess I just get irritated when I see you setting yourself up for rejection. You're so anxious for her approval." She turned the small bronze child over in her hands. A girl playing a flute. "Look at that; I can almost hear the music. Now that's one hell of a gift and if Jayne doesn't like it…okay…don't get your storm warnings up. It's your business how you handle your daughter…and your feelings about your daughter. I'll mind my own business."

"But…" they said simultaneously, and Paul laughed.

"I know you so well, Stephanie. There just had to be a 'but' added onto that. Listen, you're right. I don't have much objectivity where Jayne's concerned."

"Well, everyone's neurotic about something."

"Thank you, that's comforting to know. Now will you do me a favor and wrap this while I start the coals?"

"No need for coals. I'm doing sukiyaki."

"Oh, good. She'll like that."

"She'll like it or she won't. All I promise you this evening is a spectacularly well-prepared sukiyaki." She gave him a pat and took the sculpture to the desk to wrap it.

Better watch yourself, Lady, she thought. The last thing the evening needs is for you to get uptight too. It was in moments like this that she was almost glad that she couldn't have children. Paul's daughter, Jayne, well…Stephanie was glad she had chosen a career instead of adoption. *Kids! Who needs them?* she thought. But she knew that Paul did, and she did, too, sometimes. She had tried to be a mother to Jayne, when she and Paul first married, but that hadn't worked. She had tried to buy her, too, she realized now (and realized also that this was what made her so angry when Paul did the same thing). She had tried to buy Jayne's affection with good intentions and an open pocketbook and none of it had worked. Nothing was enough. She was a bucket with a hole in the bottom, always wanting to be filled with love and acceptance and possessions as well. But the hole let everything run through and she was always empty.

The bow on the top of the package was perfectly tied, the tips shredded and elegant with its magenta and silver stripe. There. It really looked lovely. She hoped Jayne would like it…and when she caught herself in the thought, she laughed out loud.

The package wrapped, the last-minute preparations completed, they waited. Nothing new about that. Half an hour. Then more.

Finally, they heard the car pull into the drive and moments later, Jayne's voice called out "How about turning the light on? It's dark!"

"Sorry, it's burned out. Watch your step coming in." Paul went down the driveway and helped her out of the car. His arms reached around the tall slender girl and he felt the stiffness in her body the moment he touched her. "Hi, Sweetie, Happy Birthday!"

"Hello, Dad, hope we're not late."

"No problem."

Paul looked at Jayne's husband, Mark, slowly getting out of the Porsche. As soon as he saw Mark's face, Paul knew that something was wrong. Tension grabbed at the fine muscles around his eyes and pulled them tight. The set of his mouth was taut, and the aloofness had begun even before the evening started. Paul sensed the tension in Jayne, but it wasn't anywhere near as apparent as it was with Mark. *They must have been at it again*, he thought.

"How are you, Mark?" The men shook hands and Paul was aware of the cold damp palm against his.

"Fine. Yourself?"

"Come on in. Stephanie…will you please add light bulbs to the market list?"

"I already did," Stephanie said. "Happy Birthday, Jayne. Hi, Mark."

"Well, aren't you the lovely one," Mark said, admiring her simple kimono made of fine golden silk. Mark's face softened when he spoke to Stephanie. At least there was one member of the Tabor family he could get along with. No matter how surly he was with everyone else, Mark never took his anger out on Stephanie.

"Where did you find that kimono?" Jayne asked.

"A woman in Westwood has a boutique in her guesthouse. She has a fantastic antique fabric collection—most of it is museum quality. And she has a few outfits; this one's from China—about 1890-1900. I'll slip it off before I start cooking but I just had to wear it to celebrate your birthday."

"No wonder I never see silk like that in the stores," Jayne said.

"I'll give you her number, if you like…"

"If she takes credit cards, I'm in trouble!" Mark's words may have been meant for humor, but something in his tone only implied criticism.

"If Mark had it his way, I'd buy all my clothes from Sears," Jayne said, with a haughty flip of her head. The birthday girl was California chic in her tie-dyed shirt and bell-bottom jeans. Faux hippie. At twenty-three, she liked the funky look but also loved her fancy lifestyle. Her golden blonde hair was so straight it looked like she must have ironed it. "Have a seat; I'll get the drinks," Paul said, moving toward the kitchen. He removed the French champagne from the refrigerator. Dom Pérignon, 1969. Very dry, very good. Very expensive. He put the bottle on the butcher block counter and took four long-stemmed Baccarat glasses from the cabinet, placing them on a wooden tray.

Paul brought the tray from the open kitchen to the living room. He watched Jayne take the champagne with long, slender fingers. There wasn't a flaw noticeable to the eye; it was to the ear that she was usually such an offense. Jayne was Beauty and the Beast in one. The Beast was internalized.

Stephanie sat with her legs tucked beneath her, thanked Paul with her eyes, and listened to Jayne talk about the new white over-the-knee boots she absolutely loved.

Paul looked at his son-in-law and his concern was more than casual. Mark looked terrible. The olive color of his skin was yellowed in tone. *Not jaundiced*, Paul thought, *but sallow.* Usually his movements tended to be agile, almost startling by the quickness of his responses. But tonight, he seemed wary and a bit tenuous as he took the delicate glass from the tray. His dark eyes were impenetrable. *A guarded man*, Paul thought. More so tonight than usual.

"You feel okay, Mark?" Paul asked as he sat beside him on the sofa.

"Just having some trouble with my stomach, again. It's been acting up a lot lately."

"Have you seen a doctor about it?"

"Not recently. I'll do that if it gets any worse. I see you got a new backgammon set," Mark said, abruptly changing the subject, as he always did with Paul when the conversation became personal. "When Stephanie shops for antiques, she really goes all out, doesn't she? This set must be quite a collectors' item."

"She's come out better buying antiques than I have buying stocks. When I play the market, I never seem to show a profit; all the antiques Stephanie's bought have tripled in value—at least tripled."

Mark ran his fingers along the smooth coffee table made of pear wood. Paul noticed they were shaking. "I'll challenge you to a game after dinner, Paul." Even the invitation sounded hostile.

"You're on."

"You're due for a win; I seem to remember beating you rather badly the last time." Mark's mouth curved into a broad smile, but his eyes remained coldly distant.

"So you did," Paul said, lifting his glass. "Well, here's to Jayne! Happy twenty-third." Paul liked the pungent bouquet of the champagne. The texture danced well on the tongue and carried a dry tartness down the throat while a lingering aftertaste remained. It was as fine as Paul had expected it to be. He saw Jayne's face, her mouth puckering in response to the taste.

"That's a bit dry, Dad! The top of my mouth just withered."

"Try it again," Paul suggested. "It's a Dom Pérignon and has just a little more acidity than you're used to in California grapes."

"That acidity has quite a kick."

"There's nothing wrong with the champagne," Mark said. "Paul chose a fine one. You just have to get your taste buds educated enough to enjoy it."

Jayne's voice was a whine. "I'm really not interested in educating my taste buds, Mark. I just want to enjoy my drink. Besides, it's my birthday. Not the best of evenings to pretend I like what I don't. Dad, would you mind fixing me a Scotch and soda?"

"If you'd rather." Paul went back to the kitchen while his champagne warmed in the glass.

Jayne's voice drifted into the open kitchen. "Will you go to the conference with Dad?"

"Probably just the opening reception. But there's plenty to keep me busy with all those art galleries in the area."

"Be sure you buy enough for your own gallery to make your trip a write-off," Mark said.

"I'd be stupid to pass up a chance like that, wouldn't I? Besides, I've been trying to get some Swiss graphics for my gallery."

Paul returned, handing Jayne her drink. "Lausanne is one of my favorite places."

"Why Lausanne?" The tone of Mark's voice was tight. Hard. "I thought you were happy with Geneva for the conference last year."

"Geneva was fine, but Lausanne's a fascinating city too. It's smaller and we have a great place for the meetings. The Hotel Palais de Beaulieu has one of the best facilities I've ever seen and will be perfect for the small group that will meet on our first evening. Then Wednesday and Thursday we'll be at the larger facility at the conference center. Incidentally, Mark, your alma mater's hosting one of the evening functions." Paul was watching Mark, thinking the man wasn't well. He should have canceled tonight, even if it was Jayne's birthday. He looked like hell sitting there with his hand pressed against his stomach.

"Mark, I'm seriously worried about you. I know it's none of my business, but…"

"You're right, Paul. It's none of your business."

While Paul was deciding what to say, it was Jayne who redirected the conversation to safer ground. "What's the matter with your heel, Dad? You keep rubbing it."

"What? Oh, nothing, just…" His eyes met Stephanie's and they both smiled. "My Achilles tendon seems to be a bit touchy."

"Speaking of heels," Jayne said to Stephanie, "did you see the new line from…"

Mark interrupted before the sentence was even finished. "Jayne, please…I want to hear more about the conference. Paul, what does the Conference for Innovation have to do with the medical school?"

"Well, it's an unusual conference. University of Lausanne Medical School wants an association with it. I admit, we were a bit surprised because the University of Lausanne is a very conservative school. This conference is going to make quite an impact, I think."

"Oh, come on, Paul, it's your baby and I know you're proud of it—but I don't see how it's going to be all that different from other conferences."

"I think it will be. This may be the beginning of a new experience in researching a very important subject…"

Mark shrugged. "Seems to me it's been done before."

"But Mark, this is a totally different approach to the subject." Paul went on to explain that the conference would have only fifty active participants carefully chosen. Then a hundred others will be observers to the program who would come mostly from the United States and Western Europe. Although Ulinov would come from Russia and Kline from Israel. "In this one place," Paul said, "we'll have some of the world's top experts in the field."

"So, what are they going to do when they get there?" Jayne asked, rearranging the tortoise comb in her hair.

"Work directly with the artists. We chose painters, sculptors, musicians, writers, choreographers—even scientists in the creative end of brain research." Paul gestured expressively, his enthusiasm building. "We want to consider the correlation between innovative thinking skills and stimulation to specific areas of the brain. Is it possible to stimulate a specific part of the brain that enhances nonlinear thinking?"

"And what will that prove?" Mark asked.

"I don't think we're there to 'prove' anything, but to learn from each other. The artists will discuss how they consciously stimulate innovative thinking skills. What do they do when they feel blocked? How do they explain the impact childhood experiences have on their creative thinking ability? What happens in childhood to spark creativity? What happens to stifle it? How does trauma in early childhood drive creative forces or hinder them?"

"Good luck with that," Mark said. "It's a subject people have toyed with for years. There's a Nobel prize waiting for the one who has an answer to all that!"

"I seem to have been on my soap box again. Why don't we drop this conversation and have some dinner? Jayne, I know you like sukiyaki. Stephanie, anything I can do to help?"

"It's all done. Thanks anyway."

They moved to the dining area and sat at the table, which was set in blues and white. In the center, a Japanese wok stood waiting. Paul carried the tray of uncooked ingredients from the refrigerator to the table. Stephanie, now sans kimono, brought the salad, which was carefully and artistically arranged. She enjoyed using the electric wok, which was hot now, and the oil sizzled when she poured it in the pan. Then the onions, the bean sprouts, the thin slices of meat, the wine, the condiments, the huge fresh mushrooms. Paul poured the warm sake into the Japanese cups, then returned the bottle to the warmer.

The phone rang and Stephanie went to the kitchen to answer it. "Mark, it's for you. It's the exchange."

"Someday," Jayne said, "we are going to get through a dinner without a patient calling. I keep believing that, but it never seems to happen."

"Come on, Jayne, you knew that was part of the package when you married a psychiatrist," Paul said. "That's one thing a doctor's daughter ought to have plenty of experience with."

"Yeah? Well, I always thought you were just the exception."

"There are lots of us 'exceptions,' contrary to popular opinion."

Stephanie stirred the wok; the drone of Mark's voice came softly over their conversation.

Paul's voice was quiet, and he spoke rapidly. "Jayne, Mark's really in bad shape. I wish there was something you could say to get him to see a doctor. I don't know how he can even see his patients—the man's sick!" Paul looked up to see Mark standing at the door, his face hostile and defensive. *Why was he so angry?* Paul wondered. From the intensity of Mark's resentment, Paul began to think that he regarded his illness as something shameful. Too threatening to even discuss. It didn't make sense.

"I take care of myself—and my patients—very well, thank you."

Paul wanted to explain, then let it go. It was an old pattern. Mark took everything as a personal attack on his abilities. It was a shame he never worked through his own problems in a therapeutic analysis before he started seeing patients. And again, Paul regretted that there were so few controls regarding the psychological health of therapists.

Paul had to admit that even with Mark's problems so blatant, he did have a good reputation for helping abused children. Word had gotten around about his results with them and now his practice was primarily composed of young people; the more troubled they were, the more he seemed able to help. With men, his reputation was that he tended to set up competition between them. How he dealt with women, Paul could only imagine.

Stephanie had moved in, changing the subject, smoothing the edges of the awkward moment. She served the plates, setting them on blue hand-loomed mats.

"This looks great, Stephanie," Paul said.

With a deep sigh, he leaned back in his chair. He hated to insert today's concerns into his daughter's birthday celebration, but it had to be done. "I wanted to tell you all about a young woman who came to see me today."

"About a patient?" Jayne asked. "I've never heard you talk about patient."

"Let that be reassuring to you, if you ever decide to see a psychiatrist."

"Are you hinting?"

"Jayne, please," Paul said.

"Okay, I won't be defensive."

"Today a girl came in to see me and, just to relieve your mind, Jayne, I'm not violating her trust. She gave me permission to discuss it with anyone I think should know. I'm telling you because I don't want you to be surprised if my name shows up in the papers. I don't think it will, but there's no harm in preparing you."

"Dad, who is this person? What's going on? You said you weren't taking any new patients."

"She's not a patient. But there was something about her that sounded so vulnerable and so urgent, I had to follow my intuition. She called this morning, and I had two canceled sessions so I told her I could see her right away. She just arrived from Switzerland on Friday, walked into her sister's apartment, and found her dead. The police think she might have been murdered."

There were the sounds of their reactions—from Stephanie, compassion; Jayne, curiosity; Mark? Paul wasn't sure what Mark was feeling.

"If she just got here on Friday afternoon, why did she come to you? It doesn't make sense to contact a psychiatrist so fast," Mark said.

"Leah didn't come to me because she wanted a psychiatrist; she came because my name was in her sister's journal. Leah assumed I was her sister's doctor, or her friend, and might be able to shed some light on what happened."

"Why would your name be in her sister's journal?" Mark asked, obviously shaken by the story. His reaction was a surprise to Paul, who had never seen him show much concern for anyone—except his own patients.

"I have no idea. After she left, I checked the *LA Times* and most of what I'm telling you, is all there. Except about the journal and my name written inside it. But I think that, just in case they find more details, you should have a head's up that my name might be mentioned."

There was a moment of total silence. Paul looked amused and shook his head. "Well, that certainly got your attention! I decided to discuss it with you because you might be upset if you read my name in the paper or heard about this from a friend."

"You're right about that," Mark said. "So, tell us more about how you got mixed up in this."

"There's a desperate tone to a poem on a loose sheet of paper and my name is written on the back of it next to my phone number. And my name is in the journal on the date she died. The paper was folded in her sister's journal, marking the date for last Friday, the fifth, and it said, 'Call Paul Tabor today.'"

"Was there anything else in the journal? Were you mentioned any other place?" Mark asked. He kept his hands folded in his lap so his trembling wouldn't be noticed.

"I don't know. Leah read the poem, which is why she called me, but she's been so traumatized by all this that she obviously hasn't felt like reading the journal through. The poem showed some heavy feelings. Very personal content. Leah has a great need to try to protect her sister's reputation. Anyway, I told her to take it to the police."

"You what?!"

"After all," Stephanie added, "this is a murder investigation."

Paul reacted to Mark's tight, angry expression. "There might be something there that could help them solve it. I don't know, maybe not. People keep all kinds of journals. Maybe it's an appointment schedule; maybe it's an emotional log. Who knows, it might not mean anything. But that's for the police to decide."

"Doesn't it bother you that your name's in it? How are the police going to react to that? I think you're asking for trouble… telling her to turn it over to them," Mark said.

Paul looked at Mark a long moment before he spoke.

"Yes, it bothers me that my name's there, because I don't know the girl and I don't know what it's all about. And I have no idea how the police are going to feel about it, but I would assume they'll ask me some questions and want to know where I was at the time of her death. I hope it's easy for me to prove where I was. As for turning the journal over to the police, I don't see how there's any option. That book just might lead them to the man who did it."

"Man? How do you know it wasn't a woman?"

"It could have been, of course. But Leah thinks she saw a man running away from the apartment when she first opened the door."

"She thinks…"

"She thinks she saw him. Maybe she did, maybe she didn't, I don't know. She's so upset at this point she's just trying to get her head together. Anyway, I'm going to see her again as a friend, but not as a patient. We'll see what happens."

Mark got up from the table without a word and went to the bathroom.

"So, I told you this just in case the police come around—in case they're not satisfied that my relationship with her sister was nonexistent. Or in case her death came at a time I can't account for where I was. I want you to be alerted, so you won't be shocked if they come asking questions."

It wasn't long before Mark returned to the table. His pain was obviously worse, and it was making him increasingly nervous, Paul thought.

"So, where's the girl now?" Mark asked.

"She's in a hotel in Westwood. She didn't want to stay at her sister's place."

"Are her parents with her?" Stephanie asked.

"Her parents are dead. She doesn't have anyone. No one to go back to in Switzerland because she grew up in a boarding school. Her sister was her only family, and she was going to live with her and take some classes while she decides what she wants to do."

Glancing over at Mark, who seemed to be in so much pain, Stephanie suggested, "Don't you want to lie down, Mark?"

"No. I think we should just go on home," Mark said.

Jayne sounded irritated. "We haven't even finished dinner, Mark. Why don't you just go lie down on Dad's bed for a while?"

"Sweetie, if Mark needs to go home…" Paul said.

"All right! All right!" Jayne sighed. "What a bummer!" Then softly, under her breath, in her most affected way, she said, "Oh, we are *such* a copacetic family! But before we go, I think that package on the coffee table is for me."

"Jayne—I'm sorry! I completely forgot," Paul said.

"Well, I thought you might be saving it for effect, or something. Like the tension would rise and the gift would make a great and dramatic appearance."

"It just did." Paul handed her the heavy box.

"It's not jewelry," she said. "That must mean Stephanie picked it out."

"We both did," Stephanie said quickly.

The bow slipped to the table; the paper fell away; she flipped the top of the box open. "Oh. That's sweet, Stephanie. Thank you. Thanks, Dad." She held the sculpture in her hand briefly, turned it over, and returned it to the box.

"Thanks for dinner, Stephanie, that was delicious," Paul said.

"Yeah, thanks," Jayne added.

Mark was ahead of them, opening the front door of the Porsche before the others got there. The roar of the car's engine blasted the night air, covering the sound of Jayne's words, spoken softly in her father's ear as she slipped into the passenger side. And the words came like a bolt he hadn't expected. "Dad, I've got to get out of here. Please, take me with you to Switzerland!"

CHAPTER 3

MALIBU

After they came home from work Tuesday afternoon, Paul and Stephanie pushed their Hobie Cat out into the surf, Paul on one side, Stephanie on the other. The foam licked their ankles and climbed up their legs. Then froth became wave and the whiteness changed to dark ocean blue-green-gray. Beyond the breakers, the wind carried them out until all they could hear was the sound of the slapping of the waves against the boat and the flap of the sail and the call of the seagulls above them.

Stephanie lay flat on the nylon web, dropping her suit top.

Paul was lost in thought, taking them southeast, paralleling the shore. They stayed far enough out to see only mountains and shoreline and a blur of people blending into the sand.

"You feel like talking about it?" Stephanie asked, and he realized that she had been studying him.

"No, but I guess I should." He thought of the things she said to him in bed, after they made love and slept in each other's arms, when they talked about Switzerland and their plans. After the conference, they would take a mini vacation, climbing the pathways of the Alps and sharing new places and old feelings. They would have days without telephones, patients, and the demands of their schedules. It was the quality of the time that mattered. It was long overdue.

"Hey, it's not going to get any easier to tell me," Stephanie said. And her blue eyes held his brown ones and made the telling as easy as it could have been, given the words he had to say.

"It's about Jayne."

Was it the sun's glare that brought that tightening to her eyes? He watched her hook the back of her suit and sit up, without a word.

"You could tell last night that the battle's still on between the two of them."

"That's not news, Paul."

"No, but it must be worse. When I opened the car door for her, she mentioned something that may be a bit of a problem. I don't think Mark heard her, that car's so damn noisy."

"She wants to go to Switzerland with us, right?"

"How did you know that?"

"Well, it might be my ESP again. Or just that I know Jayne and know that she would rather be in Switzerland with you than at home fighting with Mark."

"How do you feel about that?" he asked.

"How do you?"

"Ambivalent. It's the eternal conflict, isn't it, being husband, father, and psychiatrist? On one hand, I really don't want Jayne to go. I want time just with you; I don't feel like sharing that with anyone. And I want a clear head for that conference without any distractions from her. But…"

"But you can't say no to Jayne."

"Well, I can say no to her, I've said no to her about plenty of things. But she's hurting now. Her marriage is falling apart; she wants to get away. I don't know, maybe she wants to talk it over with me, maybe she just wants to work it out by herself. I don't know what she wants, yet."

"And you feel like you have to meet the need, whenever it's there."

"I know how many times I didn't meet her needs when she was little. I had my head in a books all through training; there wasn't time to do anything else in those days. Any time I had away from the hospital seemed to be absorbed by her mother… that woman's needs were insatiable. Jayne paid a high price for all that. She feels that she did anyway. She's told me a dozen times how she used to want more attention when she was little and I was always running off to see patients, missing her dance recitals and her father-daughter events at school. That night she had the lead in a school play, a patient was suicidal. I had to leave and try to keep a man from jumping off an eight-story building. Of course, I had to go to my patient. But try convincing an eight-year-old."

"Try convincing a forty-seven-year-old! Paul, you are the most logical man I know on every subject except your daughter. She has you so guilty—and that's not all her fault, you allow it! She couldn't do this to you if you'd face up to the fact that Jayne has some responsibility for the kind of person she's become. She's demanding and selfish and…now don't start getting defensive; I'm not saying she doesn't have some valid reasons why she's the way she is. But she still made her own choices. When are you going to accept the fact that you were not the perfect father, and neither is anybody else! She knows where you're vulnerable. She knows that she can push that button and you'll give her anything she wants, to try to make up for how you think you failed her.

You, of all people, should know that and not let her play this same number on you all the time."

"Okay, Stephanie, it's clear what your feelings are about this trip."

"No question. True, I don't want her to intrude on our time together. And I can see her screwing up something for you at the conference, by her need for attention and…well, maybe that's not fair—I'm overreacting because of how she's going about this. It's just the same old pattern. She wants what she wants when she wants it. And you jump every time she says frog!"

He gnawed on his feelings a minute before he looked at her. She seemed hurt, but he was too irritated with her to care about her insecurity at that moment. Stephanie seemed to recognize that she'd overstepped.

"Paul, I'm sorry. Listen, you do what you have to do about Jayne. Bring her with us if you want to—if you need to. Maybe she'll even meet some friends at the parties. Maybe she won't even want to go with us after the conference."

She was fighting tears on that last sentence.

"Okay, Stephanie, I'll tell you what. I'll talk to Jayne and try to find out how serious this is. Maybe I'm seeing things out of proportion. If not—well, one thing I promise you, I'll tell her that those days after the conference ends are ours alone. She's not going to come with us when we go…wherever the wind blows us. That's no problem. But I think you should try to get in touch with why she threatens you."

"I know what threatens me, Paul. I can't help it. I'm not usually so sensitive, but when Jayne's around, she's always your first concern. It's always her feelings that manipulate everything we do. I've watched it for too many years, and you never seem to see it. Maybe you do, I don't know. But are you aware of how totally I'm excluded by her possessiveness? All the combined people of that conference won't separate us the way she will." Her voice cracked and softened, and she lay against him, holding him, needing his reassurance, wanting the healing.

He tasted the salt on her lips. His hand felt the grating of the sand against her skin. They held each other in silence. No words now, just a little time to think about what was said and not defend against the words, to try on the other's feelings, feel where the pinches were.

"Paul?"

"Hmm."

"What are you thinking?"

She looked up at him. He saw gentleness and beauty and love all blending.

"That I'm glad you can tell me what you feel, even when I don't want to hear it. And I was thinking a lot of things that you already know and are used to hearing. Such as…" But he couldn't finish the sentence because her tongue got in the way.

After a long silence, he added, "Stephanie, it's hard to have any objectivity about a problem when you're right in the middle of it." His voice softened. "And where Jayne's concerned, I don't have any more answers than the next guy. I just love her too much to be able to see the situation clearly—or to know what to do about it."

Stephanie rested her head against the hard, muscular shoulder. "I know," she said. Her voice was so quiet he barely heard it.

Paul directed the catamaran back toward the house and less than an hour later, they pulled the boat up onto the shore.

As if on cue, Jayne was sitting on the back steps when they got back to the house. "I've been waiting an age for you guys. Hey, Stephanie, do you mind if I talk to Dad for a few minutes alone? This is kind of private."

Early Tuesday evening, Mark was watching and not watching the television, seeing but not caring, marking time. Every news channel was still reporting news about that nutty woman who tried to assassinate President Ford. He kept switching channels, then gave up in exasperation. He wasn't interested.

He had been home alone for hours before he heard Jayne coming through the door. He hadn't missed her. He watched her come into the room, cast a sour look in his direction, and move in, ready for battle.

"I need to talk with you," she said.

"What's stopping you?"

"I just came from the beach house. Had a long talk with Dad." She sat far from him. "Mark, I think we need some time away from each other. We fight all the time; you're not happy; I'm not happy. What's it all about anyway?"

"Is that your father's suggestion?"

"No. I made up my mind before I talked to him. I asked if I could go to Switzerland with him."

Anger raged inside of him, churning acid, burning the lining of his stomach. "Oh, I'm sure he said yes to that! He would really enjoy taking you away from me…very symbolic, Jayne, doesn't it seem?"

"Not to me. All I see is that I'm going to lose my mind cooped up in this marriage, and I need space. I asked him if I could go."

"And Stephanie? I'll bet she wasn't so glad to hear that you want to go, was she? You've always been her biggest competitor, or weren't you aware of that?"

"You're really sick, you know that?"

"Is that what your father said?"

"That's what I say."

"Well, Sweetie." His tone was sarcastic. "Let me be explicit about this, so there won't be any doubt in your mind about how much I mean it. You are not going to Switzerland. You are not going anywhere with your father. And if you think that I don't mean that, then you know me not nearly as well as I think you do."

Her face paled as he watched her. Golden-beige Jayne, pale beneath her tan. He saw the confusion in her eyes and knew that she didn't know what edge he held against her, what specific threat was implied in his words. But she heard the tone of it.

She slammed the door as she left. Mark stared at the television, watching while the wreckers destroyed a house. A huge ball of iron rammed against it, pulled back, and rammed again. Time and again.

So, Paul Tabor wanted to take sweet baby Jayne to Switzerland with him. Mark could see it all, her walking into the University of Lausanne Medical School, boasting that her husband went to school there, flashing his name. And Paul would introduce her to the head of the psychiatric residency program at the hospital and she would say, "Oh, yes, my husband took his training here," and then Mark could imagine the man's answer to that. He grabbed the wastebasket, unable to make it to the bathroom before the retching began.

He could hear the iron ball ramming into the building, twice and then again. He saw himself falling beneath the blows.

Damn Paul! Damn his interference and his manipulation! Damn his arrogance and his eagerness to trumpet Mark's weakness to the world.

Exhausted and worried, Mark felt himself scrambling to find some way to stop his world from collapsing. He was in enough trouble without his father-in-law being involved. He had to make a plan to get out before he got caught.

What did Nicole's journal say about him? He hadn't even known she kept a journal. All he could think about was how this entire disaster had started. As if understanding the story would make the facts more malleable. How could he write a plausible story around the existing facts? The walls were closing in. He needed to make his decision, and soon.

He focused on last Thursday night, the night before Nicole had died. Already worn out and on edge, Mark had gone to her apartment resenting her all the while. He knew it was over between them. He wanted out. She had to know how he felt. Mark dropped his coat on the chair and settled himself on the sofa, placing his feet on the coffee table.

She fixed him a drink. A martini was his usual choice.

He sensed her tension, which she cushioned with the sweetness of her words. He knew that her seductiveness tonight had nothing to do with sexual desire. Bed was her bartering place; it always had been. She moved past him, up the stairs. He could hear the sounds. The closet door opening. The bathroom door closing. The silence.

When he'd finished his drink, he climbed the stairs to her bedroom. The sooner he got it over with the better. He turned the television on and propped himself up against the pillows of her bed to wait for her. He switched channels but nothing seemed interesting.

She came into the room, folds of a lavender silk nightgown draped the softness of her body, playing against the hard edge of her mood.

"You're giving a double message, Nicole. Did you get me up here to fight or to fuck?"

He saw her color rise. She groped for words, and he thought how poorly she handled anger. "So, the lady has a temper," he said. "After all these years I finally see it poking its way out of the iceberg. OK, let's have it." Mark watched her try to work up the courage, straightening the set of her shoulders, tightening the line of her lips.

He should break it off right now, he thought, but said nothing, revealing only a look of boredom with the evening news.

"When you asked me to come to LA, I didn't think it would be like this," she began.

"You knew I was married."

"I knew you were unhappily married, and I thought you were going to break it off—you said you would, or I never would have left Switzerland."

"Well, people say a lot of things. Circumstances change."

"Then why did you ask me to come?" Her voice rose, stretching out of natural range.

"What difference does it make? You're here. I'm here. If you wouldn't push so fucking hard, everything would be fine." He stared at the television, seeing Nicole only peripherally.

"I want to be married. You promised me that."

"I promised you nothing. You heard what you wanted to hear."

"I wouldn't have come here to be your mistress for the rest of my life."

His laugh reddened her cheeks again. "You're in America now; you should learn the vernacular. You came here because you wanted to come, and you stay because you enjoy what I have to offer. When you don't enjoy it anymore…the door's open."

"I'm pregnant."

"You're also naive. What's been done can be undone. It's no big deal. This is hardly the time for you to think about a child."

She struggled for words.

"Look, it's a minor problem, Nicole. If you don't screw this up, and you keep working your ass off, you can finish med school, you can be a doctor. The last thing you need is a baby! The last thing *I* need is a baby. What would you do—give it all up now because you got careless? After all it took to get you this far? Don't be stupid. Call me at the office in the morning; I'll have the name of someone you can see."

"I won't have an abortion. I want this baby."

"And I won't get a divorce. Checkmate." He cocked his head in an arrogant swagger.

Nicole's call to Mark that Friday afternoon hadn't been for the name of a doctor. She called with threats that sent him racing out of his office, calling over his shoulder to his secretary that there was an emergency and to cancel his afternoon appointments. This was a great deal more involved than just a simple pregnancy and her threats to call his wife. She threatened to call Paul Tabor. And to tell him what happened in Switzerland. He couldn't let that happen.

The kitchen door was unlocked, and he went quietly into Nicole's apartment. She must have heard his footsteps on the oak stairs for when he entered her bedroom, she was standing there, waiting for him.

"You don't think I'll do it, do you?" It was the voice of a woman who had no intention of backing down.

"I don't think you're that stupid," Mark said. "You were in on it, too, you know. If you pull me down, you come with me."

"But I can prove what you did. You only have accusations against me." Without another word, she walked out of her bedroom and onto the landing at the top of the stairs. He followed her, grabbed her, whirling her around to face him. She backed away, out of his grip.

"You can't go to Paul Tabor! You can't ruin everything I've worked for!"

Her voice was tight and controlled to a whisper. She flicked the words at him: "Watch me!"

And she cocked her chin in the same arrogant tilt that he had done the night before.

He never meant to kill Nicole. He couldn't bear to think about it.

Running away from the memory of one killing only sent his memory whirling to the past. He was powerless against it.

CHAPTER 4

WEST LOS ANGELES & SANTA MONICA

The police station was crowded when Leah asked directions to the Robbery-Homicide Division of LAPD. Dr. Tabor had been right, she thought. After all, who was she to determine if the things in Nicole's journal were important? She approached a woman seated closest to the door and asked where she could find Detective Gerald McKenzie.

"He stepped out for a minute. You can wait over there, if you want to," she said, indicating the wooden chairs along the wall. "It shouldn't be too long."

Leah sat in the straight-backed chair and thought about the man she was waiting to see. She remembered his voice, harsh and insulated from feeling—and the smell of him, like used cigars. She imagined him looking through Nicole's journal, finding her most hidden secrets, pawing over the pages that were like a part of Nicole's own person. She could hear Nicole's voice from years ago, making her promise never to read her journal. "It's a secret, even from you," Nicole had said.

And Leah heard her own voice saying, "I promise."

But times and circumstances change. *I have to do this*, Leah thought, and she longed for forgiveness even before the act was done.

She remembered the first time she saw Nicole's journal—and her own. That was many years ago. The memory of that day was swollen with sadness. How could she violate such a trust?

Leah had been given her own room in the boarding school that year; a virus had kept her in bed for a week, and finally Madame had called Nicole, suggesting that she stop by. Lying under the eiderdown comforter which was a Christmas present from Nicole the year before, Leah had waited anxiously for her sister. Then Nicole had come; the snow had melted on her coat, leaving damp spots on the shoulders. She smelled of wool and sweet perfume and her voice was music.

"What is this I hear about my lazy sister, eh? Spending all these days in bed with daydreams instead of arithmetic! Look, I brought you a present. This should make you feel better." She came over to the high, narrow bed and rested a cool hand on Leah's hot forehead; then Nicole brushed her lips across the place her hand had touched. The way Nicole had said their mother used to do.

Leah pulled at the paper around the gift and opened the box to find a leather journal the color of wine. Soft leather, filled with blank pages, except for the date on each page. The journal could be refilled each year and the pages were trimmed with gold.

"Nicole, it's so beautiful I'll be afraid to write on it."

"Make a mistake on the first page—on purpose. After that you can enjoy it without worrying about spoiling the book. This is just for you to see. You can write all your feelings and your poems and even draw pictures if you like. You can write appointments in it, if they're special, of course. But don't clutter it up too much with things you have to do. This is for all the wonderful feelings and the terrible feelings and the most secret ones."

"I could never write what I really feel, Nicole. What if it got lost? What if Marianne read what I think about her! She would never speak to me again!"

"Then leave her out of your book. Or use a code. You can make up your own words for her or just use an initial or something. Besides, no one should ever read this journal but you."

Nicole then took a book the same size, the same style from her purse. The color was dark green. "This one is mine. I won't show you the inside because that's private."

"Private from me?"

"Even from you. This is for my secrets. You must never get into this."

"I wouldn't do that, Nicole."

"Very well. I will respect your privacy and never read a page of your journal. And you will do the same for me, yes?"

"I promise."

Nicole had taken time to stay with her and listen to her feelings of loneliness. "I miss you, Nicole. Now that you're working so hard, I never get to see you anymore."

"When you're well and when I have a break at school, I'm going to come and borrow you from Madame for at least four days. We will say that we must go away on very important business, which it will be, because you and I have some very important skiing to do and nothing is more important business than that."

"Would you really do that? Would you tell Madame a lie?"

"What would be a lie? It is most important that you and I stay close, even though we cannot live together. That is more necessary even than your lessons."

"Nicole, I love you!"

"Now get some rest and start building your strength back. Start thinking about where you'd like to go. Grindelwald maybe? You decide. Bye-bye, my dear. I love you too."

But that was a long time ago. Pieces of other memories were loosened by these thoughts and fell from the past like boulders too large to dodge. Leah's sigh was audible, filled with anguish.

She saw a policewoman turn and look at her. Leah acted on her feelings. No matter what she promised Paul Tabor, her promise to Nicole took precedence. She hurried toward the door, grabbing the knob and pulling it toward her. Standing in her path, just coming in, was Detective McKenzie.

His stocky build was like an immovable wall before her. The sagging muscles of his jaws had hardened into sullen jowls.

"You want to see me?" he asked.

Leah could feel the power of him confronting her; she hesitated a moment before saying, "Yes."

"Come on in my office." He led the way and she saw no option but to follow.

"What can I do for you?" he asked as the door to his office closed. The room was functional. Lacking character. Leah didn't notice. She was reaching for some way out, for some excuse she could give for coming.

"I wondered if you had any news about my sister's…" She couldn't form the next word. "I mean, about my sister's case."

Penetrating, experienced eyes evaluated her carefully. "Nothing yet," he said.

"I thought you might have some information." Her voice was thin, diffident.

"Have a seat, Miss Vassaux."

Reluctantly Leah sat on the black vinyl chair across from the Formica desk cluttered with papers.

"Maybe you've thought of something that might be helpful," he said, in a way that she was sure he could read her mind, or at least her attitude and that was tantamount to the same thing. She couldn't fool him; Leah knew that. She was a rotten liar.

"Yes," she said, her voice soft. "When I went to the bathroom, I found something that I took with me. It was very private, and I wanted to hide it so that no one would read anything so personal. But I think you should have it."

Leah felt the tension in the room, the anger in the man's lowering brows and wished desperately that she had never come.

The detective just stared at her. Holding back his anger. Then finally he said, "Let me have it." He extended his hand, but in a way that seemed to Leah like a threat.

She reached into her purse, felt the cool, smooth leather against her fingers, and drew back. The detective's hand was inches from the journal. She felt for the paper that was stuck between the pages, the paper with the poem and with Paul Tabor's name. Pulling it from the book, she placed the single sheet of paper in his hand.

He read it first quickly and then again, as his eyes narrowed over the words.

"And just why did you think you had the right to take evidence out of the apartment?"

"What evidence? I took my sister's poem, or maybe it wasn't my sister's, how do I know? I only know it was there." From the moment she withdrew her hand from her purse, leaving the journal inside, some small part of her had begun to fight back. And that small rebellious part was beginning to grow and now she was stronger than she could remember feeling, ever before. He wasn't going to intimidate her. She chose not to allow that, and the feeling of choice was good.

"I was afraid you would assume Nicole wrote this," Leah said. "Which may not be true at all. I was concerned because she wouldn't want something like this to come out in the newspaper. Can you promise me that it won't?"

"I can't promise you anything. This is a murder investigation."

"But the newspapers. Printing the poem won't help you solve the case. You don't have to let them see it."

"I'll think about it," he said, but she took no reassurance from his tone. "Where did you find this?"

"In the bathroom. With a stack of books on her vanity."

"Folded this way?"

Leah felt his eyes wander across her, searching for what else might be hidden there, probing for something left unsaid. "No, I folded it to fit into my purse." Leah looked him straight in the eye and held his gaze, closing the door to her secret by strength of will.

"It's against the law to remove evidence from a crime scene. Did you know that?"

"No." Still she held his gaze and let her defiance show in her eyes.

"Do you know who this Paul Tabor is?"

"Yes. He's a psychiatrist."

"Do you remember your sister mentioning him before?"

"No. I went to see him, thinking he might be a friend of Nicole's…"

"He might also be her killer; did you think of that?"

"I wasn't thinking very clearly then. But he's not the man you want. I'm sure of it."

He laughed and there was condescension in the sound. Palms upward, he gestured in exasperation. "And how do you know that?"

So many thoughts raced to make words that for a moment they jammed in her brain, and she was speechless. Then she said, "Trust me," and the tone of it was as caustic as his own.

"Is there anything else you have that might be useful? Or anything you remember?"

"No," Leah said, hoping that he would believe the innocence she was pretending, trying not to think of Nicole's journal hidden in her purse.

"What did you tell Paul Tabor?"

"That Nicole is dead. I thought he might have been her friend, that he might become my friend. But he didn't know Nicole."

"Or he *says* he didn't."

"He didn't know her. He told me he didn't and I believe him."

The detective had short, thick arms that he flung toward the ceiling. He shook his head and then stared at Leah.

She gave him an enigmatic smile and walked toward the door.

"Oh, one more thing." His tone was flat. "Did you know that Nicole was pregnant?"

Leah put her hand on the wall to steady herself. Did she know Nicole was pregnant?

She was beginning to wonder if she knew Nicole at all.

CHAPTER 5

WEST LOS ANGELES & SANTA MONICA

On a sweltering Wednesday morning, Sharon Miller was sitting at her reception desk as she was every morning, five days a week. September was always hot and there were difficulties with the air conditioner. She worked for all the doctors in the suite, typing case histories, answering phones, doing the billing, the insurance, and all the other chores that go with office management. She was efficient, and at this moment, concerned.

"Dr. Favre, I didn't expect you in. When you called this morning, I thought you wanted me to cancel your patients starting today. I've already called them."

"That's fine, Sharon. I just stopped by because there's something I need to do before I go to the hospital for a few days. This won't take long."

"Oh, I'm sorry, Doctor. If there's anything I can do…?" She followed him into his office.

"No thanks, I'll be fine," he said, dismissing her with his manner. Once the door to his office was closed, he removed the passports from the drawer where he had placed them for safe keeping. He just had to check them, one more time. The money was there with the passports. Of course it was. He knew Jayne used to have her own key to his office, but she lost it. It wasn't likely that she would know where to find it now.

Mark looked up a telephone number and dialed it. The line was busy. He leaned back in his chair and waited, tapping the ends of his fingers together, feeling that he had won, even before the game was started.

Mark decided his stomach problem had come at a good time, after all. He could use it well. *Nothing like the manipulative powers of the sick*, he thought, and dialed the phone again. This time he could ring through.

"This is Dr. Favre calling. Is Dr. Martin in?

When he came on the line, Mark said, "Hey, Bill, it seems you were right all along. I must do something about my stomach."

Mark tried to make his speech slow, depressed. He fought the sound of excitement that would have come so naturally now.

"No, the Maalox didn't help, and I've had just about all I can handle. I want you to go ahead with a complete workup…yeah, I remember, you suggested that before. Well, you know how it is; it's hard to get away from patients. I really feel bad not being able to give them any notice…yeah, I know, well, I'm doing that now…I'll be taking a lot better care of myself from now on; I don't want another week like this one. I'll go on over to the hospital, I didn't have anything to eat or drink this morning; you think they can get started right away? Okay, Bill, thanks a lot, I'll see you there."

Still trying to keep the energy out of his demeanor, Mark left the office with a final word to his assistant. "Everything set now? Did you talk with Dr. Barton?"

"Yes, she said to tell you she's sorry you're not feeling well, and she'll be glad to cover for you."

"I don't know how long this will take, Sharon. It depends upon what they find."

She looked away from him; he could see her concern and knew her mind ran down the possibilities, as did his own. Her apprehension had triggered his. Mark had been so intent upon using his physical condition as part of his strategy that he had given little thought to the fact that the tests might reveal something more serious than just the ulcers. "I'm not sure when I'll be back in the office. I'll call you when I have some answers."

The drive to St. John's Hospital took less time than it took to fill out the forms in the admissions office and to be shown to his room. He didn't have to feign worry now; the reality of the hospital and the possibility of serious problems weighed upon him.

The feelings of euphoria had been short-lived.

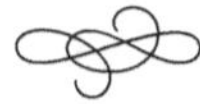

On Wednesday afternoon, Paul arrived a little early for his meeting with Leah at Sam's Café. "The space is yours, Doc. Coffee? I have some chocolate chip cookies the wife made, and I'll add those, too, if you want something sweet," Sam said, as he seated Paul in the small garden with the director's chairs that were more comfortable than the wooden ones inside.

"Perfect," Paul said. He had a weakness for Maggie's cookies and after all the years he had been going there, he was treated like family. Sam made a round trip to the kitchen and returned with a plate of cookies, two mugs, and a carafe of coffee.

Leah showed up right on time. She was clearly distressed and trying not to show it.

Sam made an exit as quickly as he could, closing the door behind him.

Leah seemed different today. Paul could see that from the moment she arrived.

"Hello, Leah, it's good to see you."

There was a kind of energy in the way she walked when she entered the space, in the tilt of her head when she greeted him, in the quick, jerky movements when she sat down. She didn't say a word.

Paul leaned forward in his chair. "Leah? What's going on?"

"I don't want to talk about Nicole."

"Okay." He nodded.

"You think you know someone and then you find out you don't."

He waited.

"I need to just get on with my life! There's nothing I can do about what happened."

"Do you want to tell me what made you so angry?"

"No, I just want to talk about my life, my future, my getting through all this!"

"Well, that's what I'm here for. Where should we start?"

"I don't want to talk about Nicole."

"I understand. What comes to mind when you think about your future?" It was a leading question. "Just say the first thing that you think of."

Leah closed her eyes, then quickly opened them and said, "The first thing I think about is that I don't know how to stop thinking about Nicole. I feel so angry with her. I want to stop thinking about her, trying to solve her murder, when I don't know how to do that. I went to the police, just like you told me to. And I met with Detective McKenzie."

Leah changed her position quickly, crossing her legs, folding her arms in front of her. "You know it's hard to understand why the police are so insensitive. Why do they have to be so abrasive? This is all difficult enough without their hatefulness."

"Someone must have been pretty hard on you to make you so angry."

"That detective didn't care at all about my feelings."

Paul didn't comment.

"Sometimes it's better not to talk about things that hurt too much," Leah said.

"Is it, Leah?"

"Yes. I don't know. I don't know anything right now. Except that Nicole was pregnant!"

The words formed sharply on her tongue.

Paul waited a moment before responding. "Did the detective tell you that?"

"Yes, and then I read some things in her journal."

So. That would mean Leah still had it.

Paul frowned. "What was it that Nicole wrote that hurt you?"

Paul watched her frustration, her desire to tell him, her fear of telling him.

Paul sat back in his chair, respecting the distance she seemed to need.

"When I left your office, I had some new feeling…of control…or power…I don't know what to call it. But I felt that I could handle that. You see, I was strong when I left you on

Monday. I was in touch with some inner strength that I no longer have.

"But then…I went to the police station, and I wish I'd never gone. It made me want to…"

"Made you want to…what?"

Silence. And he answered the question for her, "Made you want to cry."

She was trying to push the feelings away, trying to stop an avalanche with sheer strength of will. Her eyes challenged him. Tears brimmed and held without falling.

He went on. "It's easier to get angry than to give in to the tears. I know the feelings are painful but trying to avoid them will only make it harder in the long run." He watched her considering that. "Do you want to tell me what was in the journal?"

Slowly the decision came. Slowly she let down her defenses and the feelings surfaced. It was hard to form the words, harder still to trust another person with something so devastating.

At first it was a whisper. "She didn't want me." Then again, the same words, but with rage propelling them.

"She didn't want me. All the years she took care of me, I was just a burden, a responsibility. All the times she acted like my mother and pretended to love me and care about what happened to me, it was just an act! Just her fine noble values. She never loved me. Never wanted me!" Leah fought against the emotion that flooded the words. Her body, stiff and rigid, raced against the feelings.

"Leah, give me your tears," Paul said softly, and the comfort of his voice was more than she could defend against, and she wept.

He knew she must resent Nicole at that moment, and she would want distance from anyone who offered to help her, who might also betray her, as Nicole had done. Leah trusted him enough to let him see the extent of her sadness. Still, guards were posted in her mind, keeping watch for unexpected dangers.

When the tears stopped, Paul began to question her. Easily. Gently. "Leah, you don't have to tell me anything you don't want me to know. But remember, there might be some other interpretation."

"There are no other interpretations. She said that I was always a responsibility that she couldn't escape. Always a problem. Well, why didn't she just tell me she didn't want me to come? All she had to do was say she changed her mind. I didn't have to come here! I've gotten along just fine without her all my life, without anyone! I didn't need her. I don't need her now. I can take care of myself! Nicole just thought of me as a responsibility. And there's no other way to interpret what she wrote."

"I'm not so sure about that. Tell me, what was she writing about just before she wrote about you?"

"I don't know…why?"

"Was she writing about her pregnancy in the preceding pages?"

Leah thought for a moment. "I think so. Yes, it was right after she wrote about the baby, and how much she wanted it… but she didn't know if he would marry her. Why wouldn't she write his name! Nicole sounded frightened about the child and didn't know what to do…yes, she was upset about the baby. But she still meant what she said about me. She couldn't have written that unless she meant it."

"That's the way it seems to you."

"How can you possibly read anything else into that?"

"I was thinking about the fact that she was so good to you when you were little and if she didn't love you, I don't think she could have made you believe she did. Not for all those years. And then I was wondering about what else Nicole might have been feeling, just before she wrote those words. She was pregnant and apparently wanted the baby. But if the man refused to marry her, then she might have had some ambivalence about the pregnancy. What would she do if he refused? Would she give up the child? Have an abortion? The problems might have seemed overwhelming. And, at that time, she might very well have wished she hadn't asked you to come. It wouldn't have been easy for Nicole to tell you that she was pregnant by a man who refused to marry her."

Leah was absorbing every word, weighing it, doubting, hoping.

"When Nicole seemed to be rejecting you, it could have been a combination of all kinds of insecurities on her part. All those years that she took care of you, emotionally anyway, came long before the age when she was naturally ready for maternal responsibilities. It couldn't have been easy, no matter how much she loved you."

"You really think she loved me?"

"Yes. But I also think she sometimes felt overwhelmed. That's natural."

"Oh, God, I would love to believe that."

"Leah, even mothers get angry and say things—write things—that they feel when they're upset. That doesn't mean that the anger expresses their deepest feelings. It's only fairy-tale characters that are all good or all evil; Nicole was capable of loving and caring and taking on a great deal of responsibility. But she was a real person, and sometimes she felt angry and rejecting and thought that her own problems were all that she could handle. Her feelings sound very normal, Leah, very human."

Leah kept her eyes away from him, her dark hair fell across her face, hiding her response. Paul gave her time to process what he said.

"I need to think about that awhile," Leah said, leaning back, letting him see her again.

"I'm sure you do. When feelings have hurt that deeply, they don't just go away, even if you understand them." For several minutes Leah made no effort to move. She looked emotionally drained, leaning back into the chair, her eyes closed, her breathing slow and heavy. She took her time. When she opened her eyes, she seemed better. Her energy was lighter.

"Good. So don't lose that doctor's phone number I gave you. You shouldn't have to deal with all these feelings alone. And listen, I don't leave for Switzerland until next Friday. Let's meet again on Wednesday?"

Paul knew he was sounding like her therapist, but when she started seeing her own psychiatrist, he could pull back. The look of gratitude on her face showed him that sometimes rules were made to be bent.

CHAPTER 6

WEST LOS ANGELES

Paul went back to his office for his afternoon appointments. While he was seeing his five o'clock patient his buzzer rang during the session. The interruption came at a bad time; for months this patient had blamed everyone but himself for what happened to his wife one night five years ago. Now that he was on the verge of talking about his responsibility in the matter, the buzzer had sounded like an alarm pulling him out of his reverie and he closed down again.

"Go on, Carl, they can wait," Paul said, and turned a switch that silenced the buzzing. The man fumbled through his thoughts but couldn't find what he wanted to say. Paul wondered how long it would be before he could come back to that point again, when he would risk facing whatever it was that haunted him.

"Carl, will you tell me again what you were feeling that night?" And the knocking on the door began. Even through the soundproofed door, they could hear the hard, demanding sound against the wood. And Paul could hear his name, muffled through the insulation, but discernible.

"I'm sorry," Paul said, "let me see what this is about." He closed the office door behind him and then opened the second door to the outer office. Before Paul could even say a word about the pounding on his door, the larger of the two men said, "Are you Dr. Paul Tabor?"

"That's right."

"I'm Detective McKenzie, Homicide Los Angeles Police Department." He reached into the pocket of his brown polyester suit and showed Paul his credentials.

Paul made a quick assessment. McKenzie looked like he was at retirement age. He seemed disgruntled, even surly. Next to him was a young rookie. Looking green. They could have been straight out of central casting, both of them.

"I've been expecting you," Paul said. "I'm with a patient now and can't see you until I have a break."

Detective McKenzie made no effort to conceal his irritation. Paul watched the furrows dig deeper into his leathered face.

"I'll have a ten-minute break in about…" He looked at his watch. "About another fifteen minutes. If you think you need more time than ten minutes," Paul said, "you can see me at seven, after my last patient."

"We won't take long, Doctor. Let's just sit down over there for a minute. I'd like to ask you a few questions."

"I understand that, but this is my patient's time. I'll be glad to see you if you care to wait. Or you can come back, if you'd rather. Excuse me. I really have to get back to this session."

And with that Paul turned and walked out, irritated by their aggressiveness, concerned for his patient.

When he walked back into his office, he knew his hunch had been right; he could see on the man's face the resistance, the denial. "I'm sorry, Carl."

"No problem. I was getting off the subject anyway."

His defense had by now been so well developed that Paul didn't try to take him back to the former thought. The rest of the hour was of little value; his patient used one avoidance mechanism after another and seemed glad when the session ended.

Paul watched him go out the back entrance.

The interruption really annoyed him. If they had called first, the answering service would have taken the number and Paul would have returned the call between sessions. He never kept a receptionist in view of patients or shared an office with another doctor. He liked the reinforcement of the confidentiality of the sessions. Rarely had this system proved to be a problem.

Paul opened the soundproofed door and entered the waiting room. The men were still there. They looked irritated for the inconvenience; Detective McKenzie leaned against the wall with an arrogant stance. Paul could tell even before they started the questions why Leah had felt intimidated.

Paul invited them into his office, motioned for them to sit down. He never sat with the desk between a patient and himself, not wanting the symbol of authority to enter into the relationship. Today he chose to put the barrier between them. He sat behind his desk and motioned for them to take the two chairs he had pulled to the opposite side of it. He resented their attitude and was aware of how much their intrusiveness irritated him.

"Now what is it you want to know?" Paul asked.

"We have some questions regarding Nicole…eh…Vassocks?"

"Vassaux." Paul corrected his pronunciation of the name.

"What was your relationship with the deceased?"

"Nonexistent. I never heard of her until her sister came in here on Monday asking if I knew her."

"And you told her you didn't."

"That's correct."

"Did you see your name written on that poem?"

"Leah showed it to me, yes. Judging from the poem I'd say that Nicole was going through a devastating time."

"Why do you think your name was on that paper?"

"I have no idea."

"Speculate."

Paul's eyes narrowed a moment. "The obvious assumption is that she was upset and intended to call for an appointment. The name of a psychiatrist on an emotionally troubled poem doesn't seem particularly mysterious."

"Can you tell us where you were at the time of the murder?"

"Not until I know what time she was killed."

"Friday afternoon. Around two o'clock."

"I had lunch alone at one and saw a two o'clock patient."

"What was the name of the patient?"

"You know better than to ask."

"Doctor, I don't think you realize that you're an important name in a murder case. It's to your benefit to cooperate."

"It's to my patient's benefit not to be bothered with this."

"That doesn't give you much of an alibi then, does it?"

"I don't need an alibi. I wasn't involved. And I'm sure you realize that if I had killed Nicole, I wouldn't have told Leah to give you that poem. If you have any more questions, please call through the exchange and I'll get back to you as soon as possible."

Paul stood up and reluctantly the other men did also. Clearly, that conversation was over.

Paul struggled to keep the hostility he felt from permeating his office. Usually patients can sense a change in mood in their therapist and many of them assume the change has something to do with them.

There was more than just his aggravation about the meeting with the detectives that bothered him. Mark had called from the hospital, asking Paul to come by to see him after he finished at the office. His voice had been tremulous; he sounded vulnerable. And Jayne had called, sounding indifferent. She also wanted Paul to stop by to see her that night. He telephoned Stephanie at the gallery and told her to have dinner without him.

CHAPTER 7

SANTA MONICA

With some reluctance, Paul walked into Mark's hospital room. "Hey, thanks for coming, Paul. You've been working late tonight. I don't know how you do it. As you can see, I took your advice," Mark said.

From those first words, Paul sensed that something was going on; Mark never acknowledged another man's contribution to his decisions.

"I'm glad you're taking care of yourself." Paul pulled a straight-backed chair close to the bed and sat down. The stiffness of the chair matched his feelings. Damned strained it was, this relationship with his son-in-law.

"Well, I guess I'm in for a full battery of tests. Yesterday I had an upper GI. They're checking for chronic ulcer disease and a hiatal hernia and anything else they may pick up in the process. I don't relish having that tube run down my throat. They'll biopsy the ulcer just to be sure…" His voice trailed off leaving the fear unspoken.

"I suppose they'll do a colonoscopy, too," Paul said.

Mark tried to cover his anxiety with a laugh. He changed position in the bed. "I don't know which will be worse—the tube down my throat or the one up my ass. When I think about these next few days, I'm sorry I came."

"It's going to be a bit unpleasant, that's for sure. But considering your history it's a good thing you're checking it out." Paul stretched his legs, trying to get comfortable in the stiff-backed chair.

"They're doing a chest plate, EKG, and blood chemistry. But I doubt if they'll find anything except the ulcers."

"When's the last time you had the tests done?"

Mark looked away and then said, "I've never had any of this, except the upper GI. When they found the ulcers, years ago, I started taking medication and controlling the pain with diet. Since there wasn't any sign of internal bleeding, I never let them run the other tests."

It bewildered Paul that a man could be so careless about his health—but then he knew that doctors frequently deny the seriousness of their own symptoms.

"Lately, nothing seems to help," Mark was saying, and Paul heard the anxiety creeping into his voice.

"Have you been under more strain than usual?" As soon as he had said it, Paul wished he hadn't, thinking Mark would take it as prying and that wasn't his intention.

But Mark didn't react as usual. He seemed ready to open up, ready to share some of what was going on inside of him, other than just the fact of his illness.

"Yeah, Paul, a lot's going on." He hesitated. "It isn't easy to tell you about it."

Paul waited.

"It's about Jayne," Mark said. "Things have been going badly for so long. Worse lately. I'm sure you could tell at dinner the other night."

Mark leaned forward, his gestures seeming to plead for understanding. "It's my fault really. I've felt terrible and I've taken it out on her, which made it worse, of course…for both of us. I haven't been much of a husband lately, in a lot of ways. Jayne has every right to want to leave me." And his voice faded out on the last sentence.

Paul didn't want to commit himself to any statement at the moment. There was something about this entire conversation that didn't ring true. It was too out of character. But Mark was watching him now and he had to respond somehow.

"Do you think Jayne wants to leave you permanently? Or does she just need to get away for a little while and sort out what she's feeling?"

"Oh, she knows what she's feeling. Resentment. Bitterness. I need your help, Paul."

Paul squirmed uncomfortably in the chair. *Now he's coming to it*, Paul thought, and then caught himself—suddenly aware that he was judging everything Mark said with suspicion. Maybe he was so hostile himself that he couldn't deal objectively or even fairly with Mark. His son-in-law was trying to confide in him, and he was analyzing every sentence as if there was some duplicity involved. Paul took a deep breath, determined to be more objective regarding his son-in-law.

"Jayne tells me she wants to go to Switzerland with you."

"I know. It might do her good to get away for a while."

"No, Paul, not now. It would be disastrous. I know she's so full of all that's happened between us, and all that hasn't happened between us, that she's ready to flush this whole marriage. I know if she goes away now, she'll never come back. I need her, Paul;

she can name the marriage counselor and I'll agree to get some help. She suggested that once, a long time ago, but I was too proud to see it. But I don't want to lose Jayne. And another thing, I don't know what they're going to find in these tests. I can't handle a separation on top of all this."

"I can't stop her from going, Mark. If she's made up her mind…"

"She listens to you."

And Paul's laugh crept up on him unexpectedly.

"No, Paul, I mean it. Jayne pays more attention to you than you know. She makes a lot of noise about doing things her own way, but she respects you and values your judgment. She doesn't show affection easily, but Jayne loves you; she'll listen to you."

Paul wondered about that. Weariness was all he felt now. Suddenly. Just very tired. And not at all pleased to be involved in this problem between the two of them. "Have you talked with her about what you're feeling now?"

"She didn't even come to the hospital today." His voice developed a whining sound that Paul hadn't heard from him before.

"I'll suggest that she come by in the morning and you two can talk this out."

"In the morning, they're running more tests. I can't have my marriage hanging on a thread while I go through all this. Talk to her, Paul. Tell her she doesn't have a right to leave me now—not like this. When I'm stronger, I'll talk to her. Then if I lose her, well, it won't be without a fair try. Tell her she can't go with you and Stephanie."

"Mark, you might remember it wasn't too long ago that Jayne wanted to leave you and she asked me to help her financially, which I did. I was very much in favor of the two of you going your separate ways. Remember that? With my help, she left you. When she went back to you, she blamed me for meddling in her life and for causing the problem. I won't go that route again."

"Paul, there's not enough money in our joint account for her to go without some financial help anyway. Tell her you won't contribute to the trip. Tell her anything, Paul, but I'm begging you, make her stay."

"I won't try to influence her decision. I'll tell her you really need to talk with her. Whatever decision she makes from that point on is her own. I won't get in the middle of it." Paul realized he had done exactly that.

"But will you tell her that you think she should stay with me?"

"No. You know I can't do that. But I will tell her I think the two of you need to talk. But the decision is hers. You understand that I'll tell her how I feel but I won't try to manipulate her."

"But you'll tell her you won't pay for the trip? You promise that?"

"I promised myself I won't pay for the trip, Mark. Not because of a commitment to you. I won't help Jayne financially when it comes to this decision. There are plenty of places Jayne could go if she just needs to leave you. I just won't be an enabler. Her decision about your marriage has nothing to do with Switzerland. Let's keep the two issues straight. I won't try to convince her to stay in this marriage, but I will encourage her to talk with you. She asked me to stop by to see her this evening. I'll tell her about our conversation."

Paul saw Mark's face relax and wondered how he could be so sure that Jayne wouldn't work out her own solution if she really wanted to go. "I'd better let you get some rest now," he said.

"Thanks, I really appreciate your help."

Mark's smile seemed to contain a strange mixture of gratitude and victory, Paul thought, and criticized himself again for his own cynicism.

The elevator at Jayne and Mark's condo was constructed of glass on three sides. It scaled up the outside of the building to the top floor. Paul looked at his watch and sighed. As it climbed, slowly and steadily above the city, Paul stared out over the clear shimmering lights below to the expanding horizon and realized that Mark had made a good investment when he bought the penthouse condominium. Some Oklahoma oil stock became valuable, and Mark inherited it when his parents died. He sold all the stock and spent most of it for the purchase of the condo. For a young doctor not long in practice, the purchase of the luxurious condominium had seemed like an extravagance. But land values had soared, and inflation had turned self-indulgence into a solid business investment; it had tripled in value in just four years.

If Paul thought it looked more like a pretentious movie set than a home, he never said so.

Tonight, Mark had said they didn't have enough money in the bank for Jayne to pay for a vacation. *They must be living it up with every dollar he made,* Paul thought, and he wondered now what Jayne would do if they got a divorce. She had avoided all preparation for a career, as if not planning for work would mean that she would never have to hold down a job. It would be a challenging time for her—if she really did intend to leave Mark.

The elevator in Jayne's penthouse condo slid open on the top floor and her music flooded the entry. If he hadn't been so exhausted, Paul would have laughed at her choice of songs. "These boots are made for walkin'..." Nancy Sinatra's declaration of power filled the space.

Jayne turned the music off when she saw her dad enter the room.

She was wearing jeans and a tie-dyed shirt. Her hair was pulled back the way she wore it when she was a child.

Jayne wasn't wearing any makeup and looked like a little girl, until Paul was close enough to see the hard lines already forming across her forehead and her mouth. She was making such an effort to look young and vulnerable. Psychiatrist that he was, he couldn't stop noticing the subtle message she was sending. This one was obvious.

Jayne held a wine glass in each hand. Holding one out to him, she said, "Now when did you ever get such service?" Her smile seemed to erase the hardness, and her kiss on his cheek lacked the usual coolness of an obligatory gesture.

"I'm glad you came, Dad. I really need to talk to you."

In the room, dominated by chrome and glass, Paul looked around for a place to sit. He had never managed to find a chair that was comfortable. The sofa seemed the best choice, but it was so low his knees crackled when he sat down. The seat was firm, and Paul was reminded of how much the furniture of the seventies ignored the basic comfort needs of anyone older than thirty. A stiff arrangement of dried flowers sprang from a tall metal vase on the coffee table in front of him. In all the years he had been going there, Paul had never seen a newspaper left out or a magazine not in alignment in the rack. No projects were ever left uncompleted on the floor, no coffee cups half-finished and forgotten on the table. The sterility of it disturbed him. It always had.

"That's a nice wine, Jayne. I like your choice."

"I bought it from your wine merchant. He said you like that one. It's a 1967 Sauvignon Blanc."

And Paul found himself suddenly on guard.

"That's not your typical ask-Dad-by-for-a-chat kind of wine, Jayne. What's up?"

"We're celebrating."

Paul looked at her, trying to hold back his wariness. He felt like Jayne was about to try a little daughterly manipulation. "How about filling me in."

"I've told you many times I wanted to leave Mark, to think things over. Well, I've done all the thinking I need to do. It's finished. I told him I want a divorce."

"Yes, you've told me many times, and you always changed your mind. I'm not here to influence your decision, just to let you know he would like to talk to you himself.

"It's hard to believe he wants to try again. Mark is as disenchanted with our marriage as I am."

"Jayne, I don't feel comfortable being in the middle of this. The decision is yours whether you listen to him or you don't and whether you leave him or not."

"You mean Mark made you the messenger boy? According to him, I'm the one who's always manipulating you."

"It's not a matter of manipulation. He asked me to come to see him, so I did. He looks like hell. He's scared of what they're going to find in the tests, and he's terrified of losing you. I'm just reporting what I see."

"You've been suckered and don't know it."

"What do you mean?"

"I don't know exactly. But I know one thing—Mark didn't change overnight. And he's had plenty of chances in the last few months to let me know if he cared about salvaging this marriage. I don't know what game he's playing, but I know him well enough to know that there's more to it than just what shows on the surface."

Jayne's words underscored some deep conviction within Paul. Something wasn't settling well. But what? "Mark asked two things of me, Jayne. First, to tell you that he wants to make the marriage work. How many times have you left and then came back?

"Is that what you think I'll do?"

"I don't know what you'll do, Jayne. I'm supportive of any decision you make."

"I want out," she said. "You can't make me feel guilty about the timing. I've given him every chance. I've suggested marriage counseling. He wouldn't do it. Well, I don't want him anymore. The final decision came when I talked with him about leaving and realized how much of this power struggle goes on all the time. He wants to control me. And he wants to be sure that you don't make any decisions for me. Which is interesting when you think about it…he hates the thought of you telling me what to do. He always has. He doesn't want me to ask your advice on anything. And now, now when he knows it's all over, you're the one he turns to for help!"

Jayne seemed very much in control. Her temper had changed from the usual hot fire to a cold and calculating demeanor. She went on: "When a relationship's dead, there's no point in holding on. I don't want him or anything from him. I just want out."

"Jayne, how many times do I have to say it: I'm not trying to convince you otherwise. Listen to my words! I've never pretended I thought he was a good husband for you. If you want out, I'll support your decision. But if you decide to leave him, I hope you'll find a way to do it without total warfare. We've been through this before, Jayne."

Jayne crossed over to stand closer to Paul, her arms gesturing emphatically. "Is everything always like that with you? Is it always what's fair to the other guy? Don't you understand? I don't give a shit what happens to him! He can stay in that hospital until he rots for all I care. I'm not here to take care of him; I'm taking care of myself." She folded her arms tightly, locking them into position.

"You seem to know exactly what you want. But I know from experience that if a person feels they have been heard, it will make the process easier for everyone. But that's your call, not mine."

"Yes, I know you don't want to take the blame again if I change my mind later. But if I stay, and if the results prove serious, it would be even harder to leave. Or would you have me stick it out longer because he needed me, or said he did?"

"Jayne, I said how I feel. Do what you think is right. I've had my say."

She whirled away from him, returning to the chair. "You said there were two things Mark wanted from you. What's the second?"

"I told him I wouldn't finance the trip. He seemed to think that would be necessary if you went."

"What about the promises you made to me!" Now the cold anger turned hot again; the rage started. Now the old Jayne took hold and her words spewed from an angry mouth like lava erupting. "You promised me I could go. The money isn't that important to you; it's just an excuse."

"Letting you come with us is one thing; subsidizing your trip is another. I'm not going to have you look back years from now and think I was a party to your decision. You have to make this choice on your own, Jayne." Paul leaned back wearily trying to rest his head on the back of the sofa, but it was too low.

"You never asked me about my relationship with Mark. Today you listen to some shitty argument from him, and now you're on his side."

"I'm not siding with anyone. I'm trying to stay out of it. Can't you hear what I'm saying? My decision has nothing to do with Mark. And I won't be manipulated by your anger."

Frustration pushed her to her feet again. "Just butt out, will you, Dad? Just butt out of all of it." The tone was familiar.

"Jayne, have you forgotten you were the one who asked me to come by?" She was on her old ground again, where the customary reaction to not getting her way was an extension of the tantrums she had as a child. She paced in her anger across the hearth and back again.

"I'm sorry you feel this way about it," Paul said, and he put his half-finished glass of wine on the coffee table and stood up.

Jayne's voice was as hard as her words. "Just go on to Switzerland with Stephanie and have your little vacation. I'm sure you won't waste any time worrying about me. It's the same old story, isn't it? You have responsibilities to everyone else but just can't be bothered with my problems. I don't need your help." She ran into the bedroom and slammed the door so hard a picture twisted on the wall.

Things Paul wanted to say to her were left sticking in his throat. He walked out the door and closed it hard behind him. He pushed the button for the elevator five times before it finally came. Once inside, he shoved his hands into his pockets and stared at the dark wood flooring until the door opened to the lobby. With long and rapid strides, he walked to his car and started for his home in Malibu.

The drive didn't take long. Partly because there wasn't much traffic, partly because he drove faster than usual. Less than twenty minutes away from his conversation with Jayne, he was still angry and chewing on words not spoken. He thought of the ease with which she hurled her accusations and decided he was tired of getting kicked in the ass every time he tried to help. Jayne didn't see his concern as help anyway—only as interference. Even after his explanation, she thought of his refusal to pay as a rejection of her. It had always been that way with Jayne. She refused to see the logic of any position that wasn't sympathetic to her own point of view. It was this lack of fairness—lack of reason—that frustrated him. As well as her obvious attempts at manipulation. He thought about the sweetness that she turned on and off so easily, the careful choosing of the wine, the little girl attitude that was reminiscent of closer days between them. Paul felt his irritation intensifying with his thoughts. He was angry with Jayne for the type of woman she had become, and with Mark for involving him in the middle of their problem. And at himself for allowing it.

Paul pulled into his garage and slammed the car door behind him. His mind was still gnashing on the anger that refused to subside.

Paul was hardly inside the house before he collided with the mass of suitcases and boxes that Stephanie had brought from the storeroom sometime during the day.

"Stephanie! What the hell did you leave these fucking things at the door for? I damned near broke my neck!"

Stephanie leaned over the stair railing, looking first surprised and then amused. "Well, good evening, Dr. Tabor," she said softly. "Why don't you come in and tell me what you really tripped over today?"

CHAPTER 8

SANTA MONICA & MALIBU

"Looks like we can't do the lower GI today, Dr. Favre." The radiologist held Mark's X-ray to the light. "Quite a bit of the barium that you drank yesterday hasn't passed through."

"After what you all put me through, I don't see how anything could be left up there."

"You know it's not unusual to have to wait a day between the upper and the lower GI. I'll order another enema and you can go ahead with the colonoscopy today."

Mark sighed, dreading the procedure. It was degrading. He tried to ignore his reaction and think about how this could work to his advantage. It might mean that the tests couldn't be completed before Monday, so his internist wouldn't be able to make an evaluation before then. Mark went down the timeline of events.

Tomorrow night he would ask Paul to stop by again. By that time Paul might have seen Leah, although Mark was still puzzled, wondering why he wasn't seeing her professionally. What could that possibly mean?

He might have more information about the journal. Paul told Leah to turn it over to the police. If she had done that, then they probably would have read it by now. Since they hadn't come around asking questions, did that mean that Nicole's sister still had the journal? Or that the police had it and he wasn't mentioned?

Even straining for optimism, Mark knew that he must have been mentioned in that journal. Wasn't he the pivotal point in Nicole's life? How could he possibly have been excluded from her journal? His stomach tightened and he pulled his thoughts off the book. He considered Leah's statement that she had seen someone leaving the apartment. Paul might know more about that before he leaves town.

Returning to his room, Mark waited. He spent the time trying to keep his mind off what was happening to his life. More immediately, to his body. He tried to think of something that was going right for him…like the meeting last night with Paul; at least his father-in-law was reacting as he had hoped.

"Good morning, Dr. Favre." The nurse's voice was loud and jovial. He hadn't heard her enter the room, moving silently on her cloud of thick white rubber.

"Hello," Mark answered listlessly.

She was about fifty. A sharp-faced woman with a firm body stuffed into the tight nurse's uniform.

Nora Jackson, her name tag stated. She hung the plastic bag on the IV stand. He turned his head away from her.

"Okay, Doctor, over on your side. Knees up."

"I hope you have a softer touch than that girl last night; she really shafted me with that nozzle." A harsh sound, to ward off his embarrassment.

"Nurses don't come any better than Doris. Honestly, you doctors make the worst patients; you complain about everything!"

Mark heard the door to his room swing open and someone, heels clicking, approached him from behind.

"All right, Mark, what did you do with my passport?" Jayne demanded, ignoring the nurse.

"You'll have to wait outside!" Nurse Jackson said, sounding startled and angry. "Didn't you read the 'DO NOT DISTURB' sign on the door? You can't just barge in here like this!"

"Up yours!" Jayne said and turned her attention toward Mark again. "I just left the bank, and the passports are gone. I want to know where you put them!"

Mark sounded tired, his voice straining for control. "Jayne, who knows? We took them to Tahiti. I haven't seen them since. As you can obviously see, I'm a bit tied up at the moment. Now will you go get a cup of coffee or something and then come back so we can discuss this?"

For the first time, Jayne seemed to realize the indelicacy of her presence. "Sorry," she said, more to the nurse than to Mark, and walked out.

An hour later, when she returned, Mark was reading in bed.

"How are you feeling?" she asked, her anger diminished since her earlier visit.

"Not very well, thanks. How are you?" And he asked the question with a great deal more feeling than usual.

"I'm upset, as you can see. Mark, there's no reason for us to fight like this. You know you can't hold me with these kinds of tactics."

His voice disarmed her. "If I thought those kinds of tactics would hold you, Jayne, I'd use them. But I'm telling you the truth—I didn't have anything to do with those passports. You'll probably find them in the safe at home."

He saw her thinking back to the last time she had the passports; he could watch her face and see her retracing her steps, questioning her memory, then dropping it. For now.

"Why did you drag my father into this?"

"You got him into this, asking him to take you away with him. I know that it seems unfair of me to have talked with him, but I was desperate. I had this terrible feeling that you'd just disappear out of my life, and I'd be stuck here in the hospital not able to do a damned thing about it."

Mark watched her carefully, anxious to know her reaction. Jayne sat in the chair by the bed, her legs crossed, her hands folded across her breasts. He saw the closed body language and knew this wasn't going to be easy. On the other hand, she had sat down without his asking her to. That was a positive sign.

"You're a hard man to figure out. I thought you'd be as glad to get a divorce as I am."

"I can't blame you for thinking that; I've been hard on you lately. I'm really sorry."

"It's not just lately, Mark. I know you've been hurting and that makes anyone act miserably. But even before this attack, things were the same. When was the last time you really cared whether we were together or not? We haven't said an affectionate word to each other for months."

"You're right. I don't know, Jayne, rotten habits reproduce themselves; half of the fights were over nothing at all. But when I thought you were really leaving, well…I guess I realized how much I love you."

The words flowed from him, smooth as poetry on an actor's tongue. He watched her face soften in response to the words she had so rarely heard from him, even in the early days. Her hands dropped to her side, but she said nothing.

"I really need you, baby," he whispered. "I'm going to make it all up to you—I promise."

Jayne looked suspicious and was trying to read his thoughts. Then the words: slowly, cautiously she said, "All right, Mark. One more chance."

Mark smiled at the victory. But something was dragging down his elation. Something so elusive he couldn't put his finger on it. In spite of her words, Mark knew that Jayne was feeling something that was making him strangely uncomfortable.

All day he was restless, tossing ideas back and forth, weighing everything that could go wrong. Making Plan A, then B. Then C.

CHAPTER 9

SANTA MONICA

The shot that Mark was given on Friday morning contained ten milligrams of Valium and one hundred milligrams of Demerol. Drowsiness followed and then a feeling of being out of touch with reality. Vaguely Mark knew he was being moved from the bed in his room onto the gurney and then rolled down a hall to a room where other voices spoke about him with words he couldn't remember, saying things that disturbed him, but he didn't know why. And someone laughed. He was lifted off the gurney and he heard a voice say, "Careful how you move him; watch out there, you'll break his neck!" He saw Nicole's neck, broken in his hand…he could feel strong hands moving him onto the table…his own hands grew large in his mind…he had the sensation of falling, of being thrown from the window…he saw Nicole falling down the stairs…he cried out and voices reassured him, telling him where he was and he almost remembered, but not quite…his head was tilted back, they opened his mouth wide enough to allow the gastroscope to be pushed down his throat… he heard her words pounding in his head and he hated her with a passion that overwhelmed him…the flexible plastic tube moved down his throat, continuing down his esophagus into his stomach and there was pain…he moved toward her, forcing her to step backward, pushing her off balance, watching her fall…

he screamed, but the tube in his throat gagged and silenced him and voices tried to console him…her body crumpled at the foot of the stairs…he heard voices and words that he no longer understood: chronic ulcerated condition—biopsy—words that had no meaning, something was hurting his stomach but he couldn't cry out, the tube was at last removed from his throat. Hands touched his body, moving him again, and in time the drugs began to wear off.

Desperately he wanted it all to be a dream; he knew better.

Hours later in his room, alternately sleeping and waking, dreaming and worrying, Mark could not stop thinking about Nicole or the feeling of his hands pushing against her. There was no doubt that at that moment he had hated her and wanted her dead. He couldn't have let her destroy him. How did he get into this! Why didn't he make the break with Nicole long ago? If only he had. He wept. And, in his despair, realized that he couldn't keep running forever. Not from this—not from all that went wrong in Switzerland. Eventually someone would find out.

They wouldn't listen to him. Wouldn't even try to understand how he felt. He could smell the tight, dark room in his childhood. Feel the isolation. And he knew that no one was ever coming to let him out.

No matter what he had to do, Mark couldn't let that happen. He sat straight up in the bed; his heart was pounding. And the thought settled in and took form and became a plan. *The story wasn't told yet*, Mark thought. *Not by a long shot.*

Suddenly a line he vaguely remembered from a literature class in college came to him as a warning: "This only is denied the gods: the power to undo the past."

Later, he remembered how he revised the thought: *mere mortals, on the other hand, can sometimes create illusions that reframe how the past is perceived.*

"You're a stubborn man, Mark Favre." The voice of the surgeon was friendly on Saturday morning, but it was edging toward exasperation. He stood at the foot of Mark's bed, his wiry grey hair puffing over and around his ears. His expression was perceptive and, at the moment, somewhat chastising.

"Now let's not be difficult, Bill," Mark said laughing. "It's my stomach and I don't want surgery."

The expression on the older man softened. "Mark, I know you're apprehensive. Surgery is the last thing I'd recommend to you if I thought we could control the problem with medication and diet. You've tried that. For years. Now, do you want to spend the rest of your life dealing with the pain and letting it get worse?"

"You didn't find anything in the tests that we didn't know when I came in."

"That's not exactly true; we knew you had the ulcer, but I had no idea it was as seriously developed as it is. I'm certainly not quick to recommend surgery for ulcers, Mark. But look at the facts: You have intractable pain and a pyloric duodenal obstruction due to the scarring from the ulcer. I suspect you have a perforation and the black tarry stools are an indication that it's bleeding."

"What about the biopsy?"

"We did a frozen section immediately after the gastroscopy. It's a good screening process for malignancy but it'll be two or three days before the full report comes in."

"But nothing has shown up so far?"

"I'd have told you if it had. There's no indication of cancer. And you know this type of thing is usually benign. But what are you going to do? Wait until peritonitis sets in or you get a massive hemorrhage or a complete obstruction? It ought to be treated surgically, Mark."

"It's not the surgery that concerns me so much; it's that I had to leave the office without giving any warning to my patients. I don't want to be gone any longer than is absolutely necessary."

"Mark, you know the statistics…the average doctor dies ten years sooner than the rest of the population. It's just your kind of thinking that makes that true. You're not omnipotent—you're sick and need help. And your patients will get along fine for a little while longer without you. Plenty of doctors would be glad to cover for you."

"Tell you what, I'll check out on Monday. That should give you time to get the results you're so hot about. Okay? If I'm not feeling better in two weeks, I'll notify my patients and we'll set a time for the surgery."

"Okay, Buddy, I've had my say. It's your life. But you'll be checking out of here against my advice. I'll put that on the chart. You should have that surgery."

He waved an exasperated gesture and started for the door.

"I'll call you for tennis within a week," Mark hollered to the back of his coat.

The last thing Mark wanted now was more days in the hospital. These few days had served his purpose quite well, he thought. Since Jayne didn't have her passport, she wasn't going to Switzerland; that was one less thing he had to worry about.

"Mark?" The voice came from the door, accompanying the knock.

"Come on in, Paul. I really appreciate your coming back this morning. I had a hard time last night or I wouldn't have called you."

"How are you feeling now?"

"Other than a raw throat and a burned ass, I'm better. Sorry I bothered you."

"It's not a bother."

"But I do feel a bit disoriented. Probably from the meds."

Paul said, "I can see that you're not quite yourself. I saw Bill down the hall; he was getting into the elevator while I was coming out. Looked like he was in a hurry. What did he say about the tests?"

Mark's voice dropped and his face clouded. "My surgeon and I had a chat and, of course, he thinks I should have the operation. I told them I'd think it over."

"He's a good man. He wouldn't rush you into surgery, you know."

"Maybe. Pull that chair up and have a seat," Mark said, changing the subject. "How are plans coming along for the conference?"

The chair made a screeching noise as it scraped across the floor. "There's not much more I can do from here. Good people on the other end make my job easier."

"Well, I hope it goes just the way you want it to."

"Any messages for some of your old professors?

"You mentioned that before. No, I never was particularly close to the teaching staff. I don't know, something about faculty turns me off. They probably wouldn't remember me anyway; I was a shy kid in those days."

Paul laughed. "You, shy? And what do you mean by 'in those days.' You haven't been out that long, you know."

"I guess you're right. It feels like a long time. I just never seemed to fit in too well, over there. Always a foreigner, you know. I stayed pretty much to myself. Never got into personal relationships with any of the other students. Well, with anyone at all, for that matter." Mark's expression closed that conversation. "By the way, Paul, I appreciate your talking with Jayne. You must have leaned on her pretty hard."

"Not at all. Jayne makes her own decisions. As you well know." They both smiled. "Now I'm the one she's not talking to!"

"Want me to put in a good word?" Mark asked.

"No, she'll come around. In her own time."

Mark wanted to cut through all the banter and get to the point. But he took it slow, gentling into the words he wanted to say. "Hey, I meant to ask you before, but I forgot…how's that girl you started seeing? The one whose sister was murdered?"

"Leah? Oh, I told you. She's not my patient. She's just a friend."

"Okay, if you say so. Are you worried about her now? She must be feeling pretty upset if you're the only person she knows in this country and now you're leaving her."

"Of course, I'm concerned about her. She's had a terrible loss."

"What about the man she saw leaving her sister's place? She have any more recollections about that? The police must be pretty anxious to get that out of her."

Mark watched Paul's face carefully. Was it nothing more than just this fluke of memory? Or could Paul be covering up? He wasn't a devious man. Mark didn't think Paul could have any suspicions and play it this cool. Relaxing now, relieved of his major fear, Mark took a deep breath. His sigh was heavy with relief. He saw Paul watching him and tensed. Had he shown too much? Would Paul catch the association?

"The police have any suspects?" Mark asked.

"Not that I know of."

"Nothing in that journal you mentioned gave them any leads? You'd think something would come out of that; journals are pretty personal."

"Yes, some of them are," Paul said.

"Well, if she has the journal, you can probably talk her into giving it to them. I have great confidence in your persuasive abilities, after what you did with Jayne."

"I didn't do as much as you think."

Now that the subjects of their mutual interest were discussed, words came slower, and Mark allowed his fatigue to show. "I'll check out Monday morning. The test results should be in by then. I'm going to need a few more of their hefty pain shots before I leave. A few test results are still not in, but since I decided against the surgery, there's no reason to wait around here." And then, Mark offered the less-than-subtle invitation to leave. "I really appreciate you coming to see me, Paul."

And he did. Now Mark knew exactly what he had to do.

CHAPTER 10

WEST LOS ANGELES

Saturday and Sunday were both hard days for Leah. She spent hours trying to understand more of Nicole's journal. It was a composite of poetry, prose, sketches, and intricate geometric designs that reminded Leah of a highly sophisticated form of doodling.

The emotional content of the book was explicit. Nicole's bitterness was uncensored in the poetry; earlier writings of her relationship with the man she loved were expressive in terms of her feelings, but strangely lacking in the usual use of names, places, and events. Nicole had logged only her emotions; the omission of obvious names gave them even greater significance. Except for Paul Tabor and Leah, all names were excluded. Why? The question rankled Leah and she, who hated mysteries, was even more outraged at the possibility that this one would never be solved.

It was a strange book, filled with innuendos and the suggestion of some secret too ominous to detail on paper. *What was it that haunted Nicole?* Leah wondered. What could she possibly have done that was too terrible to mention, even in the safety of her private journal? Apparently, it was the memory of something Nicole did in Switzerland that depressed her.

References to it throughout the journal indicated how deeply she was troubled by this incident from her past.

Leah's mind searched back through the years, trying to find some memory of a time when Nicole seemed troubled. It was a futile effort.

The image of the Nicole that Leah once knew was crushed under the weight of the journal. Where was the strong confident Nicole? Where was the sister who was so warm and loving? Left in her shadow was a bitter woman, resentful of her responsibilities, pregnant, abandoned, guilty of some shameful deed, rejecting, and depressed. Leah stared at one of the sketches: a lonely girl staring out a small window at the rain. The face bore a vague resemblance to Nicole, except the expression was one Leah didn't associate with her sister. But she realized that it was an expression that belonged to this other Nicole—the secretive, mysterious Nicole, who lived only in the pages of her journal. Across the page from the girl were smaller sketches—parts of a swing set, a child, a flower, some numbers.

Leah saw the numbers clearly now; she had missed them before. It was strange the way they were drawn as part of the design. Nicole had taken the numbers and formed them into a border pattern. She used to do that with Leah's name when she was a child and it had always delighted Leah to find her name half-hidden in a larger pattern. Once, when she was still in high school, Nicole had done that with needlepoint and given it to Leah for Christmas. Her name had become part of the floral pattern repeated again and again in the design, hardly noticeable unless one looked at it carefully.

That's how these numbers were formed—a half-hidden secret in a border of flowers and vines. It occurred to Leah that it could be a phone number. It was too late to call then. She had to wait until Monday morning before she could try it.

At precisely 9:00 on Monday morning, Leah picked up the telephone and dialed the numbers she found in Nicole's journal. She was suddenly aware of how cold her hands were in the warm room and how loud her heart was beating in the silence. She slowly dialed the numbers, wondering if her hunch was right, wondering who would answer and what she should say.

"Doctors' exchange," the voice said. "Hello…hello…" It hadn't occurred to Leah that the number could belong to more than one person. She wondered how many doctors used that number and who they were. And which of them knew Nicole.

She thought quickly, trying to make her voice sound calm and businesslike. "I'm sorry, I'm having trouble reading the name of a doctor I was asked to call. Can you tell me, is there a Doctor Franklin or Frenlin…? I can't make out the writing."

"No, you've reached the offices of Doctors Green, Favre, and Barton."

"Sorry. I must have the wrong number."

Leah considered the information she had just discovered. They were all doctors. One of them so important to Nicole that she used his phone number as part of that carefully designed border. Leah thought back, considering the other times that Nicole had treated words that way: the name of her first boyfriend, the name of her medical school, what else? Leah couldn't remember. Nicole had always been private about her journal.

Studying the twisting and turning of the pattern, Leah was fascinated by the meticulous, detailed work. Nicole had only been playing with the numbers, but they might lead Leah to some information about her sister. She had to find out which one of the doctors knew Nicole. She wondered where their offices were, and she wished she had asked the exchange but didn't want to call again.

Taking the West Los Angeles telephone directory from the table by her bed, she looked up the name of the first doctor. Green. It was a common name, apparently, for the list was long; she went on to the next name, Mark T. Favre, MD. Checking the number in the telephone directory against the number in the journal, Leah saw that they were the same. She wrote the address down on a piece of paper and began making plans. Green. Favre. Barton. The names decorated the scratch pad beside Leah's bed. Using various forms of calligraphy, she had played with each name as she formed the letters. Stalling. Working up her nerve. "I'm sorry," the secretary said, "Dr. Green is on sabbatical at Harvard this year."

The field narrowed. "Then could I make an appointment to see Dr. Favre?"

"I don't expect him back until later next week. I can set up an appointment for you after that."

"No. I need to talk with someone right away. Is Dr. Barton available?"

The voice hesitated. Leah felt embarrassed; who chooses a doctor by just going down a list?

"Dr. Barton is with a patient now; do you want to set up an appointment to see her?"

"Thank you, yes." No sooner done than regretted. "No, I'll have to call back. I'm sorry." It would have been better just to go to the office and talk with the secretary. Leah was too restless now to sit and wait for a call that might not come for hours. Why should she wait? she asked herself. She could go to the office and probably be there when Dr. Barton finished her session. Leah had located the building on her map of the city; it wasn't far.

Walking rapidly in the warm September morning, Leah wondered about Dr. Barton; was she Nicole's friend? Her doctor? Nicole took hours forming that pattern. For a friend? Doubtful. It had to be a man connected with that number; she felt sure of it. This visit with Dr. Barton would lead her no place. Still, she walked on.

Inside the Westwood office building, written on the door, were the names:

DR. ALVIN R. GREEN, PHD, CLINICAL PSYCHOLOGIST
MARK T. FAVRE, MD, PSYCHIATRIST
ELAINE SCOTT BARTON, MD, PSYCHIATRIST

The names, in large brass letters, identified the offices. So Nicole was seeing a psychiatrist. Leah's mind grabbed at the fact and then dropped it. Nothing seemed to follow the obvious anymore.

No one was in the waiting room. The clock announced the time in digits—12:32. A string of neutral-colored chairs lined the walls. There were photographs of a calm sea, a spray of cumulous clouds, a cluster of flowers, and finally, an abundance of trees. Leah sat in the reception room, waiting for Dr. Barton to come out. It was almost one o'clock and still there had been no sounds or signs of people. Leah thought maybe the patient had left through a back door and the doctor wouldn't even come to the waiting room.

A man entered and crossed the room to a locked door. Leah watched him as he fumbled for his key. He was not a tall man, his posture slightly bent. His movements sharp. He looked tense. The name on the office door was Mark T. Favre MD, in small brass letters.

"Pardon me," Leah said.

His dark brown eyes were impersonal, observing her.

"Are you Dr. Favre?"

"That's right."

"My name is Leah Vassaux." The words hit him like a fist. He paled and she felt her own body responding anxiously. Confusion rocked her. He knew Nicole, all right. But in what capacity?

"You were a friend of my sister." She would play it without the questions. There was no doubt in her mind at all; she wasn't going to give him a chance to deny it. She had had quite enough of people saying they didn't know Nicole.

"Leah, come in, please," he said tentatively.

She saw his hand tremble slightly when he fit the key into the lock.

His office was spacious, furnished simply, with functional things. A low table and chairs, the kind made for children, were in one corner. Motioning for her to take the chair opposite his desk, he sat in the huge executive chair that dominated the room.

"You knew my sister," Leah stated again, intentionally repeating the past tense. "You were a friend…"

"…Yes."

Leah could feel the beating of her heart. Her mouth was dry. How would he have known that she died?

She watched his face drain of color; his eyes looked troubled. She hoped that he would say something, but instead, he left it to her to continue. Leah realized that even after all her thinking, she hadn't prepared herself for this moment.

One thing had worked quite well for her; she had spoken as if she knew for a fact that he and Nicole were friends and he had not denied it. If she had put that as a question, she wondered what he would have said. The silence weighed heavily between them; this was awkward for him, too, she could tell. If only he would say something…anything…to give her something to go on.

"I was terribly sorry to hear what happened to Nicole. She was a fine woman," Mark said.

"How did you know she died?" She watched closely and he didn't even flinch.

"Westwood is a small university community in the middle of Los Angeles. A friend heard it from someone who lived in the building and apparently thought I would want to know. Then I saw the story in the Times."

Leah covered her temples with her hands, letting her fingers hide her eyes, lowering her head, as if it was grief overtaking her again. She hadn't thought to look in the paper.

"This must be very painful for you, Leah," he said, interpreting her gesture.

Psychiatrist line, she thought. "We were very close," Leah said, trying to keep the conversation going, thinking her statement revealed nothing. She was wrong.

"I know you were. Nicole spoke of you often."

"Nicole talked to you, about me?" She was holding her breath.

"Quite often. You were very important to her."

Leah's mind raced with questions; logic told her to be careful, to let him think she knew more than she did.

But the question that demanded asking wouldn't be silenced by logic. "Why did she talk to you about me?"

"You seem surprised. Don't you think it's natural for Nicole to tell her psychiatrist about her only sister?"

"I didn't know you were her psychiatrist. I didn't know Nicole was in therapy!"

His eyebrows arched. "I see. You mean she mentioned me in some other context?"

How had she lost control of this? Leah wondered. Now he was in charge.

"My sister had a journal. I haven't read all of it," she lied. "But from what I did find there, you were very important to her. I just didn't know that she was seeing you professionally."

"I can see how shaken you are. Nicole's death must have been a dreadful shock to you. She was a gentle person; what happened to her was monstrous.

"Yes. I did take the news quite hard. I was in the hospital at the time," he lied. "As a matter of fact, I just checked out of St. John's a few hours ago."

"Oh, I'm sorry,"

"Don't be," he said. "Actually, two weeks in the hospital wasn't even long enough," Mark said, before he regretted the words. Then reconsidered. This was a lie that could work to his advantage.

Two weeks? Leah thought. If so, he would have been hospitalized when Nicole was killed. Some of the tension eased. Maybe she really had found someone who could help her understand more about Nicole; perhaps he even knew the name of the man she had loved. "Have you talked to the police?" she asked.

"The police? I don't think that would be very wise, under the circumstances."

"I don't understand."

"In the first place, there's nothing I can tell them that will help them solve her case. And…well…I know things about Nicole that she wouldn't have wanted anyone to know. As her psychiatrist, I have the legal right not to reveal any information about a patient without a court order." He hesitated, preparing the words carefully. "But if I tell them I was her therapist, they could demand to see my records. Even if I refuse, they could get a court order.

"I'd hate to see that happen. Privacy was important to her. I know Nicole wouldn't have wanted that. She would have hated that everyone knew the situation she was in," Mark said.

"He might have married her."

"She didn't seem to think he would."

"You must know something about him that could help the police; they should question him at least…"

"Leah, if I knew the name of the man, don't you think I would have volunteered that information?" His face seemed open; she looked into his dark eyes. "Nicole never told me his name."

"Why? Why wouldn't she tell you? If she trusted you and you were her psychiatrist, why wouldn't she have told you his name? How could she have talked with you about him without calling him…something? It doesn't make any sense!"

"It doesn't make sense to you because you don't know all the facts. It makes a great deal of sense to me, knowing Nicole as well as I did. If I chose to tell you the reasons, Leah, I'm sure you'd understand. But frankly, I'm in a dilemma…you see, I cared about Nicole; I respect the trust she placed in me. Now do you really think it would be fair to her if I didn't honor that confidence?"

Leah watched him carefully. His dark eyes were hard to read, but his concern came through in his words, in his attitude. He walked around the desk and sat next to her in a chair similar to her own. His voice was comforting, no longer impersonal as it had been at first. If Nicole trusted him, then Leah decided that she would trust him also. She would ask the question that she was aching to have answered.

"Dr. Favre, will you tell me what Nicole said about me? It's very important."

"You're asking me to break her confidence."

Leah's own strength had returned to her. And her new assertiveness. She drew upon it when she said, "Life is for the living. I need to know. There are questions that will haunt me the rest of my life if they're not answered. I think I have the right to ask."

"I think Nicole would have wanted me to tell you that she loved you very much, that she cared more about you than any person in the world. She worried about you a great deal; it wasn't easy for her to leave you when she came here from Switzerland."

"I know she worried about me; she made that clear enough in her journal. But the way she wrote about me, it seemed that I was just a burden that she resented."

"She wrote that in her journal? What did she say exactly?"

Involuntarily Leah's fingers went toward her purse. Aware that his eyes had followed her hand to the soft leather bag, she reached inside for tissue—not yet ready to show the journal that lay there. Dabbing her eyes, she said, "There's not much more than what I told you; she thought of me as always being a burden. She resented my coming—my complicating her life." Leah heard the bitterness in her own voice.

"When was it that she wrote that, Leah? Can you remember the date?"

"It was September 5th. The day she died."

"I'll always regret that I wasn't able to help her those last days. But…" He went to his desk and unlocked a drawer, withdrawing an empty file. He pretended to find the page. "Let me read you my notes after our last meeting: 'Her anxiety about her sister possibly moving here. Arrival is related to her fears about the baby. Obsessively concerned with care for both of them. Leah, the child she had always mothered—now this child, her new charge. Wants them both, feels inadequate, rejects the responsibility. Feels she will be unable to effectively help either Leah or the baby." His voice trailed off as he looked at her from behind the manila file. Leah felt the tears spill and wiped them away quickly, regaining control.

"Leah, ambivalent feelings are part of life." His voice was soft, consoling. "It was because Nicole loved you so deeply that she could feel that intensity about her inability to give you the kind of life she wanted for you. She was planning to keep the baby. I'm sure you understand the shame she would have felt when she had to tell you about the pregnancy. About the home that she was offering you being that of an unwed mother. In our society, that wouldn't have presented a stigma for you. But in her mind, it would. She thought she had failed you terribly—and she hated herself for doing that. And resented you—for the moment—for the fact that your possible arrival confronted her not only with her guilt but with her inadequacy."

Leah let the words console her. Hope commingling with doubt. She wanted to believe it; she would make herself believe it. She would try to accept the ambivalence that both psychiatrists stated so matter-of-factly.

"You're sure she didn't tell you anything about this man that could help the police locate him?" Leah asked, moving the subject away from herself.

"No. There's nothing in my files that could have helped them at all. But I can tell you this—and I'm just emphasizing what I said before—if the police find out that I was her therapist, they won't let those records alone. And I know you're as concerned about that as I am. Now let me ask you this: do you think there's any other way they could find out that she was my patient?"

"They've already finished searching her apartment. I'm going there after I leave here and try to get some things in order. But

I'm sure there's nothing there that they haven't already seen. Wouldn't they have called you by now if your name was in her papers?"

"I think so. Apparently then, the journal is the only thing that could lead them to her files."

"That's right. I'm glad I didn't give it to the detective. I almost did."

"You almost gave her journal to the police? Knowing how much she treasured her privacy?"

"Finding her killer seemed more important than protecting her privacy. But I couldn't do it anyway. I decided to read it first and then determine if it would be helpful. If I'd found anything important, I would have given it to them. Anyway, I think I'm the only one who can decipher the journal. There are still things about it that I don't understand, and I knew her better than anyone."

"Leah, no one knows a woman as well as her psychiatrist; would you like for me to help you with the journal? Where is it now?"

"Yes, I will share it with you if you tell me what you find. Even if it's breaking her confidence. She is dead, you know."

"Well, you've got me there. I can't promise. I won't interpret anything in the journal for you if I think that doing so would be against Nicole's wishes. She's entitled to that from me. But if I know something that can help and revealing it doesn't betray exceedingly personal material—yes. Yes. I'll tell you the best I can."

What terrible thing could have happened to Nicole? Dr. Favre was so withholding. She resented it but she had to respect him because he kept his promise of confidentiality to her. He was ethical without being ruled by the letter of his law. "I appreciate that," she said. She could see the weariness and knew that his time in the hospital had taken its toll. He looked worried, perhaps even in pain.

"If I bring the journal here, will you go over it with me?" Leah asked.

"Yes, I just offered. Or we can go get it together now. I don't have anything scheduled for the rest of the day."

Leah was touched by his concern. Here he was, offering to take time for her today, when obviously he should be home in bed. What difference did a few days make? She wouldn't be that selfish. Then she realized it wasn't Dr. Favre she was protecting, it was herself. Much as she wanted to know what was inside the journal, she dreaded turning page after page, trying not to cry in front of a stranger. Discovering things she might not want to know. She imagined exposing Nicole's most personal thoughts, maybe some she never even shared with her doctor. Leah wasn't ready to face what might be there. Not today. Not tomorrow. "I appreciate that. But can we meet on Wednesday?"

"Aren't you curious to know what's in that journal? I am. How about we do it tomorrow. Let's say in the morning about ten. That's the best time for me."

"It's just that…" Her eyes filled with tears.

"I understand it is hard for you. But you'll feel better when you face whatever you may find there."

"Oh. Well, then. Okay." Then she said, "No, I just can't! Not yet."

Mark saw her look toward the door and knew she was about to leave.

"I understand," Mark said. "When would be the best time for you?"

She took her time. "I can do it on Wednesday. I'm sure I can by then. I really do need to know what's in that journal."

"Let's meet on Wednesday morning, then. We can go through this together. If that's okay with you?"

Leah nodded, holding back tears.

"We'll do this on your time frame. You'll be the one to decide what time we meet and how long we take. I suggest we meet at The Garden Room; it's a quiet restaurant about a block from here. We can have an early lunch. How about eleven. Is that okay with you? Unless there's another place you'd rather go."

"No, that's fine. I'm glad you understand. I'm staying at the Camille Hotel, if you need to reach me." She stood up to leave and said, "I can't tell you how much it means to me to find someone who knew Nicole. There was another psychiatrist named in her journal also. But he said he never knew her."

"Really? Who was that? Do the police know about that?"

"Yes. His name was Paul Tabor. It was on a piece of paper and I gave them that." She started to say more but hesitated. *No need*, she thought.

"Well, for Nicole's sake, I hope he wasn't someone she ever confided in. But don't worry about that; I'm sure she would have mentioned it if she'd seen anyone before coming to me. Now, Leah, do be careful about telling anyone that she was my patient. That's very personal information and I know you want to respect her right to privacy, even now. And one more thing. I don't have a good relationship with Dr. Tabor, so I'm asking you not to mention my name when you meet with him. He might be less accessible to you if he knew we have talked."

"Yes, of course. There's no reason I should mention you. Thank you, Dr. Favre. I'll see you at The Garden Room Wednesday morning, about eleven." As she walked toward the door, she noticed the picture over the sofa. It was a primitive, hundreds of tiny animals crowded into a large canvas. Wild animals mostly, in extraordinary detail. Diminutive but perfect.

"You must love animals," she said.

"Oh, I do," he said. But his smile was forced.

In the lobby downstairs, Leah went straight to the telephone booth. Her instinct told her that Dr. Favre was a man to be trusted, but logic advised her to be careful. What hospital did he say? St. John's. The operator found the number in Santa Monica. "Mark Favre, please," she said to the nasal voice that answered.

"Is he a patient?" the operator asked.

"Yes. He's going to check out today, I need to get a message to him before he goes."

"One moment…I'm sorry, Dr. Favre has already checked out."

So. He was telling the truth. Now feeling slightly guilty for her doubts, she also felt rather foolish for not trusting him. But under the circumstances, she was only being responsible by being wary of everyone. After all, whoever killed Nicole was someone she had trusted. Trust was for children. And victims.

When Mark entered his condo, he saw a note on the coffee table. "Hi, Mark, I decided to take a week at the spa. That will give both of us a chance to relax. I hope you're feeling better." Jayne closed it with a heart sign. Maybe she did go to the spa and maybe she didn't. He didn't care where she went, so long as it wasn't Switzerland.

Mark took some painkillers and, knowing better, but not caring, he fixed a stiff drink and tried, without success, to stop thinking about Leah. He was restless all Monday night, and all day on Tuesday. He was concerned that Leah might change her mind. He couldn't risk losing control of that book, but he couldn't risk pushing Leah too fast either.

Trust what you know, he told himself. You saw her face; you watched the changes. Don't lose sight of what you know; don't let the fear control you.

Hadn't she said she would show him the journal? And hadn't he heard in her voice the need to be reassured that Nicole loved her? He had said the words he knew she wanted to hear. How old was she anyway? Early twenties, maybe. He was giving her too much credit.

The girl was more delicate than Nicole. She was like a young doe, with those extraordinary eyes. Just a kid. It would be easy to get that journal. But why did she have to put him off? He wished she would come back today, let him get his hands on it. Once he had it, he could convince her to let him study it alone. How could he have let her put it off? It would have been so easy to convince her to come back today. He could have pushed for it.

If she was so easy to convince, then perhaps someone else could convince her of things too. She said she had appointments today. Who did she have those appointments with? Maybe that was an excuse to stall. Might have been.

Would she keep quiet about the journal? If one of the meetings was with the detective, she might have this on her mind so much that she would let it slip. Like a child, told not to say something, tries so hard that the words come out unwittingly. Mark couldn't risk it. He had to get his hands on that journal.

CHAPTER 11

WEST LOS ANGELES

Tuesday was a miserable day for Mark. It was the waiting, then wondering, the fearing, and the planning that kept circling around and around. It felt like there wasn't enough air to breathe and there was nothing to think about that didn't stir his physical pain and the emotional panic.

He wondered why Leah didn't want to see him today. Why wait? What could she be doing that kept her from him? He stayed in bed most of the day, staring at the television, not watching anything. Anxiety fed on itself, pulling him deeper into despair. He stared at the clock, as if watching it could push the numbers higher. It was 2:00, then 3:00, then 4:00. His imagination created chaos in his thoughts.

Leah spent her entire day on Tuesday with the journal, seeing into Nicole's thoughts and letting the drawings stimulate her own memories going back in time, one memory stirring another. She spent the day reliving what nourished her, turning the pages when the memories were too painful to bear.

When Leah arrived for her meeting with Mark on Wednesday morning, he was already sitting in a booth, pensive, as he seemed to be reading tea leaves in a large mug. He looked at his watch. It was almost 11:00 a.m. Then he saw Leah come into the room, right on time. He made sure his manner was friendly and relaxed. He didn't rush through all the conventional conversation. Did she sleep well? Was her hotel comfortable? Not in any rush at all. Finally, he handed her the menu. "Eggs Benedict are especially good here, if that appeals to you."

"Oh, yes. That will be fine." He called the waiter, placed the order, and tried to sound casual in the process.

"Did you bring the journal?" he asked.

"Yes."

"Unresolved questions must make this time all the more difficult for you. I hope I can help you sort out some of the answers," Mark said.

Watching her hesitate as she reached for the journal, Mark knew she was still ambivalent. Even so, she brought the book from her leather bag and gave it to him.

Mark knew how to control his own nonverbal communication. Slowly he took the book from her, denying his excitement by the way he touched it. Casually he leafed through the pages, forcing his voice to remain calm. "There's so much here. Somehow, I didn't expect it to be so detailed." Every page was crowded with words or pictures or designs. She had left no margins, using all the space from top to bottom, from side to side. As if to cram her life into the confines of a book too small for the purpose. Without using a single name, her journal reflected a lifetime of abandonment and grief. It was a collection of wounds that never healed.

"Where is the part that bothers you?" he asked.

"There are several parts really. I have such a different picture of Nicole from this book. She doesn't seem to have been the capable, self-sufficient person I thought she was.

"And look, starting on this page. There are all those references to something that she did in Switzerland. Something that she thought was wrong. She seemed to feel so guilty. I can't imagine what Nicole could have been involved in."

Mark read through the pages, anxious to know how much Nicole had revealed. Terrified that he would read about that night before she died, when they argued, when she threatened him. "I'd like to spend some time with this, Leah." Was there a tremor in his voice? A slight hint of personal interest? *Careful,* he thought. "There's so much here, and before we discuss it, I'd like to read it through." As he spoke, he was looking at the pages of small, meticulous handwriting. "It might even help if I compare some of this with my notes of her therapy sessions. Putting them together, I think we can satisfy your need to understand this."

"I don't feel good about giving it up, Dr. Favre."

A crumbling sensation, hidden quickly. "It's up to you," he said. "Please, call me Mark. I'm just trying to be helpful. It's going to take some time to go through all of this. But if you'd rather, I'll just look at it now; that's okay with me."

"Do you really think your notes will make that much difference?" Leah asked.

"I don't know. Maybe not. On the other hand, if I can compare what she wrote in her journal with what she told me on the same day, you can see that we might get some additional insights."

"How long would you want to keep the journal?"

"It shouldn't take long. I could go to the office after I drop you off this afternoon and take her file home with me. Then tomorrow I could go over them. We could get together after that and I might be able to help you understand some of the things she was feeling."

"All right then," Leah said reluctantly.

Tension drained from him. He had won, after all. "Why don't we go for a drive so you can get your bearings in your new city. Then I'll drop you off at your hotel."

"I'd like that. Here, since this is too big for your pocket, I'll keep it." She reached for his hand, putting determined fingers securely around the journal.

"Thanks," he said, as if he meant it. "Don't let me forget to take it with me when I take you home." Mark couldn't wait for lunch to be over and the bill to be paid. Then to stop making small talk that meant nothing to either of them.

Mark showed her around Westwood, pointing out the best restaurants, the movie theater, the stationers. He was exhausted and his stomach was killing him.

"Mark, I can see that you don't feel well. I have another plan. Why don't you take me back to my hotel now and we can get together tomorrow? If you get your notes from the office, we can meet at the hotel coffee shop and go over this together. I know it doesn't make sense, but I still feel uncomfortable letting that journal out of my sight. I know that sounds stupid…"

Manipulating bitch! he thought. *She never intended to give me the book! Keep the voice relaxed, objective,* he told himself. "It doesn't matter to me either way, Leah. But I don't understand your hesitation. What is it that you're afraid of?"

"I don't know. It's just a feeling I have about this book; I have a sense of loss when I even think about giving it up. I just don't want to do that."

"Then you shouldn't. Do you want me to forget it then? Or do you want us to go over it together? It's your choice."

"I do want to go over it with you. I just don't want to turn loose of it. Not even for a day or two. It feels like it's a part of Nicole."

"Okay. I'll tell you what. I'll get her file from the office and we can work on it this afternoon or…after dinner, if that's better for you. There's no rush."

"Could we do it another time?" Leah asked. "I'm just so tired. All that tension and the lack of sleep has really caught up with me. Once we start in on the journal, I know it's going to be a long, involved session."

What was her real reason, he wondered? "Okay," he said. "I won't be going back to work for a few days. We can spend all day together if that's better for you."

"That's good. I just feel so…drained. Maybe tomorrow I'll feel better," she said.

Frustration permeated every part of Mark's body. His stomach burned. His hands sweated against the wheel. How had he let her get control of that book again?

Was she suspicious now? *Was that the real reason she wouldn't give up the book?* He thought not. Her reason sounded valid. But he couldn't be sure what she might do with that journal.

Leah suddenly remembered to look at her watch. Half-an-hour ago, she was supposed to meet Paul Tabor.

"Oh, Mark, I completely forgot! I'm so sorry! Would you drive me to Sam's Café? I'm late for meeting a friend and completely forgot the time."

Mark was thrown by the word "friend." "You have a friend? I thought you didn't know anyone here!"

"Well, I don't." She hesitated. "Except for Paul Tabor. I know you don't like him, but he's been very good to me."

"Leah, be careful. I have my reasons to tell you Paul Tabor is not a good man. Do not mention my name. It will be in your best interest to just let our conversations stay between us." She put her face in her hands. Tears raced down her cheeks and she brushed them away. Wasn't there anyone she could trust?

"Leah…"

"I'm sorry, Mark, I can't do this! It's just too soon for me to go through her journal. I feel raw. Everything is torn away. I'm so sorry, I really am. Just give me time. Please… I'll call you when I'm ready." Leah got out of the car and ran toward Sam's Café.

She knew Dr. Tabor wouldn't be there, he wouldn't be waiting. Why would he be? She had been so rude at their last meeting.

Sam was standing near the door of the café, as if he expected her.

"Is he still here?" she asked.

"Sorry, young lady, but he did leave a note for you."

Leah took it with trembling hands. "Leah, I hope you're okay. Please call me when you get this message."

She slipped into the closest chair and both her hands covered her eyes.

"Take your time," Sam said, "I'll get you a cup of coffee on the house. And just in case you're wondering, he didn't look angry when he left. Just concerned. Here. Have a cookie. The wife just baked them."

Leah had always been able to do what must be done. Today was no different, she told herself. And told herself again, as she walked from Sam's Café to the apartment house where her sister had lived. She focused her attention on the swirl of patterns in the sidewalk, on the tufts of unfamiliar plants that rose out of the fertile earth. In the distance, horns honked; life moved on in the city. Closer by, a child cried.

Moving against the dread, Leah walked on. She stopped at the door of the apartment. Nicole's name was typed out in raised block letters on a shiny green label above the doorbell. Leah touched it. Called on her courage. Then she took her key and unlocked the door, waiting only a few moments before she was able to open it. Memories of the last time she opened that door overwhelmed her. She tried not to look at the place at the foot of the stairs where Nicole had fallen. Leah noticed the word that came to her: not murder but fallen. That was easier to accept.

What she really wanted to do was to just take Nicole's journal and fly back to Switzerland.

It was a longing, not a plan. Upstairs, she entered Nicole's bedroom. It seemed like the best place to start organizing the things that must be done. Where to begin?

Leah looked carefully at the room. The colors were the ones she saw in magazines and that surprised her. Nicole was never one to care about decorating trends. An olive-green rug, thick and shaggy; autumn golds in a geometric pattern on the bedspread; walls that were dark brown and looked almost like wood. The mark of the 1970s made an imprint on the room, and puzzled Leah, because Nicole had never cared about being stylish. She never would have imagined that this was her sister's room.

Leah began with the desk. Did it belong to Nicole or the landlord? They would tell her when they discussed her responsibilities toward the lease. Opening the desk drawer, she saw there were bills, unpaid. This month's only. And there, secured by a thick rubber band, were the letters Leah had written to her. She had saved them. A child sound: "Oh," tumbled from her lips. She picked up the letters. *Wasn't this the sign? Wasn't it as Dr. Mark had said?* "She loved you very much." As Nicole's psychiatrist, wouldn't he know? And wasn't this the proof of his knowing? Leaning now against the solace of his words, she allowed herself to feel comforted.

In an empty overnight bag she found in the closet, Leah put letters and a checkbook, bills and other papers. She would take these with her when she left. There was another box marked "letters from Leah #2."

In the closet, clothes hung perfectly. Skirts here. Blouses there. Dresses together. Shoes all tidy in a row. In the dresser, perfectly folded sweaters rested upon one another. Leah put one on; the soft wool felt good against her skin. Nicole had worn that blue sweater and Leah took comfort in that. In the bathroom, there were a few cosmetics, the usual accoutrements.

Leah could face the downstairs now, though she still avoided looking at that place where Nicole's body was found. In the kitchen, she found a set of white dishes decorated with blue flowers. Some pots. Some things she would throw away. A quiche pan that brought back a whirl of memories about the time Nicole taught her to cook.

There were things to be done. *Bills that must be paid, what else?* she wondered. *An attorney. But who?* She moved on. She should notify the manager that she wouldn't be staying in the apartment. Was there a manager living among the tenants? *Yes,* she remembered.

In the living room, Leah sat on the sofa, now forcing herself to look at the place where Nicole's body had been. She chose that moment to stand her ground, to face the hovering thoughts, to do battle with the terror that had been and the fears of what could be. Long after dark, Leah was still there, her grief work in process.

The next afternoon, as Leah walked toward her rescheduled meeting with Paul Tabor, she felt embarrassed. He had been so kind, so understanding when she called him. He wasn't even angry that she stood him up. How could he not be upset with her? It seemed too good to be true. He didn't yell at her or cut her off or say he was too busy to give her another chance. He just said, "I'll see you tomorrow at Sam's, three o'clock." His compassion seemed excessive. Sometimes a person can seem just too kind. She was still embarrassed, and guilt showed itself in her aloofness.

Careful. Leah kept the word in mind as she entered Sam's Café. She wasn't going to be taken in by those eyes that reached through her defenses, touching her thoughts, feeling for sadness. She wasn't about to let the tenderness of him influence her now. She sat down across the table from him and avoided looking him in the eye.

"Do you want to tell me what the anger's about, Leah?"

"Why do you think I'm angry?" She observed him carefully. Coldly. It was hard not to trust Paul Tabor. Warmer than anyone she had ever known, he was. Or seemed to be. *Careful.*

"You didn't answer me," she said, suddenly uncomfortable with the silence.

"I'd like to know why you're feeling so angry. If you want to tell me."

Leah wanted to tell him what she was feeling, and about meeting Nicole's psychiatrist, Mark Favre. She couldn't tell him that, after she promised Mark Favre not to mention his name.

Nicole had trusted someone, Leah thought. Was she so much shrewder than Nicole that she couldn't be fooled by a man trained to deal with human emotions? If Nicole, with all her wisdom, could be taken in by trusting the wrong man, then Leah knew her own intuitiveness wasn't reliable.

"I'm not in touch with everything I'm feeling now," she said.

"That's very good, for openers. There's a lot going on, certainly some ambivalence about letting me help you."

"It isn't easy for me to trust people."

"You told me that before. It's easier to hold back and try to handle it yourself. People you trust keep letting you down—as you probably feel I'm doing now by leaving town. You feel I'm deserting you too."

So that was part of it also. She did feel angry with him for going away; she realized that now. But confusion was the real cornerstone of her anger. There was so much she didn't understand. This was too much to carry alone; she had to trust someone. Not the police certainly. Paul Tabor? *No man with eyes like that could kill anyone,* she thought.

Mark Favre? Remembering his pain when he spoke of Nicole, she didn't think that he could have been the one either. And hadn't he been in the hospital when Nicole was killed? And besides, if Dr. Favre had killed Nicole, wouldn't he have denied knowing her?

As Dr. Tabor had done.

"What?" His voice startled her in the long silence. "I can't read your mind, Leah."

"You're sure of that?"

His smile was so kind she had to look away or she would be drawn right into it. *Stay cool,* she thought.

"I'm upset that you're leaving. It was hard enough to come here and tell you the things I did. Now that you're going away, I don't feel like exposing myself anymore. That's all." It was the truth, too, of course. But not the truth that was at issue now. If she knew for sure that she could trust him, even the fact of his leaving couldn't make her stay quiet. Where could she turn? Tears brimmed and retreated.

Paul sighed. "This is a hard time for you."

"There's nothing to say."

"Not even about the feelings?"

Silence. And at last…"Yes. But I'm afraid to tell you."

"What are you afraid of?"

When she didn't answer he said, "Is it about the journal, Leah? Did you keep it?"

Why did he bring up the journal? Leah wondered. Was he just trying to get her to talk about it? She wondered. "Of course, I gave it to them. Why do you think I didn't?"

She felt his eyes holding hers and she pulled away, studying the detail of the bricks on the wall.

"It would be difficult for you to let anyone see that journal. Especially the police. And I know there's something you want to tell me now and are afraid to tell me." He waited and continued when the silence grew heavy. "If you have the book, I'd like for us to talk about it." A pause, then…"And I won't be angry with you, Leah."

The warm, gentle voice wrapped around her; she tossed off the comfort with a shrug. "I gave it to the detective yesterday." Remembering that he had told her to give both the poem and the journal to the police the first day they met, she suddenly felt ashamed. If he had been afraid of what was said about him there, he certainly wouldn't have told her to turn it in. She felt stupid, angry with herself for doubting him. He couldn't possibly be guilty. How could she have been so confused, ignoring obvious facts? Anger at herself increased. And fear. Why couldn't she think clearly anymore? She had to think clearly; there was no one to lean on but herself.

So. If it wasn't Paul Tabor, could it have been Mark Favre? She was not so sure. And then another possibility crossed her mind: could it be a third person? The man Nicole loved, the man who might have killed her, would have known about the book. When Leah came into the apartment, he could have panicked and run, leaving the book behind. It seemed far-fetched but not so improbable as thinking that either of the two doctors was guilty. She was beginning to question her sanity. "You said you're going out of town. How long will you be gone?"

"We'll leave tomorrow for a couple of weeks."

"Is it a vacation?"

"Only part of it. First, I'll attend a conference in Lausanne that's very special to me. Then my wife and I are going to go wherever the wind blows for a few days. Lausanne is where you lived, isn't it, Leah? It's such a fascinating place and I'm looking forward to revisiting some of my favorite spots."

Wasn't that too strange of a coincidence? Maybe he knew Nicole. Maybe there was some kind of connection.

Why should she tell Dr. Tabor anyway; wasn't he going to leave her too? What good would it do? It was better to trust only herself, for now. There would be time enough to discuss these things when he came back. If she wanted to.

"I'm sorry, Dr. Tabor. I'm confused and I really don't want your help right now. I just want to be by myself for a while. We can talk after you get back from your trip." She walked out the door, decisively. He made no move to stop her.

Paul gave himself a few minutes to release his disappointment. He wasn't surprised by her decision, but he had wished for a smoother transition. With a conscious effort, he shifted his thoughts to Switzerland. It was a skill psychiatrists had to learn for the sake of their own mental health. Sometimes that was easier than others.

Their flight would leave from LAX early the next morning. Tonight they would sleep at a hotel close to the airport. Stephanie always laughed at Paul's anxiety about missing a flight. Once he missed a plane when a five-car crash blocked traffic to the airport for hours. She teased him about his coping skills but found his vulnerability endearing.

It was dark when Leah went back to her hotel and into her room. She felt a soft breeze when she opened the door. Crossing over to close the old French doors that swung open into the small garden, Leah reached for the knob. It was then that she saw the broken pane of glass. The small French pane on the door was shattered; there was a hole large enough to reach a hand through, to undo the lock, to open the door, to enter the bedroom.

Don't scream, she thought. *Don't!*

Leah ran to the phone and called the manager. Together they waited until the police arrived. She looked in the closet and saw that someone had opened her suitcase and her clothes were tossed on the floor.

"Is anything missing?" the officer asked.

"Missing? What could be missing? I mean, I don't have anything that anyone would want."

"No money left in the room?"

"No."

"No jewelry?"

"I don't have anything valuable."

"Will you check your things, please?"

Leah opened the door to her closet. Two long dresses hung in one small corner. They made a strong statement of the seventies. The rest of the rod was bare. What would anyone take from her… worn dresses? "I have nothing more," she said, half whispering.

"Wait a minute…wasn't your sister murdered last week?"

Did the spoken words make the fact more real? Why then should her knees weaken and the blood rush so quickly from her head? These words from a stranger formed a rope tightening around her throat, making it difficult to breathe. "Yes," she said quietly.

"Can you think of any connection between what happened here and your sister's death?"

"No."

"You weren't a witness, were you? Did you see anyone or anything like that?"

"No, I wasn't a witness." That man she saw outside Nicole's apartment was only a shadow from the past, running through her life in another place and time.

"Well, I think I'd better notify them in homicide. They may want to talk to you about this. You're sure nothing's missing?" He was making notes.

"I'm sure."

"You'd better move into another room, tonight." The policeman turned to the hotel manager. "Even better, let's get her on another floor, okay?"

"Certainly," the manager said. "I just hope there's no more trouble here. For her, I mean. I didn't know she was the one. I read about it in the paper, poor dear."

Leah sat on her bed, hearing, not listening, staring at the table beside her, realizing suddenly that something was missing: her own journal. She had left it there on the bedside table. Now it was her own privacy that lay exposed to strangers. Her own secrets naked in unknown hands.

"You okay?" the policeman asked.

She looked at him, needing to tell him, desperate to tell him it was her own journal that was gone.

No one even knew she kept a journal...then she remembered. Two people knew. Paul Tabor and Mark Favre.

"I'll get you some water," the officer said, and he returned with a glass. With an arm around her shoulder, he held the glass to her lips and seemed more compassionate than she thought policemen could be.

"I'm all right," she told him. Should she tell him more? What if she said that her journal was taken?

Wouldn't he tell the detective, and wouldn't she then have to listen to his interrogation, and wouldn't he find out about Nicole's journal and how she hid it that day in his office? Then they would know it wasn't Leah's journal he wanted, but Nicole's. And she would be forced to give that up also. Her thoughts raced, tumbled together, until they collided into this one reality: She would keep that knowledge to herself.

The two policemen spoke between themselves. The woman hovered. "I'll help you, dear. What an ordeal you've been through! Here, let's get you all packed up and we can move you right upstairs."

"I can do it, thank you. I really don't have much."

Alone, some minutes later, Leah still tried to get her thoughts together. She clutched her purse where Nicole's journal was hidden. Could anyone else have known about the journal? No, only the two psychiatrists, both of whom she trusted. Could one of them have loved Nicole…have killed her? And if so, which one?

Maybe there was someone else. Maybe someone had been following them when she checked into the Camille Hotel. She decided not to tell anyone. It was safer that way.

CHAPTER 12

WEST LOS ANGELES & MALIBU

Leah walked along the streets of Westwood on Friday evening, trying to acclimate to her new home. She decided she didn't need help from anyone. The thought became a mantra every time she felt fragile. She made up her mind that she was perfectly capable of taking care of herself.

In the window of the bookstore on Westwood Boulevard, a poster announced a dance concert. It was the photograph that first caught Leah's attention. First casually, then intently, she stared at the picture. The woman, costumed in a luminous white fabric, appeared suspended in air. Her arms stretched taut, extending toward the male dancer who wore something dull and black; only his face and hands separated him from the black background.

Only on second look did the third dancer become noticeable. Also clad in dull, black fabric, he supported the weight of the woman, lifting her body high into the air, his face in shadows, his hands hidden by her costume. Leah studied the poster for a long time, feeling strangely drawn to the theme of the dance.

At the bottom of the poster, the place and time of the performance was listed. Tonight, at eight at UCLA's Royce Hall. Leah looked at her watch. An hour and a half away. There was time. It seemed strange to go to the theater so soon after her sister died. But the thought of going back to the hotel alone seemed unbearable.

Leah would have time for dinner. She went into the first restaurant she found, ordering as much as she thought she could force herself to eat, finishing as much as she could, paying her check.

Leah asked directions and walked north on Westwood Boulevard for two blocks until the street became part of UCLA and led her into the campus. A crowd was gathering at Royce Hall, but tickets were still available. Leah bought the best seat possible and was pleased to find herself sitting in the third-row center. Reading the program carefully as the theater filled, she was glad she had seen the poster. It helped her keep her mind off Paul Tabor. It was only with intense concentration that she could avoid reliving their last meeting.

Knowing that she overreacted, her suspicions now seemed ridiculous. She had thought about calling him several times when she was at Nicole's. Twice she had gotten as far as lifting the phone. But something stopped her—pride perhaps. Or latent doubts.

The theater darkened; music began. Then the dancers. Leah lost herself in the dance. They presented a startling performance of combined dance and gymnastic techniques. A strange company—bold, modern. Dramatic and intense beyond anything she had ever seen before. Wild, primitive dances, then quiet, soulful dances, all of them powerful enough to break the pull of her problems and give Leah time away from the pressures. When the lights came on at intermission, it seemed as if only moments earlier she had entered the theater.

Leah walked into the lobby. Smoke stuffed her nostrils, burning her throat. She walked into the warm September evening, taking in the fresh air. Outside the theater, Leah saw a bulletin board holding announcements of apartments to rent, bicycles for sale, roommates needed, jobs wanted. She read them with interest, using them to help her get the flavor of this new environment, trying to get some hint of what life was to be like here in America.

"I think you dropped this…" The resonance of the voice cut through the silence. "Sorry, I didn't mean to startle you."

Leah looked into the face of a tall man, about thirty, illuminated by the same light that flooded the bulletin board. He was holding out a program.

"That isn't mine," Leah said. "I have mine…here…" She was holding it so tightly that her hand perspired beneath the slick paper, making a resistant sound when she moved her fingers. There was no malice in the man's face but with Nicole's journal inside her purse, Leah's anxiety wouldn't let her relax her vigil. It was her purse she clutched tightly now.

He continued to try for conversation. "Nice program, isn't it?"

She nodded. "It is." She didn't make eye contact.

There was a bell from Royce Hall, calling the audience back for the last half of the program. He walked beside her as she started back to the theater.

"You're here alone tonight?"

"Yes. Well, not exactly, I have friends inside. I'm alone for intermission…" He smiled. "Hey, I'm not the bogeyman, you know. Just trying to be friendly. Good neighbor and all that."

"Sorry." And she managed a smile in return. "It's a built-in reflex."

"Give me another chance, will you? Meet me here after the show."

He turned without waiting for her answer. The palms of her hands smeared the black ink of the program.

Through the second part of the performance, Leah thought less about the dancers, more about the man who spoke to her. He was, most probably, exactly as he represented himself to be: a friendly man. An aggressive one, to be sure, a little too anxious to pick up a girl alone. *Or was that typical here? Wasn't it everywhere?* she thought. But what did that mean to her now, this moment? Either he was a harmless guy looking for a pick-up, or a not-so-harmless guy who knew who she was and what she probably carried in her purse. Which was it?

The dance moved on. Figures whirled in and out of her concentration. Mostly she thought about the man who wanted to see her after the performance. Nicole's old adage: before you gamble on something, consider what you have to lose. If he was nothing more than a man on the make, she could handle that. But of all the people here, why had he chosen her? She, who seemed younger than most people thought, until they knew her. Unless of course, he had come here for that purpose. She couldn't afford to be careless. More dancers now, leaping, twirling. *What if he was the man who broke into her room? Well, what if...*She argued the matter from both sides, backward and forward. *Stay careful*, Leah thought.

The house lights were still off, the performance almost ended, according to her crumpled program. Crouching as much as possible, she moved out of her seat, past the others in her row, up the aisle to the back of the theater, and out onto the street. *Stupid!* she told herself but kept moving. It was silly to leave, her logic said, but emotions pushed her on. She walked back across the campus toward the boulevard. The Gothic buildings loomed from hilly points, the paths crossed and twisted across the campus. Dim lights cast shadows around her. She shivered and walked on.

Leah's foot slipped on the uneven path. She stopped. And then heard the footsteps behind her. Her pulse thundered in her temples. "It's just my imagination," she said to herself. But her body didn't respond to reassurance. "Walk," she told herself. "Don't run. It's probably nothing. Don't look back. Just keep on."

Why had she left! There, among the crowd, she would have been safe. Here, she was alone on a deserted campus with dim lights around her. The footsteps behind her were soft, almost negligible sounds against the path.

Don't look back. Careful. She was at the beginning of Westwood Boulevard now—the part of it that extends into the university grounds. Leah could see a figure there. Not too close. But someone, nonetheless.

She hurried toward the lights of the village. She could run for it from here, she thought. Maybe. Maybe not. A little more patience, she thought. Get closer first. Did the sounds behind her quicken? If he was going to make a move, it would be before she reached the shops. Had the footsteps changed pace, moved faster?

Without her conscious will, she ran, now letting herself give way to the fear and the overpowering need to get to a safe place.

Racing as fast as she could run down the deserted street, she reached the corner. The red circle of light stopped traffic. She didn't care. Not looking, she didn't slow her pace. She ran against the light. Tires screeched. Horns honked. A man swore. Aware of people watching, she tore into the first restaurant she saw. Out of breath and pale, she asked the hostess for a table. Her cheeks were wet. Fingers trembled as she wiped her face. She put her head on her hands, elbows propped against the table. Trying to recover.

"You okay?" the waiter asked.

"I'll be all right in just a minute. I'll have a glass of wine. Any California white will do."

She wished she could call the police. But what would she say? That some man talked to her at intermission? That someone followed her from the theater? What would they think? Hysterical female probably. She could almost see the cynical face of the detective belittling her.

"Leah?" The voice was soft, the touch of the hand on her shoulder was gentle. But the wine spilled on the table.

She turned toward a familiar face.

"Hey, Leah, hold on there!"

"Mark!"

He looked concerned as he helped her clean the spilled drink.

"Mind if I sit down?" he asked. His calm, easy manner reassured her.

"I'm so glad you're here!" Leah said.

He slipped onto the chair, facing her. "It took me a while to find you."

"Really? You were looking for me?"

"I needed a distraction and thought the theater would help. I was halfway back, near the aisle. I was surprised to see you there and then I saw you leave in the middle of a scene. You looked upset. Then a man got up and followed you out. I didn't like the look of it, so I left too."

"I'm glad you did."

"Well, something about it set me off. I don't know. Maybe he had his own reason for leaving when he did. Anyway, he seemed to be following you, so I just came along after both of you. When you started running, my attention was so much on you that I lost sight of the guy. He could have taken a path toward UCLA, I guess. I saw that dash you made through the traffic; I wasn't sure you were going to make it."

"I didn't even notice the traffic. I was so afraid of the man behind me."

"Can't blame you. That's unsettling…particularly after what you've been through. By the way, why did you leave like that, before it was over?"

"Because of a man who tried to pick me up during intermission. He wasn't offensive but…well, I'm really running scared lately." She almost told him that someone broke into her room and stole her journal but instead she said, "Anyway, I've been pretty edgy, blaming everyone I meet for killing Nicole. I know I'm not being logical. This afternoon I even thought that Paul Tabor was guilty."

"Tabor and I have been on opposite sides of a lawsuit and it did not end well. I told you to be wary. Why did you think he was involved with Nicole?"

"If I told you, you'd have me committed! I try not to react like this, but I'm scared. I even checked the hospital to be sure you were telling me the truth about being a patient there."

"You're really something, know that?"

She watched the slow smile; he was amused, accepting.

"Well, I'm sorry," Leah said defensively, "but I have to be careful. Someone killed Nicole. Now someone followed me out of the theater. It isn't easy to know who I can trust."

"I know it isn't. And you did the right thing, checking me out. I was just impressed that you thought of it. Satisfied now that I'm not the one?"

"Absolutely. If you were, I don't think you would have reacted like you did when we talked about Nicole. And I certainly don't think you would have let me wait to bring you the journal."

"Ever think of setting up a detective agency? With those brains and your big brown eyes, you'd have it made. Hey, you're blushing! That's lovely." There was even more admiration in his eyes than in his words. "Have you ordered yet?"

"Not yet. I had a little something before the show."

Leah ordered a dessert, and Mark chose a full meal. They stayed talking until hours passed. She told him about Switzerland. About Nicole. About the fear. About the strange feeling she had sometimes, like she was walking in a dream, and then overreacting like when that man at the theater was probably just trying to pick her up.

Mark debated about changing the subject. Then took a chance.

"Leah, I know you don't want me to see Nicole's journal, but it might help you make sense of what happened to her. I cared about Nicole, too, you know."

"That's different. You were just her therapist."

"What do you mean just her therapist? That's one of the most intimate relationships there is. I miss her too."

"I could see you cared when we talked about her in your office. I just don't want to take advantage."

"Leah, my friend, I don't let anyone take advantage. I want to help you, or I wouldn't have offered. And another thing—I'd rather you didn't come to my office."

"Why?"

"Because there's a code among doctors that we don't socialize with pretty girls who come into our offices. How about that?" he said, touching her hand.

"Oh. Okay," she said. Considering his intentions.

"Let's go somewhere and take a look at that book. We can't stay here all night." Once on the deserted street, Leah felt her nervousness return, and moved closer to him. "My car is in the lot over there," he said.

"Why did you go to the theater when you are still in so much pain?" Leah asked him.

"I needed a distraction," he said, which, of course, was a lie. He squeezed her arm and held the door open to the small sports car. Leah slid into the Porsche as gracefully as she could, given the awkward position that entry demanded.

"Now we need a quiet place to work on the journal. How about your place?"

Where? she wondered. *In her room?* "It's awfully late," she said. "Would you rather we go over it tomorrow?"

"Would you?" He signaled for a turn and she didn't answer him until they stopped in front of her hotel.

"It might be better if we wait until morning. I'm really tired."

"Anything you say. Why don't I pick you up around nine."

"I'd love that." A car was idling not far behind them. It served Mark's purpose. "I have a feeling we've been spotted," he said with a sigh.

Mark knew he could use this to his advantage. Just as he could use her fear about the guy who tried to pick her up at the theater. It was a timely coincidence. Why wouldn't a man approach a beautiful young girl who looked alone and vulnerable?

It was Mark who had followed her when she left the theater, and it was his footsteps that she heard. She was so anxious; she saw everything as a potential danger.

"Leah, I don't want to frighten you, but there's something you should know. That car that stopped not far behind us has one headlight that shines off to the right. It's clear that's the same car that pulled out behind us when I drove off the lot. Turn for turn, he stuck with us. I'm sure he's tailing us. You can't afford to be careless."

A small sound escaped her lips and he reached over and touched her face. "Hey, it's okay; I'll take care of you. Just relax. Now, the important thing is to get you some place safe. Obviously, whoever it is knows that you're staying here, so we have to get you moved. I know how to handle this," he said.

Leah wanted to tell him about the break-in at her hotel. She needed to tell him, but she forced herself to keep it to herself.

"I want you to go in now and pack your things. Pay your bill and tell them at the desk that you're going back to Switzerland. Have them forward your mail back to your last address in Lausanne. You can say that an emergency came up and you're taking the plane out tonight. It's important that if that man tries to call you, he should get the message that you left the country. That will get him off your trail."

"Don't you think I should telephone the police?"

"No. After all, Leah, who else but the police knew where you were staying? Well, Dr. Tabor, I suppose, but who else?"

"No one else. But why shouldn't I call the police?" Leah said.

"You can't take chances. Once your address is in the police files, no telling how many people have access to it. It only takes one bad cop—or one office worker who takes a bribe—and your cover's shot. Let's do this the safe way. Just tell the hotel clerk that you're leaving the country. I'll get in touch with that detective and tell him that I'll relay the messages to you."

She nodded, not trusting her voice.

"That's a good girl. Now. Go and pack. I'll wait here and see if he comes around again."

In less than half an hour she was ready. He loaded her suitcase into his car. "It's done," she said. "The lady seemed curious, but I told her what you said."

"You said you were going back to Switzerland?"

"Yes."

"Said you were on your way to the airport?"

"Yes. She offered to call a cab, but I said a friend was driving me."

"She didn't see this car, did she?"

"No. She stayed at the desk. Oh, I see. I shouldn't have said that, about a friend, should I?"

"It doesn't matter. I'm sure he wouldn't call tonight—at least I wouldn't think so. Probably not until he can't pick up your trail and gets anxious. By then, you'll be safely in another hotel. Now, just in case, let's make a run out to the airport. It's a nice night for a drive, don't you think?"

"It doesn't seem to me to be a nice night for anything. Why would he still be after me?"

"You still have the journal, don't you? I have a pretty good idea what's in that book, knowing Nicole as well as I did. She wouldn't want anyone to see it. At least not anyone who didn't care about her. It could make some sordid reading when the reporters got through twisting it, don't you think?"

"Yes. I suppose so. I don't mind showing it to you, Mark. You probably know most of it anyway. Was she your patient for a long time?"

"Long enough for me to know what was going on. It wasn't a pretty story. She was too good a woman to have gotten mixed up in all that she did. Well, let's not go into all that until I see the journal, okay? Right now, taking care of you is my first priority."

A long sigh. His hand found hers in the darkness. Her fingers tightened around his.

Down Wilshire Boulevard and onto the San Diego Freeway moving south toward the airport, the car moved quickly in and out of the traffic. Close to the interchange of the Santa Monica Freeway, red taillights flashed across the lanes. An accident up ahead had trapped them. No cars could move. Time passed.

"Don't look back," he warned her for the third time. "If he's behind us, you don't want him to think you suspect that you're being followed."

"Now what is it you want me to do at the airport?" He had told her, but fear made her memory too slippery to hold on to his plan.

"I'll let you out at the American Airlines terminal. Take your bag and go inside. I think the ticket counter's visible from the street, so you should just go stand in line there, or ask a question if the counter's clear. If he follows us, he'll assume you're getting your ticket. Either way he'll drive on, convinced you're leaving, or he'll park the car and try to follow you inside. It takes time to park here, any time of night, so wait a few minutes and come out the next door. I'll circle around the airport and come back to pick you up."

"I almost wish I was going back." The longing in her voice was more than even Leah anticipated.

"You'll be just fine. Trust me," he said.

She did as she was told. Heart pounding and fear intensifying, she walked to the terminal. Waited. Came out again. Eyes searching, seeing nothing. Hurrying to the car.

"Feel safer now?" Mark asked, as he headed toward the freeway.

"When you're with me, yes."

"Don't worry; you'll be safe in the new hotel I'm taking you to."

Mark chose the Holiday Inn on Sunset Boulevard where he had easy access to the freeway. He hoped they had a room.

Leah said she was just exhausted and needed to go straight to sleep. That wasn't Mark's plan, but he didn't argue. She did look like it had been a long day.

It was the first jarring sound of the telephone that woke Leah. She sat up in bed. It was almost four a.m. There was another call at five. There was only silence when she answered.

"What do you want?" She heard herself saying the words that sounded like they came from someone else. She heard nothing but the sound of breathing.

When that first phone call had come, Leah thought it was a switchboard error, hung up, and returned to sleep. When it rang again an hour later, she began to panic.

She had started to call Mark. Then wondered if she should call the police instead. Torn between two choices, she chose neither.

How could anyone have found her? They had been so careful. She couldn't handle this alone. She took Mark's private number from her purse, grateful that he had thought to give it to her.

His voice sounded sleepy when he answered on the third ring. "Mark, I need you!" She hadn't intended to begin that way, only to tell him what happened. Only to ask him what to do. Not to be dependent, no. But the words came out on their own volition, as if she had no part in the decision. "He knows I'm here. He's been calling. Saying nothing. How could he have found me, Mark?"

"Only one way. I thought about it after you checked in. You registered under your own name. Maybe he got suspicious at the airport. I didn't think of that until it was too late; then I didn't want to say anything that might frighten you even more. And frankly, Leah, I thought it was pretty unlikely that anyone would start checking the hotels. But apparently, he did."

"What am I going to do?"

"You're going to do exactly what I tell you. You're going to pack up and check out. Now. I'll pick you up. You can stay at my house."

"I…I don't know, Mark."

"It's the best option you've got. You'll be safe with me."

"Maybe I should just call the police."

"Leah, we've been through all that. I'm surprised you're still considering it. I know it's just that you're upset now, but you must know that would be the dumbest thing you could do right now."

She didn't know why. She didn't remember. Why was it supposed to be so bad to call them? Fear pushed reason aside. "All right. Whatever you say, Mark. I'll do whatever you say. Give me fifteen minutes," she said.

"I'll be waiting for you. I'll park as close as I can."

Leah replaced the phone in its cradle and sat for a time with her head between weary hands. Waiting for that sense of logic to return. Why? That was the word that kept fighting through all the other words that surfaced. Why would Nicole's killer be tracking her this hard? Didn't he know that if his name had been in the journal, she would have told the police by now?

None of it made sense to her. But one fact emerged from the rubble of confusion: She had to get rid of the journal. It was too dangerous to keep it, no matter how desperately she needed that book. Her life was more important than her emotional need for this tie with her sister.

In her suitcase, some papers from her trustee were in a large brown envelope. Legal size. She removed the papers, putting them in the pocket at the top of her suitcase. She put Nicole's journal in the brown envelope and sealed it.

Taking a pen, Leah hesitated—then made her decision. She addressed it to herself, but in care of Paul Tabor. She copied the address from the business card she had taken from his office.

Leah was tempted to send a letter with the journal, explaining. But there wasn't much time. And the envelope was sealed. Mark would be waiting.

"Pardon, Madam," she said to the woman at the desk. "There has been an emergency and I must check out now. This package is very important to me and I wonder if you can mail it for me. You will be sure it gets to the postman, yes?"

"Of course. No problem."

"Just add the cost to my bill."

The clerk weighed the journal, affixed the stamps, and said, "Don't worry, your package will be picked up today." Leah had a strong sense of relief. She should have done that in the first place, she thought. She paid her bill just as she saw Mark pull up to the door.

Again, she put her bag in Mark's car. Again, they started out into the darkness with Mark looking carefully behind him, as before. Only this time, there was no reason for Leah not to watch also. And by the time they reached Pacific Coast Highway, even Leah had to admit that no one was following them.

"I've been so much trouble to you." Her voice had the sound of one who needed assurance.

"Yes, you have," Mark said, but the tone of his voice denied the words. "You have been one hell of a bundle of trouble, Leah, my girl."

"You must have really cared about Nicole, to be so willing to get involved in all this."

"I did care about Nicole. And I care about what happens to you."

"It would have been easier on you to have me call the police."

"We don't need the police. I'm not sure what they would do to you at this point, for withholding that journal for so long."

"But you told me you thought I was right not to turn it in!"

"I did. I still do. I just know they'd be madder than hell if you gave it to them now. And there's really no reason to. They'd put you under protective custody for sure. You'll be a lot happier at my house."

They made good time driving to Malibu. Before long, Mark turned into the driveway that led to the beach house that belonged to Paul and Stephanie Tabor.

"Well, this is my home," Mark said. "How do you like it?"

PART TWO

CHAPTER 13

LAUSANNE & GENEVA

In the early hours of Friday morning Paul and Stephanie were on the plane headed for Geneva. After an unexpected delay in Zurich and a nine-hour time change, they lost a day and finally arrived at the airport in Geneva on Sunday morning at 10:30, Swiss time. Paul had slept soundly on the overseas part of the trip, but Stephanie was not so easy a traveler. All she could think of now was how much longer before she could get in bed for a nap.

The airport was bustling with tourists and business travelers, blending with the eclectic vibrations of a variety of languages colliding in the cosmopolitan center.

There were no delays in customs. Swiss efficiency was, as usual, functioning to the advantage of the international guests. In the midst of the crowd, Paul saw his friend, Dr. Henri Armond, who waited, less than patiently, for them to arrive. "Paul! Paul, come this way. Madame. Pardon! Pardon! Puis-je. May I pass? Paul…"

Paul extended his hand to his friend only to be embraced by the enthusiastic Swiss doctor who placed a kiss on each cheek. "Henri! Good to see you my friend…this is…"

"Ah-h-h-h Stephanie! What a pleasure this is!" Henri held her hand to his lips. "You are as lovely as Paul described."

"Henri, you haven't changed a bit!" Paul said, not recalling that he had described Stephanie at all.

Henri Armond was one of the primary organizers for the conference. It had been his responsibility to manage the logistics for the entire convention.

"I got your letter just before I left," Paul said. "You've done a fine job. I never could have pulled this off without you."

"Yes, yes, of course," Henri said, negating by tone his value to the assignment.

"The care and feeding of celebrated academics isn't an easy job. I saw the arrangements and I'm really impressed," Paul said.

"Wait until you see what's planned for the opening party." He turned to Stephanie, not knowing how much Paul had shared with her about the plans. "It will be at the Beau-Rivage Palace in Lausanne. The hotel itself is superb. And the conference center has such efficient management that they have the solution before I have the problem! The icing on the cake is the medical school; they're interested in this research. In fact, they're hosting the first event. But…we can go over all this later. Tell me, Stephanie, how was your flight?"

"Long! But here we are and I'm looking forward to everything."

They made their way out of the airport in Henri's VW Golf which was the most popular car in Switzerland. The car was spotlessly clean, polished to a luminous shine. The man himself seemed to be oblivious to his own grooming, but his car was another matter. His suit, as always, Paul remembered, appeared just a trifle too large and could have done with a pressing. Henri seemed much the same as he did years ago when he and Paul first met. Perhaps some thinning of his hair, a few more lines in the face, considerably more books to his credit. And international recognition as a sociologist specializing in the variations in the creative process in various cultures. Neither time nor success had altered him much. The same manner, the same enthusiasm. He was older than Paul by ten years and more dynamic than most men at any age. His vitality was contagious. Paul felt some of his fatigue diminish just in the presence of all that energy.

As they pulled out of the airport, Henri talked, drove, and gestured with both hands, maneuvering aggressively in and out of traffic.

"Have you been here before, Stephanie?"

"No, it's my first time," she said, hoping it wouldn't be her last. "I know it's going to be fantastic."

"We will do everything we can to make it special for you. All the stores are closed today, of course. It's against the law for shops to be open on Sunday, but I have arranged for a friend of mine to spend time with you tomorrow and make sure that you see the best of the local artists. He is quite knowledgeable and was most excited about the opportunity of showing you around. You will have my car and if there is anything that you need you must let me know right away."

"I'm sure I'll be fine. I hadn't expected any help, Henri; you've gone to too much trouble about this."

"A pleasure, Stephanie. Now, Paul, what is on your agenda for today?"

"First, some rest. Once the conference starts it's going to be an intense few days. Then some serious sightseeing with some very good wine tastings. But for now…I don't know why just sitting on a plane for so many hours is harder work than chopping wood, but I swear it's more tiring."

"Why don't the two of you take this morning for a nap, then keep my car to drive around and see the city this afternoon?"

"That sounds good to me, but won't you need your car? I can rent one from…"

"Wouldn't hear of it. My wife is in Frankfurt with her sister who is ill. I can use her car when I need one."

In less time than it took them to get from Malibu to the Los Angeles International Airport, they drove from Geneva to Lausanne and went straight to the Beau-Rivage Palace.

"This is my favorite hotel," Henri said. "Even better than their sister hotel in Geneva. Old and elegant in the most formal of European tradition. I checked with them before I came to get you this morning; your suite is ready. All you need to do is give me your passports and I take care of the business at the desk. You have the most beautiful rooms overlooking the lake."

"Sounds good, Henri. We don't get away often; when we do, it's a pleasure to have such fine accommodations."

"In case you want to do any entertaining in the evenings you have a lovely suite for a small gathering. Here's your key."

"I appreciate all you've done, Henri."

Henri brushed his gratitude away with a toss of his head. "It's nothing! Nothing. Now, rest well, Stephanie, my dear."

Paul and Stephanie took the elevator to the top floor. The bellman followed with their bags. The elegant corridor led to the door of their suite; inside, the room was large and formal. A fireplace stood in the middle of the far wall, flanked by large French doors that led to the balcony.

"It is absolutely perfect," Stephanie said, while Paul paid the bellman. They walked onto the balcony and watched the boats move back and forth on Lake Geneva, the colorful sails swaying in the September breeze. Body against body, they touched and held.

"It couldn't be better," Paul agreed.

"This is going to be the best vacation ever."

"You said that last time."

"It was true then, too, wasn't it? But what could possibly be better than this, Paul—the two of us alone in this extraordinary country without your patients and my clients? It's a honeymoon."

"You are an incurable romantic, you know that."

"I do. Furthermore, I don't care. I am very much in love with you, Paul Tabor." Small kisses, playful on his ear. "Madly, passionately and..."

"Good morning," said the crisp voice behind them.

It was Jayne. The prima donna making her grand entrance as she came into the living room. "Imagine running into you in a place like this."

It was Paul who recovered first. "Jayne, what the…what are you doing here?"

"Escaping, if you really want to know. And before you say another word, I apologize for everything I said to you, Dad. You are really a very dear father and I was being a brat." The performance continued—the attitude well-rehearsed. A frothy apologetic tone. "I caught a flight to Switzerland and beat you here by a day. Have a seat! Isn't this gorgeous? I have so much to tell you! I'll bet you're just dying to know what happened."

"Just dying," Stephanie repeated quietly as she followed Jayne into the living room. Paul reached for her hand—cool and unresponsive to his touch.

"I told Henri my coming was a surprise; he got me the room on the other side of your living room so we could open it up to a two-bedroom suite! Look, your room's in here, isn't it gorgeous? Mine's just like it on the other side."

Paul looked at Stephanie and then turned away quickly. There was nothing he could say to that expression. Jayne apparently didn't notice. She went right on explaining the details of her surprise. "Come on and sit down," she said, playing the hostess, perching on the edge of the desk, lifting the telephone. "Room service please…what can I get for you? I'm having coffee and croissants."

"I'm not hungry," Stephanie said.

"Nothing for me."

She ordered and continued with the details of her story. "Mark was getting ready to play dirty. I could see it coming. He even hid my passport and tried to make me think I lost it."

"If you don't have your passport, how did you get here?" Paul asked.

"I said it was an emergency."

"What emergency?" Stephanie's voice, little more than a whisper.

"It pays to know your congressman. I told him you needed me to help with an international conference and I couldn't find my passport. He couldn't have been more accommodating. Took care of everything."

"You never did plan on a final conversation with Mark," Paul stated flatly.

"I took my own advice. I met him at the hospital and told him I'd try again. That way, he couldn't mess up my plans. Then I left a message that I was at the spa for a week. He's probably ruffled at the price, but he'll deal with it. So here I am!

"I've walked out before, you know. For a couple of days at a time. So has he. I didn't want to say anything about a real separation until I had my ticket put on my credit card and bought traveler's checks with American Express. If Mark had known I was leaving he probably would have reported the card stolen."

"What are your plans?" Paul asked.

"If you two will excuse me," Stephanie said. Her voice was low. Weary. "I really need to get some sleep. I'll see you later, Paul. Jayne." She walked into the bedroom and closed the door.

"Give me a minute, Jayne; there's something I need to discuss with Stephanie."

Stephanie, opening her bag, fumbling through the top layers of luggage, keeping her back to him.

"Stephanie…"

Facing him, large blue eyes intense with feeling: "Not now, Paul, I can't handle words right now."

"Hey, I'm your friend, remember?"

"I don't want to talk about it. Anything I say to you now would only make me feel guilty later. Just go talk to your daughter and leave me alone. Right now, I'm very tired and want nothing more than a hot bath and a few hours' sleep."

The bathroom door closed quickly behind her; the heavy metal lock slammed noisily into place. Paul stood there a moment listening to the sudden burst of bath water. Knowing that this whole week was going to be one long juggling event unless he got his act together soon.

Jayne sat on the deep saffron-colored chair, draping herself across the back cushion.

"You know, Dad, it's going to feel so good to be a free woman again. No more battles. No more of Mark's telling me how to live." With a precise gesture she removed two rings from the third finger of her left hand. She tossed the gold wedding band onto the coffee table. It clattered and rolled across the dark wood. She considered the diamond engagement ring, then slipped it onto her right hand. Her purse was on the desk; she removed the wedding picture from her wallet and ceremoniously ripped it in half, flipping the pieces onto the table, smiling triumphantly.

Paul watched her without comment, then finally said, "What are your plans?"

"Hmmmmm?"

"Your plans. What are you going to do now that you're on your own?"

"Oh. Well, I've given that a lot of thought, of course." Then the bright smile. A flash of perfect teeth. A tilt of her pretty head that sent golden hair tossing. "Now, that's something I want to talk to you about. You remember when I was at UCLA you told me that my graduation present would be a trip to Europe? And since I didn't take you up on it then, I thought that maybe you'd spring for me to do some traveling now. I'd love to spend some time in Paris—and London, too, of course. In fact, while I'm here it makes sense for me to stay awhile and see Europe.

"You promised it to me before, so I figured that maybe now you would like to help me pick up a little culture and get a vacation at the same time."

"Jayne, I promised you that trip to Europe as a college graduation present."

"So, I got married instead of finishing school. Big deal. I don't see what that has to do with it. It costs you the same whether I graduated or not. Less even—after all, Mark's supported me since I was nineteen. Look at how much that saved you!"

"It isn't the money I'm concerned about."

"What then?"

"Don't you know?" She looked puzzled. It was clear she didn't. Paul sighed. Where to start. How to set limits now when so few were set before. "I can't do that."

"You mean you don't want to do that."

"That's right. I don't want to." His voice was calm, the words were softly spoken but Jayne heard the firmness.

"Well, why not? Is Stephanie spending so much that you can't afford to let me have something that I need? Something that would make me really happy?"

"That won't make you happy, Jayne. It might give you some pleasure, but you're not going to feel much happiness until you get some things worked out within yourself. You made your choice to marry instead of finishing school. Fine. That was what you wanted. Now you want out. I certainly wouldn't try to convince you otherwise. But you can't turn the clock back and be a child again. You're going to have to think about taking care of yourself. What are your job options? What kind of life can you make for yourself now? These are the things you should be spending your energies on. Not traveling around Europe."

"What are my job options? How the hell do I know! I'm not going to be a secretary or a clerk somewhere. I need time to find out what I want to do. That's why this trip could be so good for me. I might come home with some idea of what I want."

"What you seem to want is for someone to take care of you. I'll always be here to help you get in touch with your feelings and I'll support you emotionally when you need it. But I'm not going to support you financially."

"I didn't ask you to support me; I asked you for one measly little trip. The one you promised. Now you're making a federal case out of it! All right, so I won't stay in Europe. I'll go home when my money runs out if that's what you want."

"Have you given any thought to what kind of job you'd be interested in?"

"I thought I might like to open a dress shop. I have a good eye for clothes, and I could decorate the place really well. Then I'd get to travel to New York and Europe on buying trips and besides, I could get my clothes wholesale. That's something I'd really like to do."

"You haven't had any experience in business, Jayne. You don't just open a shop without knowing anything about it."

"Well, I know I could do it. You don't think I'm capable of anything, do you?"

"It's not a question of your capabilities but of your experience. You've never even had a summer job, much less the background to open your own business. And do you think your community property settlement with Mark is going to be enough to even think in those terms? I just don't think you're being realistic."

"I don't have any idea how much a dress shop would cost. And I don't know how much I'll get from Mark. We haven't saved much. He bought the condo before we met so it isn't community property…unless he paid the mortgage from our joint accounts. Maybe I'll get something from the appreciated value. I don't know."

"It sounds like you've done some research."

Jayne shrugged. "I asked around. I can't count on how that will play out."

"So, the dress shop isn't a viable option, is it?"

"Not unless you want to help me get started. You helped Stephanie when she opened her gallery, didn't you?"

"Actually, I didn't. She earned her own money and had a solid background in the arts and in business. The point is, Jayne, you can't start at the top. If you're interested in the garment business, then go get a job selling in a dress shop. Spend your evenings in night school learning something about marketing. Start training yourself now so that later you'll be prepared if that's what you want. But you're not going to be qualified for a jump like that for a long time."

"You're not even trying to help me!"

"I am trying to help you. But not in the way you want to be helped."

"Okay just forget it then!"

"There are a couple of other things we have to talk about. About this week," Paul said.

Jayne's expression was guarded. "What about it?"

"You're welcome to be with us for lunch today and any evening that we're free. But this is a closed conference. Only the artists, psychiatrists, and sociologists will be at the sessions."

"Okay!" Jayne flipped her voice upward, crisp and angry. "What else?"

"Stephanie and I don't get many vacations and those last few days we planned to just be by ourselves."

"You really know how to make a girl feel welcome. Nice to know you enjoy my company so much."

"This has nothing to do with you. This has to do with my relationship with my wife and our need to be alone together for a few days when the conference is over."

"Well, I'm sorry! I didn't realize I was intruding. I was stupid enough to think you'd be glad to see me!"

"This isn't about you. And I want to be helpful to you. But your timing was lousy. Of all the times you've thought about leaving Mark, why did you choose this week? You knew I'd have my hands full over here. And you also knew that Stephanie and I had made some special plans after the conference. Why now? Don't you see how manipulative you've been?"

"Well, I'm sorry I came! I didn't mean to ruin your little honeymoon. I just thought I might be able to depend on you to help me, but I can see I was wrong. It's the same old thing, isn't it, Dad? If it's not patients that come first, it's the conference. And Stephanie, of course. Somewhere way down the line of your priorities you might remember that you have a daughter who has some needs also! I'll have the manager lock the door again. I wouldn't want to intrude on your precious time with your wife!" Hurling the door shut, Jayne stormed into her bedroom. Paul let her go. How long before she would claim responsibility for her own life? And Paul, who was usually rather optimistic, felt weighted down with sadness, owning the part he played in her sense of entitlement. He picked the wedding band off the floor and gathered the fragments of their photograph. How different Mark looked in the picture; Paul saw a relaxed and happy groom. Gaming tables in the background. Paul put the ring and the pieces of Mark's photograph in the table drawer beside the sofa.

CHAPTER 14

SWITZERLAND

After Jayne stormed out of the hotel room, and Stephanie retreated to her bath, Paul realized he needed space more than he needed sleep. He took the elevator down to the lobby.

"Dr. Tabor? Excuse me, sir. This message came for you just a moment ago. Do you want me to send it to your room or will you take it now?"

It was his exchange. Of course, it was. Paul had said to refer all his calls to the doctor who was covering for him. But it was Mark's doctor who was calling, asking if Paul knew where he could find Mark. It was important that he get in touch with him. Paul wasn't overly concerned; it could mean a dozen different things. He had no information to share; his thoughts didn't linger. He would call when he got back to his room. Then there was a message from Leah. His exchange had forwarded it to the hotel.

"Dr. Tabor, I hope you get this message. I'm so sorry about what I said at our last meeting. So very sorry." Leah's voice was soft; she sounded young and certainly vulnerable. She left a phone number.

Using the lobby phone, Paul called the Camille Hotel. "Leah Vassaux, please."

"I'm sorry, Monsieur, she checked out."

"Checked out? Did she leave any messages?"

"She did. She left a message saying she was going back to Switzerland."

"Are you sure?" Paul sounded bewildered. "Were there other messages? Maybe one for Paul Tabor?"

"Nope. She said to tell anyone who called they could reach her at her old address in Lausanne. Do you have that?"

"No," Paul said, reaching for his pen; he wrote down the name of the boarding school, the phone number, and the address. He wanted to know more, but before he could ask questions, the operator had hung up.

Paul tried to imagine what happened. Something to do with their last meeting? She left feeling angry; something unsaid troubled her enough to spin her out the way she did. It wasn't a good way to nurture a relationship. Unsatisfying for both of them. Unresolved conflicts in the last hour tended to strain the relationship.

She had been so determined to stay. And what was she going back to? Paul tried to find a positive side to this and hoped it would be for the best. At least she'll be in her own country and out of harm's way.

"Would you like us to bring your car up, sir?" the doorman asked.

Paul started to refuse, then reconsidered. Maybe a drive in the country would be just the thing. He was having trouble letting go of the conversation with Jayne. He didn't need any more city sounds at the moment. And sleep was out of the question.

Heading up into the low mountains, close to the eastern edge of Lausanne, Paul drove away from the congestion of buildings and homes and stopped on a bluff above the city. He walked on the road that passed through the grape country, seeing the lake far below and the colors of Lausanne splashed beside its northeast shore. He loved this city. This country. These people who dealt with life so reasonably.

In time his frustration dissipated in the presence of mountains and lake. He headed down toward Lac Léman considering what he would do next. He knew that if he were going to make any contact with Leah, it should be now. Once the conference started, his time would be limited.

Why would she even consider going back to a boarding school? Maybe it was just a temporary address until she relocated. On the other hand…Paul decided to quit speculating and stop by the school. That last meeting with Leah had been painful for her. And a disappointment to him. It would be good to see her for a moment, just to be sure she was all right. Odd, what a way she had of getting to him. What was it—her courage? Her determination to confront staggering problems and seek a viable solution? She had enough ego strength to try to pick up the pieces of her life and not expect someone else to do it for her. Paul felt an intense need to comfort her. To let her know that someone cared about what had happened to her. About what would happen to her now.

"Bonjour, monsieur." The girl who answered the door wore a typical boarding school uniform: solid blue skirt, white blouse, and functional shoes. She had the well-bred look of hundreds of others like herself who spent years raised in Switzerland's better preparatory institutions. The atmosphere was gracious, a sprawling estate set against the foothills.

"Bonjour, Mademoiselle. Je m'appelle Dr. Tabor. Je voudrais parler avec la directrice, s'il vous plait."

"Dr. Tabor." Her English was perfect, quite formal with a soft French accent. "Madame Rochet is in the garden. If you will come in, please, I will call her." The girl led Paul through the entry, into a room he thought looked like a parlor. "Please be seated, Doctor. I will tell Madame you are here."

There was an ambience of conservatism—a plainness about the decor. Swiss efficiency working and teaching by example, the value of thrift and cleanliness. Good solid structures, but no frills. The building itself, constructed before the Reformation, carried the memory of more ostentatious times, but Calvin's influence on the Swiss culture was present in all contemporary appointments.

Paul heard strong, hurried steps against the hardwood floors. He stood to greet a woman in her early fifties with a sturdy build and a grace uncommon for her size. Her hand extended toward him. "Dr. Tabor, I am Madame Rochet. Please, be seated. How can I help you?"

Paul took her hand, aware of her firm confident grip. Her dark eyes conveyed both intelligence and warmth. "A pleasure, Madame. I'm looking for a mutual friend, Leah Vassaux."

Paul felt her evaluation. "Leah? Leah hasn't been here for years. How do you know her, may I ask?"

"We met a few times in Los Angeles and then I had to leave town. I called her hotel and was told that she had returned to

Switzerland, which was completely unexpected. She left this as her forwarding address."

She frowned. Her head moved slowly sideward. "Returning here? But that is not possible. Leah graduated from here four or five years ago. Why would she use this address?"

Taking a card from his wallet, Paul handed it to her. In simple type were the words: Paul Tabor, MD and under that in smaller print, psychiatrist. Then his address and his phone number. "I am Leah's friend, Madame. Her confidant. And I am deeply concerned about her safety. Anything you tell me will only be used to help her deal with the loss she has experienced and perhaps her safety."

"Her safety? What has happened to Leah, Dr. Tabor?"

Paul hesitated. "Leah has just been through a traumatic experience. I can see by your reaction that you haven't heard about her sister."

As gently as he could, he said, "I have some tragic news." He paused, giving her time to prepare herself. "Nicole is dead, Madame."

Deep furrows appeared on her high forehead, then she covered her face with her hands and a deep moan escaped her usual composure. "Oh, no. Not one more tragedy, one more loss! That leaves dear Leah totally alone."

She took a deep breath in, trying to compose herself. "Please tell me, how did she die?"

"When Leah came into Nicole's apartment, she found Nicole lifeless on the floor at the bottom of the stairs. The police suspect it was not an accident."

"Oh, my God! This is such…astonishing news, Dr. Tabor." Her eyes watered. "Nicole was such a fine young woman. Do the police know why she was killed?"

"No. As far as I know, they have no suspects. I met with Leah several times and I'm concerned about her. She was isolated in a country where she knew no one. Unless she contacted the doctor I referred her to, she had no support system at all. I think it's important to speak with her."

Deep furrows appeared on her high forehead. "Yes, of course, I'll help you any way I can."

"I'm grateful, Madame. I know this is devastating news. Take your time, please. This is a lot to process."

Paul leaned forward in the chair, taking his time, giving her time. "I have no official information except what I heard from Leah. She's dealing with this in the most constructive way she can. If I can just talk with her, I can help her find a good therapist here in Lausanne or Geneva. Please tell me all you can about Leah."

"I hesitate because of privacy consideration. Normally, I would not discuss a student's personal matters without her consent."

"Nor would I, Madame. But she needs help. I don't know what kind of support she has had here in Switzerland, but she must not be alone. I'm Leah's friend, but I am also a psychiatrist. She needs our cooperation."

Madame hesitated and considered. "Very well." Her sigh was deep. And extremely sad. "When I think of Leah, I see a kind, fragile girl, with head down, soft spoken. So very lonely.

"Adolescent girls are not known for their compassion. Leah became a victim with her unsophisticated ways and teacher-pleasing behavior. She wanted attention…from a mother-figure, from a student, from her sister. Leah longed for a friend, but the other girls saw her as weak and a struggling student. That did not serve her well in this intellectually competitive school.

"We accepted her into the school out of gratitude. You see, years ago, her father supported us when we began this school. The school would not have made it without his help. It seemed like the responsible choice…I thought we should at least give her a chance. She would have done well in most schools. Many of the girls here have IQs around 130. And some even above. Leah did not. She would have been better in a less demanding environment. That was a major factor in her shyness and inability to form close friendships. She was immature but conscientious."

Madame seemed to look into the past; her voice was soft and she was silent for a while. Paul waited, watching the emotions that surfaced.

"With some tutoring, we thought she could keep up with the work. She did well in anything to do with the arts. Languages came easily for her. And she loved books. History and literature and poetry fascinated her. Math was a struggle. Chemistry was challenging. She failed physics. Oh, I do remember that! Leah's retentive skills are good, but not her analytical reasoning. She had no close friends and certainly was no judge of character. But she was kind and so very dear.

"After she graduated high school, she didn't want to attend the university. It wasn't convenient for her to live with Nicole at that time and she spent this last year in an arts program that was offered to girls gifted in that arena. Now that's where she excelled! She was outstanding in all of those classes, especially acting, which won her heart. When she left school, she joined a group of traveling thespians. I heard from her from time to time. She even considered going back to the university.

"I hope she sharpens her survival skills. I spent many nights worrying about her safety and her judgment."

"You sound disappointed in her choice."

"An understatement, to be sure. She's not a good judge of character. I was heartbroken when she didn't go to the university."

"Do you think she was talented, as an actress?"

"I do. I must admit, she was extraordinary on stage. In person, as I said, she was terribly shy. But I saw her play the lead in Saint Joan and she has amazing power. I am told that many actors are shy off stage. Leah surprised all of us and one reviewer said, 'She looks like a fawn, but she has the power of a tiger.' That one line says it all. After that, I didn't have a chance of getting her to go to the university."

Abruptly, Madame changed the subject and her voice softened.

"Leah and Nicole lost their parents when they were quite young. Leah was five. I think Nicole was about fifteen when it happened. Nicole took her responsibilities toward her sister quite seriously. I did not know the girls until I arrived almost ten years ago. When her sister, Nicole, was in university in Lausanne, she would take Leah on weekend vacations. She tried to make her life as normal as it could be. Nicole was so young for that responsibility, but she was always available when Leah needed her.

"Nicole was a lonely girl. I think she drew as much support from Leah as Leah gave to her. Her actions seemed extremely maternal. But there was something about her that seemed so…unfulfilled, one might say. But now…what a terrible thing." Deeply affected by Paul's news, she still retained her composure. "Tell me…how did you come to know her?"

"That's a complicated story, Madame. But I'm not asking these questions out of curiosity. Right now, my concern is why she returned to Switzerland and I'd like to know if she's planning to stay here. I was surprised that she didn't tell me she was returning."

"I encouraged Leah to see a therapist when I first came here, but when I mentioned it to her sister, she was opposed to it; and the girl's legal guardian showed no interest in her whatsoever.

"Leah's dependence on her sister was extreme. In all the years she was here, I can hardly remember a day that Leah did not mail a letter to Nicole.

"Those letters, and a journal she was attached to, served as her confidant all the years she was here.

"Most girls her age have a need to establish friendships. Nicole seemed to be the only person Leah trusted.

"I suspect—I hope—that Leah sought you out to help her through this difficult time. I can understand your concern if she left without telling you. But what is it that brought you to Switzerland?"

"I'm here for a conference."

Her eyes brightened. "Ah…the conference on the Catalyst for Innovation!"

"There's been no publicity on that. How did you know?"

"I have friends at the medical school…that's why your name was familiar! Of course, you are the one who had the vision for the conference. It should be an exciting week for you, Dr. Tabor. A dear friend of mine told me how much she is looking forward to this."

"We all are. May I ask you one more question about Leah? What happened to her parents?"

A heavy sigh of frustration. Madame shook her head as she said, "I've heard conflicting stories about that. Leah never talked with me about her parents, but Nicole told me that they were killed in a car accident. And that's what Leah said to the other students who were rude enough to ask. That may have just been the best way for the girls to answer, if one of the more sordid stories is true. Of course, it is possible that saying the parents died in a car accident is the story that the children were told to protect them. Sometimes a lie is beneficial in service to mental health.

"Whatever it was that actually happened was apparently a source of great humiliation as well as grief. One could sense that more in the themes that were revealed in some of her poetry." She ran her fingers through her hair.

"What were the stories that circulated?"

"Gossip among the parents said her mother died two years before her father…there was violence. Something to do with a young American boy who lived in their attic apartment. Someone said she was murdered by her husband when he found her in their bed with the boy. Others said it was the boy who killed her, and the father tried to stop him. As another story goes, her husband was so badly injured that it brought on a stroke, and he couldn't speak. He lived for two years before he died in a facility. There are so many stories; I don't know what to believe.

"I wish she had talked with you about her parents," Madame said. "Nicole told me Leah didn't remember anything about their mother. I wonder if she even knows the truth. It must be terrible for her to carry so much sorrow for all these years and not share it with anyone. And now…this terrible thing…the death of Nicole leaves her absolutely alone."

Paul leaned forward, his voice consoling. "You were very close to her, weren't you?"

"Yes, she had a way of bringing out all my maternal instincts. I try to be available to all the girls, but Leah, how can I say? She had a way of making me feel…needed."

"I know what you mean, Madame. Well, I assume that Leah's somewhere in the city and will contact you as soon as she settles. If you hear from her, would you give me a call at the Beau-Rivage in Lausanne? And please tell her that I came here and would very much like to hear from her—actually, I'm returning her call. Tell her that I'm concerned about her. Please."

"Of course. It's good that we keep in touch."

When Paul returned to the hotel there was a message waiting for him from the headmistress. She said that there was a priest-turned-psychologist in the village who might have more information. "I took the liberty of telling him about you and he said he could see you in his office tomorrow morning at nine. Here is his address and phone number. Please let him know if that is a good time for you."

Paul had other plans for Monday morning, but he could change them to the afternoon. Guests wouldn't be checking in for the conference until Tuesday afternoon and Henri had things under control.

Lying in bed, weary from her hours of traveling and the emotional stress Jayne brought to the event, Stephanie stared at the molding on the cathedral ceiling. She heard the door open in the living room of their suite.

"Paul?"

"Hi. You get some sleep?" he asked.

"Not much. I tried, but I could hear you and Jayne quarreling, and the walls are so blasted thick I couldn't hear what was being said and then everything got quiet. I just kept wondering what happened and couldn't quit thinking about it. I must have fallen asleep."

Paul smiled and shook his head, then bent over to kiss her soft waiting lips. He ran his hand along the curve of her hip. "Well, what was said wasn't worth losing sleep over. I just set some limits and what you heard was the sound of a very spoiled woman/child who didn't get her way for a change."

"About what?"

"The obvious. I clarified that the days after the conference belong to us…which I had already told her in LA…and I tried to explain the restrictions of the conference, and most threatening of all, I suppose, I finally had the courage to say no to something she wanted."

"How did it feel?"

"I think we both experienced some growing pains. Long overdue. Have I always been such an easy touch?"

She answered him with her eyes.

"And has she always been that manipulative?"

Her expression intensified only slightly.

"Well, no wonder she's having trouble setting her own limits. I always felt sorry for Jayne. Always tried to make up for… whatever. I wonder how many times I've seen that in patients and helped them see it and not recognized it in my own life. I feel like a fool."

"Paul Tabor! If you do a guilt trip over this, I am going to scream! Now stop it!"

He laughed. "Your response is a bit raw, but effective. I'm not going to wallow in self-recrimination. I promise you."

"Well, that's good to know. While I get dressed, why don't you invite Jayne to lunch? Now that I know what the boundaries are, I don't resent her so much."

"Really?" His sarcastic tone made her laugh.

Paul crossed the room toward the living room and the bedroom beyond. "Jayne's had time to deal with her anger and is probably deeply involved in a Swiss soap opera."

Stephanie peeled herself slowly from the bed and started putting on her makeup. Before her mascara was dry, she saw Paul leaning against the door frame. A sheet of hotel stationery was in his hand. His expression was drawn. Worried. Taking the paper from him she read the note:

"Dad—Sorry to be in your way. I won't bother you anymore. Jayne."

"Oh shit," Stephanie said, wadding the paper into a ball and throwing it to the floor. "What a rotten bratty thing to do! I knew she'd find a way to ruin this trip!"

"She's gone. Nothing in the room but the note."

"She's not gone, Paul. She's filling this room with her presence. She has an amazing ability to absorb everyone's energies wherever she goes. Whether she's here or not here, she certainly knows how to get attention!"

"Where would she go?" The question was to himself. Stephanie stayed quiet, not trusting herself to open her mouth again. Her thoughts were becoming increasingly hostile and another sentence or two and she thought she would go too far.

Neither of them spoke for a while. Then it was Paul. "I shouldn't worry about her. After all, she's a grown woman. And perfectly capable of taking care of herself."

Stephanie held his gaze and let her face show all the hardness she felt, and her voice was cold as she meant it to be. "That's right. Now why don't you just accept that and let go of her. I traveled over most of Europe alone when I wasn't much older than Jayne. So do a lot of other kids. If she's not woman enough to handle it, she'd damn well better learn. And the sooner you let her fall down and pick herself up, the sooner she's likely to grow up. She made the first move, Paul. Maybe she's trying to stand on her own feet and just can't do it without kicking you in the shins on the way out. For God's sake, will you let her be!"

A heavy sigh. "Yeah."

Softly. "Yeah, what?"

"Yeah, I'll try to turn her loose. I'm not sorry for the way I handled the situation this morning and I'm disgusted that she reacted like she did. I'll try not to worry about what she might do. She won't go home to Mark; she certainly won't come back here. She has no close friends that I know of and she has not spoken to her mother for years. But I'll try not to consider her options."

Stephanie slipped easily into his arms. They held each other for a long time in silence. "Paul, you remember when Jayne was fifteen? The sixties were in her blood. She was living with her mother then and she ran away from home. She left a note, just like she did today. She said she was going to hitchhike to San Francisco and be a hippie. Live with all the 'free people.' Remember? And just when you were so frantic, the doorbell rang and two real hippies brought her to your door. They had picked her up hitchhiking on the highway and, kind hearts that they were, they convinced her that it was a dangerous place for her to be. They brought her home. It turned out fine," Stephanie said.

Paul thought for a minute before he answered her. "Did you ever wonder how she would have turned out if some compassionate people hadn't convinced her that she was making a dangerous choice and went out of their way to bring her home?"

"Paul, Jayne is not a child. She's a grown woman and she has to figure this out on her own. And even God never forced anybody to accept wisdom or love against their will."

That was about all he was willing to hear, right then. "Well, I don't know about you," he said, "but jet lag's really hit me. Then, I have so many things to tell you, but right now I just want to get a few minutes of shut eye. Over dinner, I'll tell you about my day."

CHAPTER 15

MALIBU

When Leah and Mark arrived at the Tabors' beach house in Malibu, it was 5:00 Saturday morning, Pacific Coast time. Mark opened the living room drapes to reveal a calm sea and stars that were fading into the early morning light.

"That is so beautiful. I'm grateful to you for bringing me here, Mark, and for…well, just for being here for me. I'm scared to even think about what would have happened to me if you hadn't come along when you did."

"Anyone in your situation would be terrified, but you'll be just fine here with me, Leah. You're safe now."

Mark saw the adoring look she gave him and thought she wanted more than a hug. Of course, she would. Wasn't he the one who saved her from the man who stalked her? If these were normal times, he would gladly accept her silent invitation. If these were normal times he wouldn't be in constant pain, he wouldn't be taking pills just so he could function. Mark reminded himself he didn't want to hurt Leah. All he wanted to do was read and then destroy Nicole's journal. How could he ever be safe until it was in his possession? He could force Leah to give it to him. But if he made her angry, she would tell the cops. He had to be patient. He didn't want to hurt her. He didn't want to have to stop her from destroying him.

Mark walked over to the wine cooler and said, "Unless I'm misreading your history, I'll bet you've never been offered a California chardonnay at five a.m."

"That's true," she smiled. "California is full of surprises."

She touched his hand when he offered her the glass.

"That may be the first time I've seen your smile, Leah. It's lovely!"

"I'm glad you think so," she said. "I wouldn't be smiling now if you hadn't been here for me."

It occurred to Mark that it might be to his advantage to give Leah the romance she seemed ready for. It was certainly predictable that she would long to be held, to be loved, to feel safe. But given his medication and his stress, he just wasn't up to it. Not now anyway.

"To a safe future…for both of us," Mark said. It wasn't long before the wine had them both relaxed enough to realize how tired they felt. They agreed the rest of the bottle would have to keep until later. He carried Leah's bag upstairs and assured her that he would sleep quite well downstairs on the sofa. "It's long and just firm enough. I've spent many nights there when I had visitors. Look, it's almost daylight. Oh, later I'll need to borrow your shower. There's just a powder room downstairs.

"One more thing…My ex-wife left some of her clothes in the closet. She was in a hurry when she left for Paris and I said she could leave them there until she decides where she wants to settle." Mark enjoyed the game he was playing. A broad smile stretched across his face as he said, "Stephanie and I have a compassionate relationship. We're good friends but not good partners."

It was hard for Leah to sleep, even though she was exhausted. Despite the hypnotic rhythm of the waves, she kept hearing the guttural sound of a large dog; maybe it was a German shepherd or a Rottweiler. Something huge. Then she heard the squeaky high-pitched voice of a miniature lap dog. Finally, the dogs quieted and she fell asleep. Dreams woke her twice with warnings she didn't even try to interpret. Her shoulders ached from the tension, and she felt as vulnerable as she did when she arrived. Too many conflicting messages caused a plethora of anxieties.

Mark was too wound up to sleep. He kept thinking about Leah. She reminded him so much of her mother, not so much in features, but in the way she held her wine glass, the way she moved, the way she smiled.

He got up and poured a martini, knowing he would pay a price for it, but it would be worth the pain. It always settled his nerves, if not his ulcers. It wasn't long before he needed just one more. And then another.

Ever since Nicole's death, his thoughts had turned so frequently to his life in Switzerland. It wasn't Nicole he longed for, but her mother, Genevieve. Lately, he couldn't stop thinking about the time they spent together.

Genevieve was his first love, and his last love. Other women were just convenient ornaments.

The June that he graduated high school, Mark took all his money from his savings account. Two summers of work with a construction firm, heavy work, good pay. Three winters of tutoring, easy work, less money but consistent. He saved all of it. He planned to stay until the dollars ran out. It would be worth every brick he lifted, every nail he struck, every dumb kid he force-fed with algebra. Hopefully he could afford to stay a month, maybe more, if he could hitch his way, trade a little work for a meal.

He got a ride out of Bern with a Swiss farmer in a truck. All the way to Thun. A few days around the lake and he moved on toward Geneva. An Italian took him as far as Spiez, then another farmer, who spoke only French, let him out when he turned off on a smaller road toward his house. It was the kind of country that storybook tales are made of. The greens, deep and vibrant. The mountains fierce in their beauty and potential violence; he had heard the stories of these roads in winter. The old farmer spoke slowly, and Mark's Bakersfield French served him better than he had expected. Four years of it in school was all he had. But his ear was good and his will strong.

He wanted to learn about everything, hoping to latch on to something that could help him stay out of Bakersfield, and the likes of it, for the rest of his life. Education was the only way. And hard work. He wasn't afraid of either. His father had resisted helping him through college. He said that Mark had saved his own money, let him spend that if he wanted an education. He had a scholarship; he could work for his keep. Starting in September.

But that was before he met Genevieve.

He met her when he walked along the road toward Lausanne, enjoying the exercise, hoping that a car would come along before he was tired. The pack on his back was heavy, complete with sleeping bag and a few clothes, his passport, and the bottom half of his round-trip ticket home.

The Mercedes could be heard in the distance, breaking the silence in the still mountain air. Mark walked backward, watching it come around the turns, over the dips in the road. He smiled before he could even see who was behind the wheel. And he held his thumb in the air and a smile on his face. The car stopped. All innocence and charm he was that day. And where was he going on this deserted road? To Geneva? Lausanne? Anywhere out of these mountains. It would be a cold night, if he had to camp.

His winsomeness caused that enchanting laugh of hers. She opened the door for him. "Come in, come in," she said in English when she heard his American accent. "I'll take you as far as Lac Léman. What a place to be stuck! How did you get here? Ah. Well, the farmer didn't do such a bad turn after all. You will be in Montreux long before dark."

Light brown hair lifted high on her head. She was elegant in an earthy way. Proud. A soft beauty, somewhere in her middle thirties, Mark guessed, more by her manner than any signs of youth slipping away.

"Are you all alone on your trip?" she asked. "No friend?"

"No friend. I'm trying to see as much of Europe as I can before my money gives out. Then I have to go home to Bakersfield. That's in California."

"A beautiful place, no?"

"No! It's out in the middle of nowhere with nothing to do and nowhere to go and nothing to see if you went."

That laugh, more girlish than her years. "No wonder you want to stay in Europe. How long have you been here?"

"Two weeks. And three days," he added, reluctant to admit so many days had crossed off the calendar since he arrived. "I should be able to last another two weeks, if I'm lucky."

She took her eyes off the road and let them rest on his face. Gypsy eyes, he thought, but corrected himself, recalling that gypsies were a darker people—or the ones he had heard about were. But she had that quality—spontaneous movements, quick and graceful. Oh, she was something, this generous woman who risked giving such a needy boy a ride.

In the next village, they stopped for hot bread at the bakery. Lunch was coming soon, Genevieve said, and only a few miles farther she turned off the road onto a smaller trail that led to a fast-moving stream and an ancient tree. "I've stopped here before," she said, "on my way to or from Interlaken. I like the view from here. Don't you…Mark, is it?"

"Yeah." He liked the sound of his name, coming from her. "The view's great. Better than Bakersfield even," he said, hoping to hear her laugh again. He did.

"Help me get things out of the trunk," she said.

A basket of food and a blanket were among the clutter, and he lifted them out while she brought the wine and closed the trunk.

Genevieve said, "Put the blanket here. The grass is fluffier, like a skinny mattress." She described each item of food as she took it from the basket. "We have the bread, not long from the oven. I brought several cheeses. So here you can taste from each—a nice French Brie that is so creamy and smooth on your tongue.

The Swiss hard cheese is a bit tart, not too much. Then we have Gruyère, that's softer, made locally." She was playful, watching the expression on Mark's face with delight. "Also we have one pear. Sorry I didn't bring dessert. I only have that at dinner. Now you will taste a very special wine; the grapes are grown right here on the hills above the lake. The wine is called Chasselas. This is one of the most popular white wines in Switzerland. I think you will like it."

"Do you always eat like this?" Mark asked, watching in awe as she opened the wine, pouring it into a single glass. "We must share," she said. "I didn't expect company!" She toasted with a gesture, "*à votre santé*," handing the glass to him. Mark's eyes were wide with amazement at his good fortune.

He gestured wildly, over the food, the mountains, the sky with cumulus clouds. He couldn't find the words.

Genevieve laughed. "It is a very simple lunch, but I love picnics. So, yes, I do this every time I pass here."

Never in eighteen years had food tasted better, had the breeze been more gentle, the view more spectacular. After lunch Genevieve brought a pad of paper from the car and while he sat there, leaning against the tree, she began sketching. "You have a good face, Mark; it's those cheek bones that are so special. The eyes are nice. Good hands, like a pianist. Or a surgeon. Look. Do you like it?"

"Do I look like that?" he asked, awed by the image that stared up at him from the paper.

"To me you do. That's the difference in sketches and photographs. This is the way you look, as I see you. Others may see you differently. But to me, there is a quality of strength—and shyness, too, something very sensitive about your eyes, though hard to understand. You have heard that before? That it's hard to get to know you?"

"I guess."

"It's because your eyes are so dark, I think. And you keep yourself so protected. You do, yes?"

"I suppose. I don't mean to."

"Do you like the picture?"

"A lot."

"Then you may keep it."

It took a minute before he knew what to say, feeling foolish and awkward in his gratitude. He would always keep the sketch; no one had ever seen him like that before. Least of all himself.

"You could use some money, Mark. And I need to hire someone like you. Would you like to work for me?"

"Sure. Oh, yeah. Sure, I would. What would you want me to do?"

"Pose for me."

"Huh?"

"I'm an artist. I recently lost my model. You should do very nicely."

"Well, I'm not a model!"

"Such scorn! My, oh my, you must have such an idea of models!"

"Guys who model are sissies."

"Not the ones who work for me, they're not! That's why I offered you the job; I can get all kinds of men to pose for me who are…what did you call them? Sissies. But I need a masculine type for my work. It's very hard, working for me. No one will ever tell you that working for a sculptor is easy. The hours are long; the pay is fair. Your muscles will ache at the end of the day."

"But I wouldn't know what to do."

"I will show you. You must be able to hold a position for a long time without moving. It is not easy. But I have a studio with an attic room above. Sometimes I rent the loft out to students. You can sleep there if you like; and there's a hot plate and a small bath. Nothing grand, but better, I suspect, than the other places you have stayed in Europe.

"I have two daughters. The little one is five and the older one is fifteen. You must have nothing to do with them. I don't want them to form attachments to tenants. You can, and must, avoid any communication. It is in their best interest."

"Okay by me. I'll be invisible. Hey, don't I need a work permit? I was told I couldn't work in Switzerland."

"That won't be necessary. Not when you are working for me. It will be our little secret."

Genevieve's studio was located on the second floor of an old house. A skylight let the summer sun burst through. There was the smell of paint and wet clay. Some sketches were on the easel and some naked bronze figures on the workbench.

He looked away. And saw her smile.

"I'm not going to pose like that!" he said.

"Are you shy about your body? You are so handsome to be shy."

"I just don't go around taking my clothes off," he said.

"The body is beautiful, Mark. Nothing to feel ashamed of. Where did you learn such things?"

He hung his head and felt anger in the memory. Genevieve noticed, so she sketched his face that day…and his hands. Over and again, those hands.

Often during the week, she sketched him by the window. When the sun was too hot coming through the glass, he removed his shirt.

"That's nice." Soft-voiced woman, smooth hands against his face, turning him slightly, looking for a certain angle.

He liked the work. More, he liked Genevieve. She was kinder than anyone he had ever known. She was gentle; she was caring.

"Tell me, Mark. What will you do when you go back to the States?"

"Go to college. It means a lot to me to get an education. My parents…well, neither of them ever went to college. I would really like to be a doctor, but I don't know how I could afford it." But as the days went on, he spent a great deal of time studying the anatomy books that she kept in her studio. Every night, he went to bed reading them. And the art books as well. And then he started thinking about how he could stay in Switzerland. Could Genevieve make that happen? He would do anything if he could just stay, just for a year, maybe. He could defer his scholarship. Or maybe she could help him get in a college here. How would he go about getting her to help him? It should seem like her idea. He would think about that. Act carefully. Maybe there was a chance.

"Were your grades good?" she asked him one day.

"All A's. All through high school. Never got anything else."

"Do you enjoy working for me, Mark?"

"You know I do. You're the nicest person…" The words embarrassed him and he stopped, his admiration stated before he knew the thought was formed.

"If there was a way that you could stay on—here with me—and go to the University of Lausanne, would you like that?"

"To stay on? How? I don't have enough money, and it's too late to apply to college here. I've been accepted at home on a scholarship. Sure, I'd rather stay here. Anyway, I don't have a work permit and you couldn't have enough work to keep me on forever."

"Not forever," she said. "Come, let me show you something." Opening a door with a large key, she led him into the next room. It was filled with blocks of clay and some things behind white sheets. "I'm getting ready for an exhibit," she said. "In Paris. The smaller works are ready. Some finished, some ready to cast." He looked around the room at the collection of bronze figures, a few in marble, some in clay. "Here is my problem," she said, lifting the sheet to reveal two figures.

"Oh, wow!" No other words would come. Mark stared at the clay figure, the exquisitely formed young woman, her bare body in such an expression of tenderness that he found it hard to believe she wasn't alive. A nymph's body, reaching toward the other form. Her bare breasts were small, anxious tips of sensuousness. The bare belly drew his eyes, pulling them down. "Oh, wow," he said again, as if those words contained the epitome of accolades.

"The woman is completed, as you can see. The man—ah. The model walked out before I could finish. He wanted more money, easier hours, whatever. He was miserable. I could not work with him. It is just as well he left. I went on to finish the woman, and now…now I must find another model. You're perfect for it, Mark. Please tell me you'll stay."

"I…I couldn't. I couldn't do that."

Of course, he could.

"Let me assure you that I have worked with many male models. I think of the body in a different way. To me, you are a thing of beauty, an object, well-designed. I will do nothing to embarrass you."

"Okay. Yeah. I could stay, I guess I could, but I have to be back for school at the end of August."

"Perhaps something else could be arranged. My husband's company provides scholarships to worthy students at the University of Lausanne. Perhaps that is possible to arrange.

"Until our work is finished, you can live here, in the attic room, like you are now. I know that would be fine with my husband. We can work through the summer until you must leave for school…or you may find yourself studying here. We will see."

She laughed when she saw the expression on his face. "Now, don't get too excited. I can only promise you that I will try.

"I'm assuming your body is as good as I think it is." Her eyes wandered again across the dark denim, admiring the muscles hidden beneath his worn jeans.

Mark sat down on the model's block. "All right." It was a whisper. "All right, why not? I'll do it. What the hell." Moving quickly before he could regain his senses, Mark pulled off his shirt and sneakers. Then the dark jeans. A small hesitation, then with quick nervous movements, he peeled off his shorts. It was done. No turning back now.

Genevieve knew how to make it easy for him. She ignored him. Getting rags and instruments together, moving the block to an appropriate position, just as she did every day.

"Come over here," she said, as if she were directing him to move a chair, as if he were not naked before her. "We will work quite well together, you and I.

"Now that I've found you, I'm really delighted that Andre walked out on me." Then her eyes focused on the business at hand, and he felt the gaze of those evaluating eyes.

"Yes. You will do very nicely," she said, and the admiration wasn't hidden from Mark, though he could hardly believe it and didn't understand why. He didn't see any grace at all in his form. But who was he to question such authority? He relaxed a little. Not much.

"You have a better muscular structure than Andre. And you are not difficult. What a pleasure it will be to work with you. We have a good rapport and that is imperative if I am to do my best work. You'll get over your nervousness, Mark. It won't take long, I promise. You are…perhaps, not too experienced with women?"

"I never had time for girls."

"Ah."

"I mean, I tried once." He blushed. Why had he said that? He had never told that to anyone.

She sat beside him on the block and said, "And?"

He didn't answer.

"She was someone you cared for? A young girl?"

"She was a slut. I hated her!"

"And she was unkind."

He was silent.

"A man's sexual education shouldn't be left to women like that. First impressions are strong; they leave scars on the emotions." She was kind in sound, in feeling.

"Can we get to work now?" he asked, longing to change the subject.

"Of course. Here, take the position that I have begun with the clay. There. Yes. Very nice. Reach out—as if you will touch the woman. It is her breast, just inches from your hand, can you see on the figure how it will go?"

She turned his shoulders, angling them to the right. A hand upon his leg, lifting his thigh an inch.

"I will begin with the shoulders and the arms," she said. Her fingers sought out the muscles along the spine. "Are my fingers too cold?" she asked. It was the heat beneath the coolness that he felt. Her hands explored his back, getting to know each bulge of muscle, each vertebra. "Oh, this will be very nice, Mark." She returned to the clay and he couldn't see what she was doing. Then she came back.

"Here, can you lift just a little higher, here, with this arm?" She stood in front of him, lifting his elbow, rearranging his fingers. He would not touch Genevieve. He would not. His hand was stretched toward her full breast that revealed the nipple beneath the artist's thin cotton smock. He would not. And he forced himself to concentrate on his hand as she held it there. He would not reach for her. Less obedient than his hand, another part of him reached instead. There was nothing at all that he could do about that. How could she ignore the enlarging phallus that stretched toward her? How could she?

And why should she? He saw her smile. "Mark," she whispered. No embarrassment, no ridicule, just the faintest whisper of his name. And her lips soft against his, and her tongue, unhurried.

"Don't look so worried, everything will be…just…fine." Wiping away his frown with warm fingers. "Take your time." Easy against his ear. His hands fumbled with her clothes. Quickly she enveloped him, anticipating the sudden explosion, saying, "Ah, what a man you are, Mark!" Saying it often enough that summer so that he almost believed it. Oh, Genevieve. It was perfection. Nothing so perfect could last forever.…

Mark knew that he was the luckiest of all guys. He had Genevieve. And before the end of August, he had her husband working the kind of magic that is common among the entitled gentry that functions in every country. Mark, after making excellent scores on the entrance exam, received an anonymous scholarship to the university. It was a win all around. Mark got exactly what he wanted. So did Genevieve. Her husband, who headed a major financial corporation and was gone more than he was at home, was glad to have another adult living on the property. The two little girls, Nicole and Leah never entered their mother's studio. They were accustomed to having tenants in the attic space, but they never met any of them. It was life as usual for them.

How could a situation so perfect have ended so badly?

CHAPTER 16

MALIBU

It was the sound of Mark in the kitchen that woke Leah.

"Time to get up. Food is on the table." Leah looked over the railing from the bedroom, "I'll take a quick shower and be right down." She would much rather be sleeping, but she got herself dressed and walked down the spiral staircase as quickly as she could.

On the table was a loaf of bread, butter, and jam. One napkin was placed askew beside a mat. A spoon was on one side of the plate. Coffee was already poured, chilling by the moment. No cream was on the table.

Leah wasn't hungry and chose to focus on the bookcase, which she loved. Mark was in the powder room, taking a long time and that was just fine with her.

Books climbed the walls on either side of the fireplace to the high beams of the two-story ceiling. An antique ladder leaned against the bookcase. A catwalk dividing the upper and lower shelves. Leah took a few steps up the ladder, then read the titles and the authors.

She became engrossed in the variety of interests reflected there. Art books covered two long rows, then there were volumes of poetry that included Anne Sexton, Sylvia Plath, and Edna St. Vincent Millay. Archeology, photography, and a myriad of subjects dotted the shelves. She had expected to find books on psychiatry but was surprised to see so many philosophers represented there. She recognized some of the names, Bonhoeffer, Kierkegaard, as well as a row of novels by authors she didn't recognize.

Then she found the shelf that held the music. Apparently, Mark had a wide range of interests. The stacks of LP's and cassettes included everything from classical to pop and she looked forward to hearing some of his Carole King and Cat Stevens. Then she found Joni Mitchell and Stevie Wonder. She couldn't wait to hear some of those. Maybe during dinner.

Leah went back to the books and removed one about chess. She opened the cover. In the front leaf was a bookplate. And the name, Paul Tabor. They must know each other pretty well to borrow books. She wondered what happened to cause such hostility between them.

Quickly she closed the book and replaced it on the shelf when she heard Mark coming toward her. "I love your house, Mark. And your library most of all. Have you lived here long?"

"Not really."

He reached out and took her hand. "You're not trembling anymore."

When he touched her, Leah realized that his own hands were less than steady.

"I feel safe here," she said. "No one can find me now. It will feel so good just to walk in the sand and take a swim. Can we do that right after you finish breakfast?"

"I'd rather not. Just a precaution. I want you to stay in, no point in letting anyone see you here. Besides, we need to get to that journal."

"Why, Mark? Whoever was trying to get the journal couldn't know I'm here. No one was following us."

"Leah, I don't want to argue about it. I don't want you going outside. I just don't want you getting any more exposure than you have to, for a while."

She started to argue but his voice had been so curt she didn't want to irritate him further. It wasn't all that important, she thought. After all, he was just trying to protect her, wasn't he?

"You have so many fine graphics, and I love that abstract glass sculpture on the coffee table. It's extraordinary. Have you been collecting for a long time?" She couldn't imagine that he had chosen it.

"Not long."

Abruptly he changed the subject. "Tell me about yourself, Leah. What do you want to do with your life?"

"Stay alive. Sorry. I can't get that man off my mind. Even when I'm talking about something else, I think of him. What am I interested in? Theater, most of all. If Nicole had moved to New York, I would have moved there long ago. I'm not interested in film. I just want to work on the stage. I doubt I could make a career of that on the West Coast. I'll find out."

"You're not considering medicine, like Nicole?"

"No." Her voice saddened again. "I couldn't be a doctor. I panic in emergencies."

"You seem to have held up admirably through this week. I'd say you're pretty capable in emergencies."

"I wish I felt that way. I just need to get through all this. Get some roots down."

"Why don't you go back to Switzerland? Or you could go to New York, if that's your dream."

"No. There's nothing to go back to in Europe and I'm here now. I have enough adjustments to make."

"Did Dr. Tabor encourage you to stay?"

"Why would he? He's not my psychiatrist. He's been very kind to me but I make my own decisions. Why do you dislike him so much?" Leah regretted asking. She knew it wasn't her business to pry.

"Now, didn't your mother ever teach you that if you couldn't say something nice, you shouldn't say anything at all?" His voice was playful, artificial. His hand gestured broadly as he spoke.

"My mother never had time to teach me much. I was five years old when she died."

"I'm sorry…For a moment I forgot about your mother's passing. Her name was Genevieve, right? Nicole mentioned her, of course. Maybe there's something about her in Nicole's journal."

"If you don't mind, Mark…I'd rather not right now."

He touched her hand. A comforting gesture that failed in its purpose.

Leah couldn't think of anything that would stop him from bringing back the past. She struggled for a moment, then said, "Mark, I'm so sorry. Thinking about what we might find in the journal now just makes me sadder than I already am. Nicole was like my mother and she was always there for me. I have no memories of my real mother, only an awareness of the void she left when she died. Now they are both gone."

Through the afternoon, into the early evening, Mark worked at keeping a conversation going. Leah tried her best, but it was hard work. She didn't want to talk about the past. She didn't want to even think about her future. Finally, she said, "Mark, I'm sorry, I'm so tired, I just have to get some sleep."

Leah climbed the circular stairs, taking her time. They were steep and she took care not to fall. She was thinking about Nicole.

Leah had dreams that warned her of danger. She ignored them. She had premonitions, the kind Nicole used to tell her to forget about and think happy thoughts. Nicole said, you had to stand strong against nightmares. If you kept thinking about them, they gained power.

Did Leah really hear Mark's voice in the night? Was there a phone conversation that upset him?

Perhaps Mark had talked in his sleep. Or maybe she had just imagined it.

CHAPTER 17

LAUSANNE, SAINT SAPHORIN & VEVEY

Paul rolled out of bed early that Monday morning, trying not to wake Stephanie. It was 7:00 in Switzerland, but his body was still on Pacific Coast time, nine hours earlier; he was longing for sleep. Paul had breakfast and a short walk before calling for his car.

Dr. Lucien had a small office that was functional but certainly not "decorated." It was also tidier than Paul's had ever been. The chairs were firm and not a stray paper was to be seen.

"Thank you for seeing me on such short notice. I really appreciate it." Paul was welcomed with a firm handshake and a warm smile. "I have some questions about a local family and hope you know the answers."

"The Vassaux family, yes, so I heard. Please, have a seat. I never saw them professionally, so I am free to share what I've heard. I hope I can help you." Dr. Lucien returned to his chair and said, "There are few secrets in our village, Dr. Tabor. You are curious about the Vassaux family…as are most people in the area. And there are many assumptions made. I think I know the truth about some of them. What do you need to know and why is it important to you?"

"Anything that has to do with Madame Vassaux or her husband is important to me. Their daughter knows nothing about what really happened to her parents. She needs to have some closure."

Dr. Lucien was silent for a long minute. Paul finally said, "I know you must think it's odd that a man who isn't a detective is asking about the death of a woman who died many years ago. I'm her daughter's friend and I am concerned about her. She needs to know how her mother died and I have many questions about Genevieve Vassaux. And her husband."

"We were never close," the psychologist said, "but I knew her casually. She was a famous artist. Everyone in the village knows her story, especially if they lived here in the sixties."

"I'm trying to find out how she died."

"It depends on whom you ask. Some people think she was murdered. I am not sure what the real story is. The gossip was that it was one of the young men who worked for her. She was very good at sculpting nudes. There was a lot of talk about a young American boy who lived in her studio and disappeared after she died. He was not arrested so maybe he had nothing to do with it."

"Do you know his name?"

"It has been a long time, Dr. Tabor. I remember seeing him, but we never spoke. He was probably in his late teens. I do not recall his name. He took off after the police said he could go. Ah, I think his family name was Hall. Maybe his first name will come to me.

"Genevieve had a series of lovers, young men who modeled for her. She was discreet but it is very hard to keep a secret in this town. I know the woman who was the governess for the girls, and I trust her report of the story. She would know more than anyone about what really happened.

"I will tell you what I think happened and you can see if my story is the same as hers. I heard that the eldest daughter, Nicole, was at summer camp. Leah was very young. I'm guessing about four, maybe five. She was staying with her governess at her house overnight and they were due back the next day. For some reason—I forget why—Leah and her governess came home a day early.

"I know Leah was the one who opened the bedroom door and saw her mother lying on the floor. I can only imagine how she interpreted what she saw.

"Part of the intrigue was that Madame Rothman said she saw a man dressed totally in black, running past the window. She could not see his face. I do not know if Leah saw him or not.

"Most of the town thought the American tenant was the man who killed Genevieve. But the police didn't think so. When they went upstairs to the attic room, the boy was sleeping. When the police told him Genevieve was dead, apparently, he was devastated. Of course, that could have been grief, or it could have been fear. They gave a long interrogation but finally they let him go.

"Days later, after an autopsy, the report came back that Genevieve had been drinking heavily and she died from an overdose of sleeping pills. So, it was either an accident or it was suicide.

"Most of the locals believed someone tricked her into taking the pills."

"What do you think?"

"It's hard to imagine that joyful woman intentionally taking her own life. She had two lovely little girls and a glowing reputation as an artist. And a husband who would give her anything she wanted. Which included the liberty to have a lover, so long as she wasn't open about it.

"Genevieve frequently had migraine headaches and perhaps too much wine brought one on. If she was high on alcohol and the migraine started, she might have reached for the meds for her headache and taken too many or taken the wrong ones. I don't know how much it would take to kill her, but an accidental overdose is the most reasonable assumption."

Paul considered that for a moment. "That sounds reasonable except for one thing: how would that explain the man who ran by the window?"

"I am sorry, Dr. Tabor, I have no answer for that. But you are just a few blocks from a woman who was the children's governess. Yesterday, I called to tell her of your interest, and she said she will be at home all day and you can stop by anytime. I'll write her address down for you. It has been a pleasure meeting you, Dr. Tabor. You have my phone number, and you can call me if you have more questions. By the way, I've heard wonderful things about your conference on creativity. Congratulations."

Paul followed the therapist's directions and walked a few blocks to the home of Greta Rothman. Maybe the governess could be helpful.

To Paul, it seemed like a different world in this quaint village. He could meet with three people he needed to see without previous appointments, and they were generous with their time. He thought of how that compared to how many days that would take in LA and almost laughed out loud.

The Rothman cottage was built two hundred years earlier, simple and charming, a storybook house with two rocking chairs on the porch. Local stones, contoured by time and wear, shaped the walkway. Paul felt like he was walking back in time. Greta Rothman was remarkably agile for being in her eighties. Her posture was perfect, and she stood to greet Paul with the grace of a much younger woman.

"Dr. Tabor, good morning. Please join me." She motioned for him to take the other rocker, which was even more comfortable than it appeared at first glance. Her hair was rolled into a French twist and it was the shade of silver that seemed luminous when the sunshine touched it. She was carefully groomed, except for one wild hair that escaped the tweezers on the left side of her chin. No makeup. No glasses.

After more coffee and Swiss chocolate cake, still warm from the oven, she said, "So how can I help you, Dr. Tabor?"

"Madame, I have several questions."

"Perhaps I know why you're asking these questions. You are a psychiatrist from the United States trying to help Leah. Now, please, do not be offended, there are no secrets, though many rumors, in small towns. I think it is the proper decision to tell you," she said. "Genevieve would want that. It has been many years now.

"Her husband was one of the kindest men I have ever known. I worked for the family from the time Nicole was born until she went off to college and Leah went to boarding school and never did I see him make a choice that was not for the highest good.

"He fell in love with his wife when they met at a showing of her work. He fell, how do you say, he fell with his heels under his head. Wait. That is not quite right, is it?"

"I think you mean he was head over heels in love with her," Paul said with the most heartwarming smile.

"That's exactly what I mean. You could see it in his eyes every time he looked at her. All he wanted to do was make her happy. It gave him the deepest pleasure. She was so many years younger and quite bored when they socialized with his business associates in Zurich. She said all they talked about was money and the market and the mergers and politics. She was young and wanted to dance and laugh and have fun. She did love her husband, but not his lifestyle.

"She could have anything she wanted, and since he was very wealthy, it was easy for him to give generously. Because she was so talented and charming and beautiful, he knew that he must create a world for her that was fulfilling, so she would be content with him. I know she loved him. But love is not always long-lived, when the icing on the cake begins to melt."

"You have an interesting way of looking at life, Madame."

"I am a practical woman. I just wish there were not so many ridiculous and contradictory stories about how Madame died. Some people thought it was suicide, some thought it was that boy in her studio who killed her."

"And what do you think happened?"

"I know what happened: Sometimes Madame would drink too much wine but that brought on terrible migraines. When that happened, she could hardly read a prescription label. She died from an overdose of pills. I think she reached for the pain medication and accidentally took too many. Some people thought she committed suicide, but that is ridiculous. She was a successful artist and always had…interesting company. There was always a twinkle in her eyes. Monsieur Vassaux was extremely generous. When he bought the house and the studio for Madame, he bought this little cottage for me. He arranged for showings of her work in Paris and Rome, and locally, of course. When she wanted a larger studio, he bought one for her. When she wanted children, he arranged for that also. Money was not even an issue."

"So the children are adopted?" Paul asked.

"Monsieur had a disability that prevented him from physical intimacy. He made sure that Madame was not a victim of the problem. He could not father her children, but he researched the finest young men in business and science and art and chose a man that had the qualities he thought would produce the brightest and most talented children. He arranged for them to stay at one of his most romantic retreats on several occasions. The girls have the same father, even though they are ten years apart. Or maybe eleven. I have such a bruised memory.

"When she did not want to have more children, she settled here and made her own choices in men, or boys, to make her happy. Once a month she would go to Zurich to visit her husband. She absolutely adored him. The arrangement was good for both of them. He even paid for a college education for a couple of her young lovers. He was quite generous, you see, and they did have the loveliest, most thoughtful marriage."

Paul was amazed, not so much at the story, but at the nonchalant way she told it. "Well, Madame, I must ask, how did he die? And when?"

"Ah. Well. The stories were wild. Once a rumor catches hold, you can forget about the truth. The stories can be much more interesting to share. Some thought he killed his wife, others said he died of a stroke. The truth is that he was not even in town. I came home with Leah and she ran to open the bedroom door. She was just five years old. She saw a man running away from the bed and out the side door. I could see that from where I stood behind her.

"Madame was not conscious. I think he might have been trying to help her. Why did he run out the door as soon as Leah walked in on them?

"I called for an ambulance, but it was too late. The little one ran to her mother and it broke my heart to see that.

"When Madame joined the angels, her husband was heartbroken. Truly a broken man. He lost interest in his business and decided to retire. He established trust funds for the children to provide generously for them, but he could not bear to see them because they looked so much like their mother. He never saw them after her passing. His depression was devastating. He stopped going out, then he stopped eating; he had no desire to live without her. The way he died—it was a blessing. One morning, he just didn't wake up."

Paul was silent for a moment. "You have been very helpful, Madame. Your explanation clears up many questions."

"You are welcome anytime, Dr. Tabor."

While Paul was busy with his meetings, Stephanie was nearby exploring local galleries with Marcel Gerard, Henri's friend and art connoisseur.

"We have a one thirty reservation in Saint-Saphorin," said Marcel. He was gracious, yet not effusive, and his company wore well through the morning. Stephanie discovered that his knowledge of art was extensive, but nothing in his personality urged him to try to impress her. *A humble man,* she thought. *Quiet. Late thirties perhaps?* He waved a jaunty *bonjour* and they were on their way.

Within twenty minutes, Marcel made a sharp left turn off the main highway that connected Lausanne with Vevey. After the quick turn, the car scaled the steep and narrow road.

"Hey, you sure this isn't made for a four-wheel drive?" Stephanie couldn't help exclaiming as she stared at the cobbled road ahead of her and the steep drop off the mountain to the highway below.

"Perfectly safe. It was built by the Romans when they conquered the Helvetians in 58 BC. This was then part of the Roman Empire. Julius Caesar marched right through here. The entire village is protected from architectural change by Swiss cantonal law. Everything looks about the same as it did when the Romans were here. The plumbing's modern. Not much else."

"Who lives here?" Stephanie asked as they reached the top of the cliff and entered the ancient village.

"Farmers. Artists. A few businessmen from Lausanne or Vevey. There are a couple of hundred people in the village. A hundred more up in the vineyards beyond." He stopped near the restaurant and opened the car door for her, keeping his hand on her arm as she stepped on the jagged stones.

"Wait, Marcel! I don't acclimate that quickly. Give me a minute, will you? What a place! This is the first cobblestone street I've seen in Switzerland."

"Let me show you the old carriage path that leads here to the west. See how the stones are worn? That's from a couple of thousand years of wear. And how do you like those arches? That is where the horses came through. Horses and carriages and donkeys, too, of course. Look at that bridge between the buildings."

"It's absolutely charming."

"I think that bridge goes to the police station. Someone put up a sign…"

Stephanie laughed at the absurdity of a police station there. It looked out of place in storybook land.

The restaurant sign swung from an ancient hook: Auberge de l'onde Saint-Saphorin. "A rather quaint tavern, yes?" he said. "Many hundreds of years ago, this structure was much the same. Only a few minor changes, none that should steal from its charm."

"I can't wait to bring Paul here; it's the sort of place he will really enjoy. He's off with some old friends for the day."

Inside, the restaurant had dark red draperies and rich wood, leaded glass, and scent of thyme. It was a tavern, in the best sense of the word. From the bar, a barrel-bellied man waved in their direction. "Bonjour, Marcel."

"*C'est bon de te voir*, Jean. I tried to reach you by phone for two days," Marcel said.

"I did not feel like answering. The work was going too well." The men greeted each other with affectionate masculine expressions of their fondness and Stephanie was introduced and instantly adored by the enthusiastic Swiss artist.

"You will dine with us? I insist, Jean," Marcel demanded and to the tavern hostess: "*Pouvez-vous amener encore une chaise?*" He was far more assertive with his friends than with his colleagues, Stephanie noticed.

And so they drank the wine of Saint-Saphorin, the dry white wine of the village, and with lunch, which involved two hours of gormandizing, they enjoyed le rouge du pays. While Stephanie knew that Paul would have found the red wine too sweet for his taste, she totally enjoyed every drop of it. She scarcely begrudged the afternoon's work that would be affected by the wine and her enthusiasm: Stephanie was much too wise a businesswoman to invest in art in the mood she was in. After two hours in Saint-Saphorin, her judgment would be influenced by her delight in the culture.

Jean was a storehouse of knowledge regarding contemporary artists. Although he wasn't particularly fond of graphics, he knew everyone who was important in the medium and a few who weren't but should be. He gave names and phone numbers, and Stephanie's hunch was that he knew what he was talking about. Cautioning herself not to let charm influence her appraising eye, she asked to see his paintings. She wouldn't close her mind to bringing home some nice oils if she were impressed.

"Yes, yes, of course. I would love to show you my gallery," Jean said. "But first...more wine and more talk." After he had heard about Paul and the conference and her gallery in Los

Angeles, Stephanie said, "Jean, did you ever hear of a girl named Leah Vassaux? She used to live in this village."

"Everyone who lives in Saint-Saphorin knows everyone else. Of course. But I haven't seen her since she was a very young girl. She had a sister, Nicole. How did you know her name? I should have thought you would have asked about her mother."

"Her mother? Who's her mother?"

"Genevieve Vassaux. A very fine artist. She has been dead for many years and her work is treasured in Switzerland. Well, all over Western Europe. A fine talent."

"That was her professional name, Genevieve Vassaux?" asked Stephanie.

"Yes, a sculptress. She had amazing sensitivity. She did some drawings as well, but most of them were just working drawings for her sculptures. She was a delightful woman. That bastard husband of hers! Everyone thinks he found out about her lover… and…." His gesture completed the sentence.

"He killed her? Dear Lord! What happened?"

"No one is sure. He was much older than she. A banker who left her alone for long periods at a time."

"How sad."

"It is indeed. Lots of rumors ran around. It wasn't just the lover, the American boy who rented the attic space; there were several before him. Maybe one of them came back and…now that's what happens with stories! I could imagine all kinds of possibilities. I don't know what became of the girls. They stayed around with a guardian until the oldest one went to college. Then the little one—Leah—went to boarding school. After that, I don't know. How did you know Leah?"

"We have a mutual friend. I just thought she might have returned here."

"Would you be interested in seeing some of her mother's work? There is a gallery not far from here that has a couple of Genevieve's pieces. I saw them last week. Most expensive but exquisite."

"Yes. I'd like that very much. Where is the gallery?"

Jean wrote a name on a piece of paper and gave it to her. "Tell Viktor Bernard you are a friend of mine. If you buy anything there, he should give you a small discount. Or a higher price, depending on his mood!"

"What kind of woman was she? Genevieve, I mean," Stephanie asked.

"I liked her. A good woman. Talented, bright, warm…too warm it seems, for her health."

"Was she known to play around?"

He swiveled his hand from side to side. "She was discreet. The marriage was bad. People assumed she had lovers. There was some speculation about the young man who lived in her studio; he denied being involved and no one could prove otherwise. There were all kinds of stories. In a small town, people like to talk."

"I can imagine." Stephanie looked at her watch. "Well, as much as I would love to stay longer, we must be going. A whole afternoon has been planned for us. Though I can't say I feel exactly like working!"

The check was paid long before, and Marcel and Stephanie walked from the cool stone structure into the summer sun, blinding in its intensity. Stephanie reached for dark glasses.

"Let's stop off at Viktor's studio first," Marcel suggested. "I want you to see his latest treasures."

"I was just going to ask if we could do that," Stephanie said as they walked past the ancient church, once decorated with gold and paintings, then washed with grey paint during the Reformation.

"I don't want to see inside the church," Stephanie said. "I can't bear to see what Calvin did to all the art."

"Don't be too hard on old Calvin. If he hadn't painted over the frescoes, they might have been totally destroyed in our damp winters. Now restoration is being done in some of the churches and they're removing the paint and finding that beneath it the art is extremely well preserved. More protective coatings are available now."

"Then it seems that time is the only fair judge. Here I've been holding it against him all these years!"

"Forgiveness, Stephanie, my dear, forgiveness."

They wandered down narrow, slippery cobblestone paths on the way to the Bernard gallery but first they came to a small but inviting shop. Stephanie wanted to take a quick look inside. The artist looked more like a young hippie than a serious art dealer. But in 1975 one could never just assume. She reminded herself that she should not make assumptions.

Unfortunately, she found his work mediocre and far too commercial for her taste. It was a sticky moment. An artist and his work are so inextricably entwined, how could she affirm the man and still not give unwarranted praise to the work? Knowing that she wasn't obligated to do either, she still struggled with the problem. Until she saw the whimsical stone cat on the mantel.

A young French artist had made it from a large garden stone, the natural curve of it suggested the animal itself. The work was sophisticated, exquisitely detailed, considering that the expectations are different when one paints on a rock.

Stephanie laughed at the cat, playfully stroked it, and determined to keep it for her own. It would make Paul smile when he saw it on the hearth.

"I'll take it," she said. "Can you arrange shipping?" And then she saw the other pieces displayed in the next room.

Stephanie bought a tiger and walrus, and of course, the cat. So much for her decision not to buy today. The stone animals were a find.

"See that house there?" Marcel asked. "Where the balcony is protruding at that precarious angle?"

"Yes, it seems ready to collapse!" Stephanie said.

"That's the old Vassaux house," he said. "No one has lived in it in years."

Stephanie and Marcel made their way to the gallery Jean had suggested. The bell on the door sang melodiously as they opened it. "Un moment, s'il vous plait." The voice came from down the hall.

Before Stephanie had even begun to examine the paintings and sculpture in the gallery, the owner appeared. "Good morning," he said.

"Are you Monsieur Bernard?" Stephanie asked.

In English then, "I am. And are you Jean's friend whom he just called me about?"

"Yes. Stephanie Tabor. I understand that you have some of Genevieve Vassaux's work."

"Yes. Yes. I have several pieces. They are not easy to come by anymore. Some of them are in museums already."

"So Jean told me."

"Come with me, please." He led them into the next room where the works were obviously more expensive. More protected from the open door. A series of pedestals, each well-lit by individual gallery lights from above, displayed the sculptures of Genevieve Vassaux.

"What a powerful piece," Stephanie said, realizing that it was an unusual word to describe the sculpture of a child. In spite of the delicate quality of the face, the finely chiseled cheek bones, the long, tapered fingers that touched her hair—in spite of the fragile youth, there was incredible strength in the sculpture. How had she achieved it? Without commenting at all, Stephanie analyzed the piece. Its mystery held. The solution was elusive. She had done it; that was all that mattered. A strong feminine woman/child of…what…three? Four? A determination that transcended innocence.

"Do you recognize her, Madame Tabor? Jean told me you were a friend of the family."

"I don't know them personally. Is this one of her daughters? Which one, do you know?"

"Her younger one," Viktor said. "It is one of the last works she completed before her death."

"A gifted woman. What a shame she died so young."

"A great loss to art lovers, Madame. And to others as well."

"Is this hers also? Yes, I can see it is, that same quality of the juxtaposition of strength and tenderness. Not an easy thing to accomplish in marble."

"This one is an old woman from the village. A peasant woman. See the coarseness of the hands, the arthritic distortion. Calloused and tough. But her expression is ethereal. In this work she has reversed the elements of what is fragile and what is powerful. In this figure, it is the woman's body that carries the strength. And her expression that carries the tenderness. Just the reverse of the child."

"Extraordinary. Do you have others?"

"I'm afraid not. I had one more of a man and woman—quite reminiscent of Rodin's work, but with Vassaux's uniqueness in the concept. I had it here last week but a collector from Paris has taken it on approval. It was quite an amazing work. Terribly expensive, even for a Vassaux."

Stephanie had already seen the price of one of the figures listed at the bottom of the paragraph about the work. It was priced in Swiss francs. Stephanie didn't have to use her calculator; she could tell quickly by the number of digits that it was beyond her reach.

"It's really impressive. I'm fascinated by her work. By the way, you haven't seen her daughter, have you? Lately, I mean?"

"Not for many years."

"Well, thank you Monsieur. I wish I could afford to own them."

Not long after Stephanie and Marcel left, it occurred to Viktor that they might have been interested in the small sketch he had by the same artist. It was only a working drawing—of a handsome nude boy with intense black eyes and a strong body. It might have been the same young man she used in the sculpture that was now in Paris.

No matter, he thought. The woman was interested in important sculpture. And the sketch was such a small work. *Not important at all.*

CHAPTER 18

MALIBU & MONTECITO

The second day Leah and Mark spent at the Tabor house was in sharp contrast to their previous days together. The energy in the room seemed to be stale, juxtaposed to the frantic, fearful days in Westwood. How many things could one find to talk about with an almost-stranger who was less than generous with stories of his life or his longings for the future? By the second day, the conversation had become hard work for both of them.

"Mark, let's listen to some music. You have quite a selection."

"No. I don't want any music now. I need to think."

Leah wondered why thinking and listening to music couldn't coexist. But she had a self-protective moment and said nothing.

She could have retreated into the books that lined the walls as she did for hours at a time in Switzerland, but her attention kept wandering.

A bronze chess set provided a welcomed retreat from personal talks that were sounding more and more strained. "It's your move, Leah," Mark said, as he stared at the chess board, irritated by how much time she took between moves.

Leah was no match for Mark's skill playing chess. "I'm sorry, Mark, I never thought chess was supposed to be a game of speed." Her tone surprised both of them; sarcasm wasn't the way Leah dealt with authority. She bit her lip, holding back what she really wanted to say.

"Well, take your time," Mark said. "We have all week. While you're thinking, I'll take a shower and when I get back you might have made your move."

It was the tone of his words, the contempt, the condescension that was jarring. He hadn't sounded that way before. What had changed? Had she said something wrong? What happened to that compassionate, patient man, who seemed so irritable now? How could she have put so much trust in him?

When Leah heard the sound of water running in the shower, she opened the sliding glass door and stepped outside. She just wanted to feel the warmth of the sun on her body and the shift of sand on her bare feet. She slipped off her shoes and walked toward the waves, just to the water's edge, and she felt the fringe of the waves play around her toes. It was a moment of peace in spite of her pain.

A woman passed by with a neighborly greeting and they spoke about how lovely the beach was and Leah asked if she lived here or was just visiting. It was a momentary exchange of strangers enjoying the same experience.

The woman had her dog on a leash and Leah bent to pet him. The large German shepherd greeted her like she was part of his pack.

"She's a good judge of character," the woman said. "It isn't everyone she greets with so much enthusiasm."

Leah wondered if that was the dog with the loud bark that kept her awake in the night.

"I'm Caroline," the woman said, then she paused when Mark walked toward them. There was a scowl on his face and his body language expressed his anger. Leah felt a strong grip on her arm.

"You have a phone call, you'd better hurry; it's long distance." He nodded to the woman and said, "Sorry, it's an emergency."

The neighbor watched them leave, saw the shock on Leah's face and the dominating power of the man who grabbed her. The dog growled, then began a deluge of fierce, angry barking.

"Mark, you're hurting my arm!" Leah said, as he hurried her toward the house.

The woman wondered if there was something she could do to help that young girl. She realized that a family argument wasn't her business. If she contacted the police, they would surely tell her that a family argument wasn't their business either. She just had a bad feeling and hoped that she misread the situation.

As they entered the house, Leah said, "A phone call can't be for me, Mark. No one knows I'm here!"

Once inside the house he said, "Don't be stupid; of course, the phone's not for you! I just had to get you away from that woman. It's not safe for you to be out there. And who were you talking with? Did she ask your name? Did you tell her? You can't be that careless!"

Leah looked bewildered. How could Mark explain that they were hiding from the neighbors as well? It was a situation Mark couldn't control. When threatened, rage was his first response. He needed a new plan.

"I think it would be good for you to be somewhere away from LA for a few days. Somewhere you can relax and walk the beach where you won't be at risk. Let's drive up to Montecito and stay a night at a hotel."

"How can you say that? I don't want a vacation, Mark. My sister is dead! She was murdered! And someone might want me dead, too." Suddenly sobs wracked her body and Mark held her until finally the tears stopped.

"Oh, Leah. Don't you know I'm just trying to take care of you?" His voice softened. "I'm not suggesting a vacation, just a bit of normalcy. You are being so brave, but I see through all that faux courage. We could be in a quiet place that your sister loved, and you can talk to me about her. I can help you with your grief if you let me.

"No one would expect you to be in Montecito. The Miramar was Nicole's favorite place for a weekend away. She talked about how much it meant to her. It's not fancy, but it is right on the beach. It's just on the edge of Santa Barbara. I'm sure it won't be long before someone comes along and buys it, puts up a posh hotel, and it'll draw a whole different crowd. But a change of scenery would be good for you. You need to be in a place where you feel safe. We can talk about those things that can help you heal."

Leah wasn't as beautiful as her mother, or Nicole, but there was a lovely vulnerability about her that he was beginning to appreciate. "We might even stay a few more days, if you like it." He started to call the Miramar Hotel for a reservation, then reconsidered. Paul might check the phone bill when he came home and that could raise questions.

The one thing Mark forgot, when he decided to bring Leah to the Tabor house, was to pack a few changes of clothes for himself.

He had worn the same shirt for three days. Now he pulled one of Paul's shirts from the closet. It was a size too large, but it would have to do. He took a handful of pills before they left but was careful not to take the ones that made him feel disoriented. They were the best of the painkillers, but he had trouble making sense of anything for hours after he took them.

Mark said, "I think we should take my ex's car to keep the battery working. I try to take it for a spin every couple of weeks, so it won't be a problem when she picks it up." Stephanie's car keys were in the same place she always kept them, on the hook in the kitchen right by the door to the garage.

Taking Stephanie's car was a smart move, Mark thought. His own car was parked in the garage next to hers. His plans were working well, so far. Mark was sure he hadn't been seen leaving Nicole's apartment. But just in case someone had heard her scream and seen him leaving, they might have copied his license plate. That was a stretch. Not likely. Just in case, it made sense to take Stephanie's BMW.

"Mark, you are so kind to take such good care of me. I'm sorry I was angry."

"Well, let's just put that behind us and try to find some peace in the midst of all this grief."

Traffic wasn't too heavy and the drive relaxed Leah enough to talk more about Nicole. Mark would rather listen to anything except more stories about the perfect version of Nicole, but he'd let her talk all she wanted. There were other things he could think about.

"Look out!" Leah yelled when a van swerved over the white line.

"Shit!" The BMW didn't handle as well as the Porsche, but Mark managed to avoid a collision. "Your story was distracting me and it took my mind off the road." He sounded more accusatory than apologetic.

Mark decided to use his therapist response, addressing her as though she were a child. "Leah, it takes time to deal with the trauma you've had. Be patient with yourself. And don't forget, the memory of one loss stirs memories of the ones that came before it. You really are strong, given the losses you've had."

"It helps to talk about Nicole," Leah said. "I want to tell you about the good times; there were many. It wouldn't be right to let the grief destroy those memories."

"They coexist and remembering them has a purpose," Mark said.

An angry driver came behind them, blasting the horn, demanding the road. Mark swerved over to the right lane. "This jerk thinks he owns the highway!"

Leah was still talking, unaware of the traffic. "Nicole was the kindest person you would ever know. She gave up so much to take care of me when I was little."

Yes, yes, I know, he thought. *How many times have I heard all the wonderful things about a woman I would like to forget.* As the stories rolled on, Mark's attention wandered. He was listening but not focusing. He did that at the office sometimes. He knew what the patient was saying but he could still think about things that were on his mind.

Now he was thinking of a white Toyota that had stayed right behind them for the last fifteen minutes. He caught himself wondering if that could mean trouble and the thought jarred him back to reality. Mark knew no one was following them; that was ridiculous. It startled him to realize that he was beginning to believe his own lies. Rationally he knew that there was no reason to be concerned. But when a police car passed them with red lights flashing, his heart beat faster and he thought for a moment that they were looking for him. His logical mind knew the difference, but his emotions drove his body's reactions.

"Hey, how about some music?" He needed to hear something, anything else. He turned on the 8-track, letting the harmonies of Stephanie's Crosby, Stills, & Nash tape fill the space. Leah remembered how much Nicole had liked this California music.

It was late afternoon when they arrived at the hotel but there wasn't a cottage available. They only had a one-bedroom suite, ocean front.

"We'll take it," Mark said. When he saw Leah's expression, he added, "I'm used to sleeping on the couch."

When Leah opened the door to the suite, she said, "I see why Nicole liked this place. It almost feels strange to be here without her." Her face clouded for a moment. She pushed the thoughts aside.

"Hey, it's just an ocean," Mark said. "I think we have one exactly like it at home." He had a proud expression, as if his remark was original. But Leah was only thinking of Nicole and knowing how much she loved the sea and that made it special to her as well. The living room was ample and included a full kitchen and the large sofa that could be just fine for Mark. There was a door separating the bedroom from the living room.

The colors in both rooms were drab and a bit worn. If she only had a large colorful scarf, Leah would have covered the picture of a small boat in an angry sea that hung over the sofa. Apparently the management didn't understand the power of a visual metaphor.

"I think I'll just take a walk by the water's edge. Nicole loved to do that when we went to the lake." Leah wasn't wearing a swimsuit, but she rolled her jeans up as high as her knees.

Mark watched her walk toward the water, then run on the damp sand. She was graceful and strong. He remembered Nicole's rigid movements, her lack of spontaneity. And although she was more beautiful than Leah, Nicole lacked her sister's warmth and confidence. He wondered what Leah would be like when fear and grief subsided.

When he compared the sisters, it was Genevieve who came into his thoughts. Neither of the younger women came close to the beauty of their mother. His thoughts reached back into the past, feeling the impact of the choices made and the opportunities lost. He was just a teenager when Genevieve had stopped her car and let him into her life.

For several years after Genevieve died, the memory of her was raw and ever present. Sometimes Mark felt like a ghost was stalking him. He imagined he saw her in a crowd on the boulevard, or in a boat on the lake, or getting on a bus that pulled away as she looked out the window, staring at him. He had loved her. And lost her. But the memory of her remained.

Mark considered the impact the three women made on his life. Without them, he would have been on a much different path.

Mark applied for extension of aid when he wanted to go to medical school and to his surprise, it was granted. Still, he needed a way to cover his other costs. Fortunately, it wasn't difficult for a fine-looking young man with a charming manner to meet an older woman in need of attention. He thought she was quite beautiful for a woman in her fifties. In her, he found a willing patron to help him get through medical school.

One evening, Mark was studying for a test in a small café near campus and he sensed someone was watching him. When he turned, he saw a woman who looked so much like Genevieve, he almost cried out.

She got up from her chair and walked toward him with a warm smile. "I'm sorry," she said. "I didn't mean to stare. I thought I knew you, but I guess I was wrong."

"That's okay. Please, sit down. I'm grateful for the company." He wanted to touch her, but instead he folded his hands in his lap. He knew Genevieve had two children; one was only a few years younger than he was. This woman looked so much like her mother; Mark was thrown back in time. This must be her older daughter. He didn't know her name.

The younger child was not even in kindergarten, as he recalled. He couldn't remember seeing either of them when he lived in the room above their mother's studio. A stone wall and lush hedges shielded the main house from a path that led to the street. Genevieve was adamant that they never meet, and the architecture of the studio made that possible. He didn't even know who took care of the girls when Genevieve was in the studio.

Despite their careful planning, perhaps he had been seen. Then again, Nicole was probably a young teen with lots on her mind, and there was no reason she would have consciously remembered him. Mark had no intention of letting her know that he knew her mother, that he had never loved anyone in the way he loved her. Or that his affair with Genevieve lasted until the night she died. At first, Mark was fascinated by how much Nicole looked like Genevieve. He was disappointed when time proved that physical beauty was the only resemblance. Nicole was more intellectual, more rigid, lacking in any sense of adventure. It didn't take long for Mark to realize that his fascination with Nicole was only his attachment to the memories she stirred. But that was enough. Transference was smooth and easy for a while.

When they took long walks or sailed boats on the lake, Nicole seemed comfortable telling Mark about her private life. That was not the usual way in Switzerland, but she had her own way of rebelling against the culture. And she felt drawn to this man, though she didn't know why.

"I took a job at the med school to keep me busy until classes start," she said. "It's so easy, and there's a lot of downtime so I may keep it through the year. It would be a quiet place to study."

"What do you do there?"

"Nothing except file records and other mundane chores. But I can use my spare time to read, so it's not all bad."

"What are you reading now?"

"One of the classics, *Man's Search for Meaning*. Viktor Frankl was a prisoner in Auschwitz during the Second World War. He wrote about life in the concentration camps and how the atrocities they endured stirred such diverse responses in the prisoners.

"Some became more compassionate, sharing food, caring for the most vulnerable among them. Others identified with the Nazis and became as cruel as their captors."

"How did he explain that?"

"Ask me when I finish reading the book," she said. It was an obvious invitation, not lost on Mark.

He thought of Genevieve and remembered when she read to him from the romantic writings by Rumi, and how much she adored the love poems of an Italian poet whose name he couldn't remember.

Nicole always read serious books. From scientific reviews to Russian history. Mark longed for the softness of Genevieve's touch, the tender qualities of her laugh.

Nicole looked so much like her mother that, at first, he assigned to her all the attributes of the exquisite artist who won his heart years ago.

"We should take a picnic today," Mark suggested to her at lunchtime. "Now that the weather is better." He remembered the taste of foie gras and escargot, the local wine, and the only woman he had ever loved.

"Oh, Mark, it's still too cold for a picnic. And the grass will be wet from last night's rain. Let's wait until we have a bit more sun. Why don't we go to the café near my apartment, then we could go upstairs and listen to some music? I went to the record store yesterday and asked them what the most popular American music was. They suggested a new recording by Bob Dylan and something by Olivia Newton-John. We could have some time alone," she said, with what she believed was a seductive smile.

Mark didn't know what to say. Genevieve would have chosen a picnic, spread a blanket, sipped local wine, and spread camembert or brie on warm bread. If she was cold, she would have curled up in his arms and neither of them would have complained about the chill in the air.

Nicole was unaware that she was in competition with the memories he had of her mother. Mark never wavered from his commitments or in his gratitude for the support of generous women. He made sure he was always available to his older patron when she called. Studies were his second priority. Third on his list was Nicole. He saw her in his spare time. Just often enough for her to fall in love with him. He never loved her, but she was convenient.

Mark set the rule with Leah: there would be no more talk of Nicole. He would take Leah to the San Ysidro Ranch for dinner. He could impress her with its history. "John and Jackie Kennedy spent part of their honeymoon there. I think you'll like it. The distraction will be good for you. You've been dealing with the past too many hours today. It's time to be in the present."

"That sounds too formal. I don't have anything to wear!"

"Actually, it's pretty casual. And the food is terrific." Besides, after all he had been through, he thought he was entitled to some fine dining.

"There's just one rule, Leah. No talking about the past. Not tonight. I want us to spend our time discussing things that make you smile." He was wearing a new shirt that he bought in the gift shop, and he didn't look nearly so undernourished in one that fit him. The circles were still dark under his eyes and his skin looked sallow. He was not well but trying hard to hide it.

The meds he took just before they left the hotel seemed to make things even worse. By the time they'd been seated at dinner, his voice was too loud, and he laughed about nothing at all. His eyes had a peculiar look to them. Leah was worried. But what could she do?

The views from the hillside dining room were even more spectacular than the beachfront hotel, with glimmers of light from houses below twinkling on as the sunset moved from apricot to orange-red then velvet black, the islands across the channel vanishing in the night.

Leah skipped wine with her dinner but chose a brandy Alexander for dessert. Mark ordered his third martini. His eyes were glassy and seemed to be scanning the room.

"Mark, are you looking for someone?"

"I always like to check out the crowd here. You never know what celebrities might be here, and you might enjoy seeing some of the Hollywood crowd. Last time I was here, Rita Hayworth walked right through that door." His arm swung out as he pointed to the door, causing a waiter to almost drop a tray.

"I've never understood you Americans and your obsession with celebrities," she said.

He had about had it with her and women talking down to him. Mark's eyes were glassy. He signaled the waiter, slurred as he paid the check and asked for the valet to bring the car.

"I'll drive, if you don't mind, Mark." And then she dared to add, "Too much alcohol and too many drugs make for more trouble than either of us should have to deal with now." She didn't wait for his answer but tried to slip into the driver's seat. He grabbed her arm and she almost fell to the ground as he pulled her out of the car. She thought he was going to slap her but he didn't. Maybe he saw the dismay on the face of the parking attendant. Maybe he just changed his mind.

"Mark, please, you've had too much to drink. I won't get in the car with you! You can leave me right here if you insist on driving this car. I'm not getting into it!" Leah backed up, out of his reach, shocked by her own sudden rush of rage and empowerment.

She saw the attendant run up the stairs toward the restaurant, probably getting help. Mark got in the car and charged out of the parking lot like a mad man, leaving Leah standing there, not knowing what to do.

"Do you want a cab, Miss?" the attendant asked when he and the manager arrived in the driveway. "Do you want us to call the police?" the manager asked.

"Not the police, no. He's just drunk, but he's not dangerous," she said, as if she was capable of discerning that. "I'll take a cab to the hotel."

She paid the cab driver before he stopped at her door. The room key was in her hand. Leah ran to the door and noticed that the living room side of their suite was dark.

She didn't think he would come for her, but she never knew what he was going to do and began to wonder where all of this was going. This man needed a doctor and probably more than one. She had no idea what the morning would bring. She wished she had never come here, never gone with him to his beach house. There were so many things she wished for at that moment.

She had barely closed the door to her room when she heard his key rattling in the lock. So quietly, she turned the bolt on her bedroom door. She immediately turned off the light.

The door between the rooms was thin and soon Leah could hear Mark's voice, slurred and angry as he shouted into the phone. "No, I told you, you have to stop this right now! What a fucking bitch she is." Leah assumed he was talking about her, but then she realized he was upset about a patient. "I saved her kid's life and she wants to sue me! You get a settlement, right now. I will not go to court. I will not give depositions and all that shit. I don't care what she threatens me with, you get this settled. Have I made that clear? Okay, I'm sorry, I'm sorry. Really. No, you don't understand. I will die before I'll go to court."

Then she heard the phone slamming against the floor, the small bell dinging once, Mark swearing. He seemed to be talking to himself as he flung open the sliding glass door so hard she could hear the grating of it against the metal track. Her drapes were open, revealing a restless sea and suddenly she saw Mark run past the window. She started to call to him but her heart was pounding. What was he going to do? He was in a manic state, and she felt afraid…afraid of him and afraid for him. Leah couldn't just ignore what she sensed. She called security and reported a man who seemed deranged running along the shore. She was sure he was drunk or high, but didn't he just say he would rather die than go to court? Was he just being dramatic? Or, would he take his own life? What should she do now? Leah checked the lock on her doors, turned out the lights, and closed her eyes. And listened. And waited.

It was later Tuesday morning when Mark knocked on the door to her room. She waited, took a deep breath, then said, "I'm coming," but she didn't open the door. "Good morning, Mark," she said as if nothing had happened the night before.

Mark's voice was sharp: "I went back for you and you were gone."

What could she say to him? She couldn't find the right words. Then he said, "Room service just arrived. I ordered French toast for you. And coffee."

"I'll be right out," she said, through the closed door. Leah took her time dressing.

Dreading what she would say to Mark. She imagined trying to get him to a doctor, but she didn't have much confidence in that. He was much too macho to let her help him.

Mark looked up when she opened the door.

"So, where did you go last night?" he demanded.

"Here, Mark. I was here. Now I think we should just go home. It's obvious that I'm not being followed, and I want to get on with my life. I need to get settled."

Mark's face was drawn and his look was stern. "I've planned for us to go to the zoo today. One of Nicole's favorites."

"Mark, I'm not feeling well. If you want to go, I'll wait here and rest. Really, I won't mind. If I feel better, I'll lie down on the beach. Or just sit outside and listen to the sea. Don't worry about entertaining me." Her hands were trembling; it was hard for her to stand her ground.

"If you don't want to go to the zoo, pack your things. We'll go home. Now!" His voice was cold. She wanted to scream but what good would that do? Leah looked at Mark's hands, curled into fists. She considered her options. Mark would never let her go. And even if he did, how would she get back to Malibu? She didn't even know the address. She didn't even have a key or enough money for a cab.

She couldn't call the police and tell them…what? What could she tell them? That she was scared of a crazy man?

Right now, it was perfectly clear what she had to do. Stay calm. Not make a fuss. Pretend she didn't know he was having a breakdown. And most of all, not make him angry.

She would get all her things ready and wait until he went to the bathroom. Whether he liked it or not, she wouldn't spend another night in the same house. Again and again, she reminded herself that Mark's mental condition had nothing to do with the death of Nicole. But if she really believed that, why did she have to remind herself time after time? But before she'd had a chance, Mark had his bag open, shoving his clothes inside before snapping it shut.

Leaving breakfast untouched, they left the suite and started toward the front desk to check out. Before they got there, Leah heard a mature female voice, loud and slightly hyper. "Dr. Favre! Hello. Oh, my, it's so good to see you again. How delightful that you're visiting this lovely little town."

Mark looked frantic. Why? It wasn't too surprising that people from LA would see each other here; Mark had told her that Montecito was the weekend playground for wealthy players who lived in Los Angeles.

The woman looked at Leah and said, "Oh, my dear, it's so good to see you again! Nicole, isn't it? I'm so bad at names. You've lost a bit of weight, good for you!"

When she heard the woman say her sister's name, Leah felt tears stream down her face. Mark grabbed her arm and said, "It's nice to see you, Mrs. Caldwell." He tightened his grasp on Leah's arm as he led her firmly toward the car. Over his shoulder, he said, "I'm sorry, we have to rush off. We're late for an appointment."

He squeezed Leah's arm even harder and forced her to walk to the car. Her thoughts were racing and none of them making sense.

Options circled around and around, making choices, changing her mind, now she was afraid to stay with him, but how could she leave?

If someone from security or even a strong-looking guest had been standing there, she would have called for help, but there was just a woman with a baby and a toddler. By the path to the pool, two teenagers were sharing a cigarette.

As they hurried to his car, Mark practically pushed Leah into the passenger seat, slamming the door. While he ran to the driver's side, she fumbled for the door lock. Then Mark was beside her and he acted like someone was after him. He started the car.

Mark said, "That woman is nuts. She used to be a patient of mine, and when she met Nicole in my waiting room, she said all kinds of inappropriate things. I sent her to another therapist, but she kept calling me. I couldn't get away from her fast enough."

"That sounds really…strange," Leah said, knowing it was a lie.

"Well, you do look enough like Nicole to confuse a stranger. You'll hear all kinds of things as we spend time together."

Could that be true? Her heart was pounding, and she turned her head away, forcing her voice to sound calm, forcing her tears to stop. "I'm not feeling very well Mark, I think I'll try to nap for a while."

All the way back to Malibu, Mark was talking to himself. At first, he sounded angry, then he laughed, then he swore at the traffic. Leah huddled close to the door, looking away from Mark, staring at the ocean. Leah didn't say anything, and he didn't seem to notice. How could she have missed the cues? She longed to get away from him, and she tried not to imagine him with Nicole. Leah longed to be back in Switzerland. She would have to hide her fear. Could she do that? She had to do that. But she knew that couldn't happen.

She would call the police. Would they believe her? Where was her proof? What would Mark do to her now? She couldn't let him sense that she knew. How could she hide her fear? Was he going to kill her too?

For a fleeting moment, Leah imagined just opening the car door and falling out, her hands covering her face. The power of the impact freeing her from pain forever. She wouldn't do that. She couldn't, of course. But the thought lingered.

PART THREE

CHAPTER 19

LAUSANNE

Right from the start, the conference on The Catalyst for Innovation was unique. As soon as guests began to arrive at the hotel reception on Tuesday evening, the participants were gathering in clusters, anxious to discuss the subject of the conference, catching up with old friends, exchanging ideas, telling stories. Seeing these people so filled with fascination with the creative process was exciting. Stephanie realized that no predetermined social structure could have contained them. Challenges grew from speculation. Words were shot by Italian artists at machine-gun speed.

Stephanie leaned back against the wall, alone for a moment, observing. Fascinated. Her mind translated the scene into her own medium; how would she paint what she was experiencing now? To put this moment on canvas would require an abstract, of course. Fierce purples and arrogant reds, vibrant yellows colliding, exploding into celebration. Wild, exquisite, provocative colors. Chaos with design. Serendipities waiting to happen. She thought of how Kandinsky would paint it and smiled.

How many languages were crashing in the air? From her place in the room, she heard English, Italian, German, French, of course, and Ulinov's interpreter trying desperately to keep up with the night's ideas and translate them into a more familiar language: A cacophony of sounds. Living research. Hypotheses over canapés. This was the night for the expansion of ideas and the exchange of insights. A moment before, Stephanie had left Paul talking with Dr. Kline about the effect of Israel's kibbutzim on the creative personality. They were so engrossed in the conversation that neither of them had noticed when Stephanie slipped away. She was having a most satisfying time, listening to bits and pieces of conversations as she walked around the room. She saw it created an extraordinary montage that absorbed her attention.

Only after the last of the Schweppes had been swigged at the bar, did they have a moment to themselves back in their suite. Paul, who had less rest that afternoon than Stephanie, gave in first to the impact of jet lag. In bed, Paul lay with his back to her. Stephanie was still too keyed up to sleep. Days and nights made war in her head. It would take a while before the Swiss time change began to feel comfortable.

"Paul, you asleep?"

"Hmm?"

"You know that doctor from the psychiatry department at the university?

"Well, we got to talking about one thing that led to another and I mentioned that Mark had graduated from med school and taken his residency here. And he said he didn't remember him."

"Big school. Can't know everybody."

"I know. But he introduced me to one of the other staff members who would have been in Mark's class, and he didn't remember him either."

Silence.

"Paul?"

"Hmm."

"Doesn't that seem sort of strange? There couldn't have been that many Americans in the program. And Mark doesn't seem to me to be the kind of guy who fades into the woodwork. Paul?" Deep heavy breathing. *Oh well,* she thought, *we can talk about that tomorrow.*

The formidable Palais de Beaulieu was only a twelve-minute drive from the Beau-Rivage Palace hotel where Paul and Stephanie were staying. It was a huge facility, with a small conference room that created the perfect location for The Second International Conference on The Catalyst for Innovation.

After making a few opening remarks, Paul took a seat at the end of a row toward the middle of the auditorium. He wanted to separate himself for a while from the organizational responsibilities and just enjoy listening to the speakers. At the podium, speaking in German, was a psychiatrist from Austria. He was so well known and respected in his field that he could afford to speak simply and directly regarding his subject. The pretentious frills of academia didn't appeal to him, and Paul was pleased that the opening speaker had gone right to the heart of the material. No pedantic bid for accolades attracted this man.

Paul was wearing earphones that allowed him to hear the speech as it was translated into English. He pushed another button and listened to the French translation, switching eventually back into his own language, which was the most comfortable for him. It was possible for the other participants in the room to press other buttons, hearing the speech in Russian or Italian. The facilities were equipped to accommodate a sixth language, but it wasn't necessary.

All participants were conversant in at least one of the five languages offered. At the back of the room, the five linguists sat in a glass booth, wearing earphones, and translating what the speakers said. Provided by the conference center, they came with extraordinary credentials.

Occasionally applause broke out from the audience. Last night's spontaneity set the tone for the day. The second speaker and the third led the participants into an enthusiastic mood that threatened to extend the questions far into the lunch break. It was Henri who insisted that they adjourn for lunch and continue their conversations in smaller groups.

Dr. Ulinov sat across the table from Paul, his translator beside him. The four women and two men also at the table could converse in either English or French. They chose English as their common language. Only Ulinov needed a translator, which slowed the conversation considerably, causing them to break into three groups after a few minutes.

"I'd like to hear about your work, Dr. Jordan," Paul said to the psychologist on his left. "I've heard some rather impressive things about your research on the creative process."

"It's kind of you to say so, Dr. Tabor, but the program is new; we are still constructing the framework.

"All I can actually assure you now is that we are well funded, both by the university and by private grants, to sustain the research for five years. We have an abundance of creative persons volunteering to work with us and as one of you Americans said,

'If we knew what we were going to discover, it wouldn't be research, would it?'"

"I've heard the quote and it certainly applies here. This field's so new that we don't have to cut through too many long-established prejudices."

"Your wife told me last night that your son-in-law graduated from our program. Is he interested in the subject of creativity?"

"Not really. Mark seems quite determined not to venture far beyond his individual private practice. I've tried to get him involved in a few things at the university where I'm affiliated, but he really isn't interested."

"I wish I could place him. Very well, I'll satisfy my curiosity when I check the yearbook."

"How could anyone expect you to remember him? After all, you must have a hundred or more students in every class."

"You'd be surprised, Dr. Tabor. When you work so closely with students all through medical school and then through their residency, as in Dr. Favre's case, and then don't even recognize the name, it's truly embarrassing! We have had very few American students in recent years, since when we began to discourage an influx from the States back in 1948. Mark Favre would have had to be exceptionally bright to have qualified for the program."

"He didn't transfer from the States; Mark attended the university here in Lausanne for his entire college education."

"Most unusual. And even more frustrating that I don't recall him. I'm sure it's going to bother me until I get a chance to refresh my memory by seeing his photograph in the yearbook. There's no chance he's from the other medical school in Lausanne? Or even from Lucerne? So many Americans confuse the two names. But in your case I don't suppose that is a possibility."

"I've seen the diploma, Doctor," Paul said, letting the nod of his head close the subject.

The woman on Paul's left had been waiting for a break in the conversation to get his attention. "Dr. Tabor, I was so impressed with Dr. Rinelich. But I noticed that he didn't refer to any political factors that promote or stifle the arts. Wouldn't you think that there would be some reference to the influence of political oppression?"

"I'm sure that's going to come up. Probably in the workshops. How much of his omission was because of Dr. Ulinov's presence, I don't know. It may be that he just didn't want to focus on that problem at the beginning of the conference."

"Perhaps. And, of course, he may have been protecting himself politically. Europeans think that Austria will be totally controlled by the Communists in another few years. Friends of mine who live in Austria say they can't even sell their property at a fraction of its value because most people think the government will take it all anyway before long."

"I hope they're being pessimistic."

"Pessimism is tantamount to survival in many cultures, Dr. Tabor. My parents left Czechoslovakia at a time when most of their friends thought they were being pessimistic."

The luncheon was served quickly and well. The workshops began on schedule.

Using the discipline required to shift from one patient's problems to another, Paul dismissed all concerns except the business at hand. He chose to attend the workshop entitled,

"Structure vs. Spontaneity: The Critical Balance." While a dozen artists shared their personal responses to the issue, seven psychiatrists took notes, asked questions, and interjected observations.

When the second day ended, there was nothing but praise from the participants about the conference. The sustained mood of expectation permeated the atmosphere. In small groups, they headed back to the Beau-Rivage.

Just as Paul was starting out the door, Dr. Jordan from the medical school motioned him to one side. The expression on his face could only mean one thing. Trouble.

"Dr. Tabor, I know what I'm going to ask is an imposition at this time. But could I speak with you privately?"

"Could we make it sometime tomorrow? I have…"

"It is most important that we talk this evening. The problem is regarding your son-in-law, Mark Favre."

As participants were leaving the conference for the dinner break or gathering in small groups, focused on their particular interests, Paul and Dr. Jordan faced each other in a quiet corner behind the podium. Dr. Jordan took a yearbook from his briefcase and handed it to Paul.

"I think this is something that cannot wait, or I wouldn't bring it to your attention now. You see, in the year you said he graduated, there is no reference to a Mark Favre. Is it possible that you are mistaken about the year?"

"I would like to think so, but the date Mark left was the same year my wife and I married. It's a date I'm not likely to forget."

"And you say that you saw the diploma? In your opinion there could be no confusion with a different Swiss medical school?"

"No. I saw it. Of course that doesn't mean it was authentic."

"Tomorrow morning, I'll go to the university and check the files for myself. Then I'll meet up with you at the conference."

"There must be some reasonable explanation," Paul said.

On the last afternoon of the conference, Paul and Dr. Jordan skipped the official luncheon and met in a quiet café nearby. They were so anxious to get to Dr. Jordan's report, they barely skimmed the menu before ordering. Paul wasn't interested in food; he just wanted to get down to news about Mark. Dr. Jordan ordered a traditional Swiss meal of Lummelbraten for both of them. A local Swiss wine was a welcome addition to the meal. Nerves were tight and they both spoke in soft voices.

Dr. Jordan said, "What I found in the records room early this morning is devastating news for all of us. I thought there was some accident that he was omitted from the yearbook so I went to the record room to see if I could find something about him. It does not help us that his name, Favre, is the most common name in French-speaking Switzerland.

"So, finally, I found the name, Mark Thomas Favre. An American citizen…high honors. Missing was his photograph, and all the records of classes taken and reports from professors. But there was a newspaper announcement of his death. The real Mark Thomas Favre died in 1969 in a skiing accident. That was two years before I taught here.

"And look at this. I brought these letters. Three copies of recommendations? Forgeries! There," Dr. Jordan said, tapping rapidly on the file. "That is my name, but that is not my signature!"

Paul took a moment to accept what was now apparent. Before he could even consider what to do about what he had discovered. "This makes no sense. If Mark took another man's name and history from here, how would that help him in California? He would still have to have a residency program in psychiatry and pass the Boards to get a medical license. Unless…unless he never took a residency or the Boards! Maybe he just opened an office, hung his fake diploma, and slowly built a practice."

"Is that possible?" Dr. Jordan looked appalled.

"It has happened. More often than you would think. Just last year the New York Times published an unbelievable story about how many people have fake medical degrees and some managed to practice medicine without even finishing college. It's easy to imagine how someone can hang a fake diploma but it seems impossible that they can get away with practicing medicine for years without a license. You have to wonder how many patients died before the scumbags were caught. The article came out the end of last year. December 1974, I think."

"That is shocking."

Dr. Jordan was watching him carefully.

"I can see this is a terrible blow to you, Dr. Tabor. I wish there were some way that you could be spared the consequences of this. But I must report it to the authorities. You understand, I have no other choice."

"I understand."

"It seems impossible to me that this type of forgery could have happened here. I can't even imagine how it could have been done. These files are secure and only a few well-screened employees have access…and the fact that a man is practicing psychiatry in the United States claiming that he was educated here…it is unbelievable! And in all these years no one—not even you—has found him out!"

"Dr. Jordan." Paul sighed deeply in the middle of his thought. A multitude of ramifications confronted him. Where to begin? "Dr. Jordan, Mark Favre is not considered incompetent in his community. True, he has kept a low profile; now I understand why he refused to involve himself in positions that would attract too much attention. He seems to have a busy practice and although I have serious doubts about his emotional stability, I've never doubted the authenticity of his credentials. He's had some training somewhere! A man can't just manufacture an education out of wishful thinking. I did wonder how he could be so young to have completed his medical requirements, but then I remembered that fewer years of schooling are required in Switzerland than in the U.S."

The older man nodded…His voice was consoling. "Indeed. I'm sure things are going to be unpleasant for you, Dr. Tabor. As well as for your daughter. I deeply regret the embarrassment this is sure to cost you."

"My daughter is in the process of a divorce. She met Mark when she was nineteen and married him soon after. I met him for the first time when they returned from their honeymoon. He can be very charming when he wants to be.

"This will be difficult for her, of course. Terribly embarrassing but I doubt she's going to be upset for the man himself.

"As far as I'm concerned, I went out on a limb for Mark in the early days of their marriage. Trying to help him get started. I introduced him to other doctors in the community. I'm grateful now that he didn't take me up on my offer to help him affiliate with UCLA."

"Let's be grateful for that. This is going to be awkward enough for you without a professional overlapping."

"There's one thing I'd like to ask of you. A favor."

Dr. Jordan raised expectant eyebrows while Paul found the words.

"Mark has just come out of the hospital. He has severe bleeding ulcers and possibly cancer, though we don't know that for sure. Surgery has been recommended. My daughter left him just a few days ago. What I'm asking, Dr. Jordan, is a chance to talk with Mark first. I no longer hold any hope that he could have an explanation...not with forged signatures and the fact that the date he claims isn't confirmed by the list of graduates. It isn't that I'm hoping for some solution. But I'd like to have a chance to talk with him before the authorities get involved in this. I'd like to encourage him to terminate his relationship with the patients himself. And arrange for a psychiatrist to be available to help them."

Paul slouched in his chair; his fingers wiped his forehead, trying to erase some of the tension. "I know I should stay out of this, but..."

"You have more compassion for him than I do, Dr. Tabor."

"Compassion isn't what I'm feeling at all. I'm appalled at what he's done. And embarrassed. What I'm asking has nothing to do with any feelings of compassion."

"What then?"

Paul stood up and walked to the window, staring out at the courtyard below. "It has more to do with philosophy than emotion, I suppose. I'd like to be constructive despite what I feel. It's going to be a great deal easier on his patients if they have an opportunity to say goodbye to him, to terminate directly, rather than just read about this in the newspaper." He turned again to face Dr. Jordan. "This is the kind of story that gets a lot of press in Los Angeles. Despite what I feel about Mark personally, I'd like to see him have a chance to give himself up. It's going to be devastating enough. Maybe now he'll get some psychiatric help himself—he's certainly needed it for a long time."

"Let me think about it. I understand your reasoning. But we can't risk having him thank you for the information, clean out his bank account, and open an office in another location. Knowing the man, would you say that there's a chance of that?"

There was a long and weighty silence. "Knowing the man, I would have to say that he might try it. Can we take a day to think this over? Both of us? Frankly I'm feeling overwhelmed."

"I will agree to that. I'm especially sorry this has to be a concern to you now, when the conference is such a successful event."

Paul looked at his watch. "Speaking of the conference, I need to get back over there. After it ends tonight, some of the staff will stop by our suite for a nightcap and a casual plan for what comes next. I'd be so pleased if you would join us."

"I'd like that. There's nothing more you can do about Mark Favre tonight. Come. Put this matter out of your mind, for now."

As if he could.

The conference ended on Thursday evening with gratitude and excitement. Paul's only regret was how much he missed of the program he had created.

Most of the attendees headed back to their homes. Others waited for a Swiss conference that would begin on Friday regarding Psychedelic Drugs and Creativity. Most of the international participants chose to spend the night before traveling. The locals stayed and rehashed the conference in the bar.

Late that evening, in the Tabor suite, about a dozen of the event planners were busy creating a plan to sustain the momentum. There was a smile on Paul's face, but his eyes showed his stress. Stephanie could see it; the others, involved in their own conversations, probably didn't notice. Paul excused himself for a moment, ran cold water over his face, then tried to flush everything he was feeling down the toilet. There was nothing he could do about it anyway. *Let it go,* he thought. Mark made his choices. It wasn't up to Paul to carry the weight of them.

He reminded himself of that several times during the next hour. He saw Stephanie watching him a few times and knew that she sensed something was up. He hoped the rest of them, if they noticed at all, would just think he was tired. Paul had a lousy poker face. What he felt was usually written all over him.

There was local wine and Swiss chocolate and an abundance of praise to Paul for the concept and the success of the program. There would be other conferences in the future.

Paul asked Dr. Jordan to stay until the last of the guests were gone. "You might be interested in seeing the face that goes with Mark's name." Paul opened the drawer in the end table, heard the wedding band roll and clatter to the back of it. Sorting through the torn pieces of the photograph, Paul removed a small particle of the picture. Mark's face was not affected by the rips in the photograph.

The professor stared at the picture, let out a string of French expletives, and folded his hand over the photo.

"Is this the man you call Mark Favre?"

"Yes."

"I know him well. Very well. His real name is Mark Hall. And now, what you told me about him makes sense. He is subject to paranoid tendencies. There is a great deal you don't know about your son-in-law, my friend. I think we will be together for quite a while longer tonight."

Stephanie stayed silent. The atmosphere was too charged to tamper with it. She would know soon enough.

Paul freshened his drink, giving himself a moment to prepare for whatever was to come. Stephanie's eyes asked the question. He answered in one sentence. "Mark's credentials were forged. He's not a doctor, much less a psychiatrist." He didn't wait for her reaction. He had to know what else Mark had done.

Dr. Jordan frowned. "He did graduate from the University of Lausanne. With high honors. I know he had at least three years in general medicine. I was his supervisor when he began his psychiatric residency. I recall being pleased—at first.

"I don't remember how much training he had in psychiatry, but I know he never finished his psychiatric rotation. The first few cases he was assigned went fine. His diagnoses were accurate, his treatment appropriate.

"And when he was asked for a textbook indication of treatment, there was no problem. It was when he had to deal directly with the patients that we began to see signs of trouble. He tended to see himself as omnipotent. I talked with him several times about it, warning him that his patients could become worse when they found that he could not provide all the comfort and salvation that he appeared to be offering.

"The problem was serious enough but could have been remedied in most students. Mark took badly to criticism. He sulked, was defensive, even belligerent.

"I began then, for the first time, to see some signs of paranoid tendencies. Looking back, I can see there were probably some earlier indications of his emotional problems, but we were all so taken with his brilliance and excited by his potential that we tended not to see what was right before our eyes."

Dr. Jordan paused, re-creating in his mind the situation that he would explain, trying to remember the details, the order of events. "A young woman was assigned to him when he first came on the rotation, and they seemed to have a good rapport. She had made several attempts at suicide which was the cause for her admission to the hospital.

"After I became aware of Mark's need to be omnipotent, his desire to solve everything for his patients instead of helping them resolve the problem for themselves, I began to worry about the patient. She was young—nineteen, twenty. She was an 'acting-out' girl who had difficulty containing any of her own feelings. So, when she felt lonely, sad, angry, or just wanted attention, she would ask for Mark and he would come to the rescue. After a while, he became disenchanted with his patient. Primarily, I suspect, because she was not improving.

"We recommended that he try her on an ataractic medication. Instead he put her on heavy sedation at bedtime, hoping to stop her night calls, which had been increasing. As she became more demanding, he just ordered more sedatives. I'm sure you can anticipate the conclusion.

"After a stormy session with her one day, heard by everyone on the floor, she walked out of the office and went to her room. And that's when she took all that medication she had been hoarding. By the time someone checked on her she had overdosed. We couldn't save her."

Paul held his head, listening. He couldn't imagine the Mark he knew fitting into that picture. He always seemed so conscientious about his patients—well, maybe he's been trying to undo what happened here, he thought.

"And Mark was expelled at that point?" Stephanie asked.

"No. Mark was called before the review board. He refused to accept any responsibility in the mishandling of this case. He blamed me for suggesting medication; he blamed the nurses for not supervising the patient more closely. And he blamed the patient!

"After lengthy examination it was determined that Mark had little insight into his own problems. A therapeutic analysis was recommended.

"We gave him an option. He could begin treatment immediately and, in a year, we would reevaluate whether he could reenter the program or not. His therapist would make that decision. If he felt that Mark had gained insight and was able to cope with his problems, he could return."

"That seems more than fair, under the circumstances," Paul said.

"We thought so. But Mark became furious—almost violent. His paranoid response ran rampant, his accusations against the board were abusive; he stormed out the door and that was the last that any of us heard of him."

Paul was astonished. "It would have been so simple to do as the board suggested. He might have lost only a year or so, but to throw it all away and then live a lie for the rest of his life, seems ridiculous. Living with that stress and knowing what the consequence would be, if he was found out, well that would give anybody bleeding ulcers! The question is, what do we do now?"

"One thing seems obvious; I must bring this to the Governing Board, and I will try to report his offense without bringing your name into it if I can. My next job is to review the names of all the people who had access to the records room when he was here."

CHAPTER 20

LAUSANNE

All day on Friday, Paul was taking care of the aftermath of the conference, meeting with Henri and trying to keep his mind on the business at hand. Stephanie was grateful for a time of quiet and although she wanted to read about the history of Lausanne, she fell asleep on the sofa. Then there was a demanding knock on her door. She put on her shoes and straightened her dress; the knocking became more intense.

She started to open the door, then paused. "Who is it?"

"It's me. Open the door."

"Jayne? Come in, what's wrong?"

"You tell me! I just heard a really sick rumor and you may know more about it than I do!"

"Tell me what you heard."

"I heard that Mark faked his medical license! That he isn't even a doctor." She plopped down on the sofa and kept gesturing wildly. Her eyes were wide. "I can't believe this. Is it really true? Tell me it isn't true."

"I'll tell you what I know. And you tell me where you heard it and let's take a breath, open a nice bottle of local wine, and share the details." Stephanie didn't wait for a response, she just opened and poured. "You first. Where did you hear this?"

"At the bar, just a few minutes ago. I heard two men talking about it and I just froze and kept listening. Obviously I wasn't going to ask them how they knew! I just tried to look invisible and hoped I'd find out. They were tying the story to Dad. Dad! The head of this conference! They didn't give any details and when they changed the subject I left. Now, you. Do you know about this?"

Stephanie told her how they learned what happened and how they found out. She chose not to mention the photo of Mark that was the last bit of news that clarified who Mark Favre really was. There was no point in rubbing salt in an open wound.

"The conference is over," Stephanie said. "I don't know what we're going to do. I imagine there are procedures for things like this and they may need Paul to be here, or maybe he has nothing more to add. I have to say this…we are a long way from answers, and we have to be prepared for whatever comes."

Jayne had trouble getting her breath. She put her wine glass down and covered her face with her hands. Then came the sobs. "What am I going to do, Stephanie? He's going to need a lawyer and a good one. We're going to run out of money before this thing is over. Even if he doesn't go to jail…his 'career' is over. What will he do? What will I do? Do you think he'll go to jail, Stephanie? Really? I mean, how serious is this?"

Stephanie moved over to the sofa and put her arm around Jayne. It would have been impossible for her not to. This time, it wasn't Jayne's fault.

She looked like such a little girl, all doubled over. What would she do now with her shattered life?

"I don't know what I'll do, Stephanie. I never should have married that bastard. I was just so mad at my mother for leaving and my dad for never being available and here was a doctor who fell in love with me. I was just a kid," she said, as if Stephanie didn't know the whole story. "I don't think he ever loved me. He just married me to have a connection with Dad."

"Don't go there, Jayne. He seemed very much in love with you when you first married."

"Yeah, for about six months. I don't know why Dad let me get involved with a man that much older."

"As I remember, he didn't know you were dating Mark until he heard you went to Vegas and married him."

"I think I married Mark to get even with Dad."

"You can't change the past, but you can start thinking about what you want to do now."

"I don't want to go home. But I don't want to lose what is legally mine. He would sell all my stuff. He would leave me with nothing, if I don't go back and fight for it. But how can I face my friends?"

Stephanie said, "I like the proverb that says, 'If they really are your friends, they'll support you. If they didn't like you before, they will probably be pretty nasty.' I'm paraphrasing, just a little.

"You can do this, Jayne. If you don't go home, it will look like you are complicit. Hold your head high, tell your truth. And protect your assets. Your dad and I will be right there with you. You need to be sure Mark doesn't make things worse for you.

And there's another thing. Although I know you didn't ask my opinion…"

Jayne just looked at her, wide-eyed and speechless. "Should I stop?" Stephanie asked.

Jayne shook her head. Then in a soft voice, almost inaudible, she said, "Why would you help me? We don't like each other."

Stephanie smiled. "I'll help you because we're family. And because I think we can change the way we treat each other and, in time, the way we feel about each other. I want to be there for you, and I'll be the stand-in for a friend, until we both stop acting like competitors and work at this relationship. I think this is a good time to start. What do you think?" Jayne threw her arms around Stephanie and sobbed.

That's when Paul walked in the door. Stephanie was smiling, Jayne was crying, and Paul was speechless.

Stephanie was optimistic about their plan. Excited even, and deeply touched by Jayne's response. She knew this wouldn't be an easy journey for either of them. Suddenly she was feeling just a little guilty for being grateful that the beach house had only one bedroom.

CHAPTER 21

MALIBU

Leah didn't know what to expect from Mark. She had planned to leave as soon as they got back to the house in Malibu, but she had to wait until that night, when he was asleep. There was no way she felt able to confront him or to escape without his knowing. She knew that all the doors were on an alarm system and Mark kept it on day and night. Fear led to unwise choices and Leah was caught between her desire to get away from Mark and her anxiety about what he would do to her if he saw her as a threat. All she could do would be to pretend he was innocent. It would take all of her acting skills to get through the days and find a moment she felt brave enough to try to get out.

Leah was upstairs, pretending to be suffering from a migraine. She could hear him on the phone. His voice was soft, like he didn't want to be overheard. She could hear most of what he was saying. The words were muffled, but she sensed fear in the tone of them, whining the same request as before. It was all about the drugs.

Leah heard the anger in his voice. He sounded as crazy as he had in Montecito. She heard the receiver of the phone being slammed down on the base.

If she had been more mature, more experienced, more knowledgeable about mental illness, she would have known to stay silent. It was not the time to argue with Mark, or to stir the rage that was intensifying.

Leah tried to keep her voice from shaking. She straightened her shoulders, took deep breaths. Imagined she was calm and not at all afraid. She came down the stairs with her heart racing but her appearance calm.

"Mark, I'm so grateful to you for all that you've done to protect me, but I really need to get on with my life.

"I barely started going through Nicole's things. I haven't even talked with her accountant or her landlord.

"Please, let me just call a cab. You've been very good to me and I appreciate it. But now there are things I have to do."

"You're bored with me." Accusation colored the words.

"This has nothing to do with you. I just want to start taking care of business. And I get anxious just staying inside."

"You're used to staying inside. The winter snows used to keep you in for long periods of time."

"I'm from Lausanne. The weather isn't so bad. You must be thinking of the more mountainous areas east of there."

"No. I was thinking of Lausanne."

"Have you been there?"

"A long time ago."

"Then you know. You know we're not isolated there."

"I was isolated there." His voice was soft. Incredibly sad.

"I'm tired, Leah. Go to bed."

"Mark, it's only the middle of the day. What are you thinking!"

He lay down on the sofa again and said nothing.

She hurried to her room, with nothing to read and nothing to watch and nothing to think about except…she was going to get out of there one way or another.

She would keep it simple and just take her purse with her passport and money, and the picture taken with Nicole. She would hitchhike to Westwood. Why not? People hitchhiked in Europe all the time. They probably did here too. Or she would go straight to the police station. She would be safe. If only she could think of a way to turn off that alarm.

CHAPTER 22

LAUSANNE

It was early Saturday morning in Lausanne when the phone rang, and Paul got it on the first ring. "Hello." His voice was gravelly and quiet, hoping to let Stephanie get a bit more sleep.

"Dr. Tabor, this is Dr. Jordan. I'm sorry to call you so early, but I wanted to be sure you didn't leave the hotel until we talked. Can you meet me downstairs in just a few minutes? I didn't sleep last night trying to make sense out of our newest discovery and maybe you can shed some light on this. I'm downstairs now."

"I'll see you in ten minutes."

He didn't even take time to shave. As quietly as he could, he dressed and hurried out.

The table where Dr. Jordan was waiting was far enough away from others that they could speak freely. They ordered coffee and croissants. Dr. Jordan drew a paper from his briefcase and handed it to Paul. "Do you recognize any of these names? These are the people who had access to the room where our records were kept, on or around the time Mark Favre's records were altered."

Looking down the paper, Paul stopped at one he recognized. His head was spinning. Trying to interpret the meaning.

Dr. Jordan continued, "One of these names is the daughter of a man who made huge donations to our scholarship fund, years ago. Nicole Vassaux. He was one of those financial tycoons who sometimes wanted to identify a specific student as a recipient. We've had a few of those.

"Just on a hunch, I asked a friend on the board at the university, and he looked into Mark Hall's record over there. I was right! Mark was a beneficiary of a scholarship that was sponsored by Nicole's father, Pierre Vassaux. However, Mark did not have a full scholarship at the medical school. I don't know how he got his financing. Personal loans perhaps for the first year. After that, rumors spread that a certain woman on the board of the medical school was particularly fond of him. At first, we heard that he rented a room in her house, later the stories became more…more…personal. Apparently there was some sort of arrangement between them. She has always been extremely generous with the medical students, and it would not be the first time she sponsored one. There was always one student or another riding through the medical school without debt because of her generosity.

"There is the connection between Mark and Nicole. That doesn't prove she was the one who forged the papers, though it would seem that she did. I've asked around to see if there was a romantic connection between them. So far I haven't found it, but it seems probable."

"I know who Nicole Vassaux is. Or rather, who she was," Paul said.

"She's dead?"

"She was murdered a few weeks ago. In Los Angeles. She was found dead in her apartment by her younger sister, Leah. Leah found a paper with my name on it in her sister's journal and assumed I was her therapist, which I wasn't. You already know Mark's story, so how does that fit in?"

Dr. Jordan took a moment before he said, "My God, Nicole was the one who had access to the records. Perhaps she helped him alter his identity and forged the papers that changed Mark Hall into Mark Favre. If that's true, we will need proof."

Paul said, "One must assume that Mark had a relationship with Nicole here in Lausanne and, it seems, while he was married to my daughter. And that would lead…and that would lead…" Paul couldn't say the words…to even graver possibilities. Then there was a rush of gratitude that Jayne was with them and she was safe.

Later, when Paul was telling Stephanie what he heard, the phone rang and it was Henri. Paul answered and passed the question on to Stephanie. "Did you lose a blue sweater?

"Someone left it at the café and Henri wants to know if it's yours. If so, he's offered to drive down and get it."

"Yes, it's mine. I've been wondering where I left it. But let's take an hour or so, just the two of us, and pick it up. This may be the only private time we have on this whole trip. In the meantime, the concierge is trying to change our reservations and get flights for us to get out of here tomorrow. Just promise me another vacation that really is one. Okay? No conference? No drama?"

"Right now, our quiet little home on the beach sounds really good to me. But maybe a short getaway before long, and next summer a proper vacation."

They drove to Saint-Saphorin and retrieved the sweater after having a fine lunch at the tavern. Then Stephanie said, "Let's see if the gallery with Genevieve's work is open."

"Sweetie, I'm not in a mood for shopping."

"I know, but this is important, Paul. I got a call from the gallery owner. This will only take a minute."

In the prime position for display was the sculpture that had been sent on approval to a potential buyer, the week before. When Viktor Bernard refused to negotiate the price, the bronze was returned and displayed in the gallery like the treasure it was.

Paul was speechless. The boy was cast in bronze; he was young and without question it was Mark. The woman, though older, was exquisite, but made no effort to look younger than her years. They were nude. Embracing. In love.

On the way home, Paul was silent. The radio was off and the windows open. Stephanie knew when he was dealing with something this troubling, he didn't want to hear any comments from anyone. When they got out of the car at the hotel, Paul turned to her and said, "I don't think this would be helpful to discuss with Jayne right now. She has enough to deal with."

"She won't hear it from me."

When they got back to their room, there was a message from Jayne.

"The concierge just called. He got us three tickets for home, leaving tonight.

"I'll fly back to LA with you. I can stay with a friend until things settle down."

Mark was restless and the sofa seemed too short, too narrow, too hard, too soft. He tried to distract himself from the pain and began to think of Leah, lying there, so vulnerable in Stephanie's bed. There was a time when he would have been there with her. But he knew he wasn't man enough to do it. Not anymore. Even remembering Genevieve couldn't erase the impact his abusive childhood had on his confidence.

Just as he was falling asleep, he heard laughter from the past. All the way from Bakersfield, like it was yesterday, like it was today.

He remembered that summer he was turning sixteen. He had a job working for his dad. Hating the dull business of packing and shipping, Mark dreaded the hours he spent doing manual work. He made suggestions to his father that would have improved the company's efficiency, but he was told not to interfere in something he didn't understand.

Mark didn't know why he worked longer hours than he needed to. He worked harder than the others, compelled to out-do the ones who earned a full salary for their work. He wanted to earn more than just money that summer. He understood that later, but not at the time. The employees were nice to him until that last day.

"You're a mighty hard worker, Mark," Marcie Adams had said to him. "Don't you ever take time off to play?"

"No ma'am." She was an older woman, at least thirty, and he was always respectful. He looked away from her when he answered so she wouldn't know where he really wanted to look. Didn't women know that men just had to look when they wore their dresses low-cut like that? Didn't women know that, he wondered, but he couldn't stop his eyes from crawling up her to the edge of her dress that stopped way short of where he knew it should.

She sure was a pretty woman. His father didn't seem to mind how sloppy her work was. And Mark had seen him once, using his eyes to feel those tits when he thought she wasn't looking. She spent most of the time filing her nails, and sometimes Mark wondered if she wanted to get fired so she could collect her unemployment and stay home. He heard one of the office girls say that as a joke, but he didn't think she was joking.

He forced himself to take his eyes from where they had been and then he looked at her face and saw that she was smiling and looking pleased as could be. She had the prettiest eyes; they twinkled when she talked and he would have thought she was flirting, except that she was so much older and all.

"Help me carry these boxes back to storage, Mark. They sent down too many this morning."

"Oh, here, I can do it," he said. "You don't have to lift anything."

"Don't mind a bit," she said and carried one while he carried two and they walked together to the storeroom. When they put the boxes down, she closed the door. He heard the ramming of the bolt into the lock.

"I think we should liven up this place a little, you and me. I think you've been wanting to see something that I have, and I may get fired for it, but it wouldn't be the worst thing that ever happened, by a long shot. You ever fuck a girl, Mark?"

Mark couldn't even answer and the more he reddened the more she enjoyed it. He was so scared his heart pounded, hard as the mound that formed in his jeans. He swallowed dry and couldn't think of anything to say.

She took her blouse off and stood there just letting him look all he wanted to and then letting him touch and she smiled at his awkwardness but enjoyed it too. Pretty soon she had him doing it just the way she liked it.

He was scared not so much of her, though that, too, but of the thought that his father would somehow break through the lock on that door and barge in on them. Or that lightning would strike on this blazing summer day, leaving them exposed to the world. Or that she would laugh.

But she wasn't laughing. She was pulling at his jeans and letting them drop. Lying on the cool floor, she invited him in. But before it was started it was over and she swore. He wanted to run. He knew he failed her but no matter how he tried, he was so ashamed he couldn't get it up for her again. He thought she would be angry, but she just rumpled his hair and said, "That's okay, kid. Don't worry about it."

And that same day he heard the laughter of the office girls. Somehow his dad overheard the story. He fired the woman. Mark got a beating. Even as his father struck him, Mark knew it wasn't so much for what he did, as for what he wasn't man enough to do well. For both of them, it was the clarifying statement of his inadequacy.

Mark felt the world closing in on him. What was his plan? He had one when he got to the beach house, on Saturday…Now it was harder to think clearly. He had to have his meds! But how could he get them?

His thoughts were like wild animals, racing in all directions; he tried to remember exactly what his plan was. Days ago he had it all worked out. It was more than about the journal now. Could he make it look like Paul killed Nicole? How was he going to do that? He didn't want to hurt Stephanie and she would be devastated if Paul was in trouble. Mark wondered how he could keep her safe and keep her from knowing? It had been so clear when he first came to the Tabor house.

If Leah had given him the journal in the beginning, this wouldn't be a problem. This was all her fault. How could he force her to give him the journal and be sure she didn't tell? Could he take it from her, force her to turn it over? She was strong, and he felt so powerless in her presence. Again, he tried to remember…what was his plan when he brought her here? Why was he so unclear now? He had to find another way to get Leah to trust him.

Later that night, Leah woke when she heard Mark whispering her name, then gently shaking her shoulder, waking her from a terrifying dream. She made a small, whimpering sound and Mark kept his hand on her shoulder, mumbling.

"Mark, what the hell are you doing! Stop it. Stop it now."

"Oh, Leah, I'm sorry, so sorry, so very sorry. I've been unkind and I didn't mean to be. I have an idea and think you're going to love it. Wake up, please talk to me. We have to get out of here!" But he didn't wait for her to answer, he just kept talking in a fast and frenzied way that made no sense to her at all. She could smell the liquor on his breath, and she knew he was already high on whatever else was in that leather medicine bag.

"Leah, I know you want to get out of here, and I just want to keep you safe. See, we both have the same need to change our plan. Let's be adventurous! We don't have to be cooped up here. I have credit cards and cash I got from the bank. You must have available money; it doesn't matter how much. We can just go to the airport and decide where we want to go! You have nothing here for you and there's nothing I have that I can't walk away from. Let's just go!

"Toss a coin! We both have passports, and we can go anywhere in the world. Where have you always wanted to go? I'm flexible. How about Fiji or somewhere in South Africa?" His intensity increased with each wild thought. A train of ideas with no direction. "We can leave right now. It won't take long to pack, and we can get out of this house! Isn't that what you wanted? I'm sorry, so very sorry, for all the trouble I caused you, but we have to be safe. That's all that matters."

Leah shuddered when she heard the phrase, "We have to be safe." She was afraid to confront him when he was in such a wild state. "Give me some time, I need to think about this."

Reluctantly, he left her alone. All the way down the stairs, he was mumbling something she couldn't understand. She spent the rest of the dark, early morning hours just listening.

Before dawn, the solution was suddenly obvious to her. Of course, Leah would agree to go with him! She almost laughed out loud. Mark was setting her up for the perfect escape, he was just too stoned to realize it.

Leah would agree to go anywhere Mark wanted to go. She would pack her suitcase, put it at the top of the stairs, and be ready to leave before she went downstairs. She looked over the railing and saw that he was asleep on the sofa. As soon as he woke up, she would tell him that she was so excited to go with him. They could leave as soon as he was ready. She knew she was a good enough actress to make him believe it. All of her theater experience was about to get her out of the mess she got herself into.

It would soon be daylight and she couldn't wait to get out of the house. She would go along with his ridiculous plan. She would improvise. How many hours had she spent in improv classes when she was still in boarding school? In Geneva, she discovered that she was very good at that. There were many options. The simple one would be to sound enthusiastic, make him trust her. But as soon as they were in the airport, she would look for the safest way to get away from him. She would wait until they were inside and then seek out the best person to run to. Wouldn't there be a security guard or the police or some authority that could help her?

Now she wished Mark would wake up so she could tell him she would love to go anywhere he chose. It would be easy to convince him.

She made as much noise as she could, but he didn't wake up. She longed to just open the front door and run. But the alarm would go off and there might be other locks, she didn't know. She waited, keeping her excitement under control. If she acted too happy about the plan, he would be suspicious. After all her acting experience she should be able to find just the right level of excitement to make this work. She couldn't risk making him angry.

It was eight, then nine, then ten. She took her suitcase down the stairs, and left it by the garage door, making as much noise as she could without it seeming intentional. He slept through it. Now she began to worry if he was…several words came to mind as possibilities. Maybe he was just hung over, or maybe the meds held him down. Maybe…she stopped her train of thought.

She spoke his name but there was no response. She moved closer. Then she heard him breathing. She touched his shoulder and said, "Mark, I think you want to get up now. We have a busy day ahead." He didn't move. She faked a cough. Cleared her throat. Then she took a book off the coffee table and dropped it on the stone floor. His eyes opened and he looked dazed.

"Sorry to wake you, but we have some big plans ahead, yes?"

His breath made her take a step back. He said, "What are you talking about?"

"I thought you would want me to wake you so we can get started."

Mark sat up, running his hand over his unshaven face. "What? What time is it?"

"Time for you to get packed. I have all my things ready to go. So, I'm ready whenever you are."

He looked at her blankly. "Go where? What are you talking about?"

Leah's thoughts were whirling. "Remember what you suggested last night, when you woke me up and told me your plan for us?"

Mark yawned. "I have no idea what you're talking about."

"Don't you remember saying we could go to the airport and pick a flight to anywhere in the world? You have some money and I have some money and we would be free from all this!"

He stared at her and muttered, "I don't know what the hell you're talking about, but you must have had one hell of a dream."

Leah was speechless, feeling the hope torn so abruptly from her. Mark was slurring his words, but she knew what he said. "I'm tired. You should get some sleep."

"Mark what are you thinking? This is no time for sleeping!"

He lay back on the couch and she could see the anger and the sadness but nothing that gave her a hint of what he planned for her. She certainly wasn't going to stay downstairs. When she got to the top of the landing, she wished she had taken one of the books. Now she would stay in a room with nothing to distract her from her own thoughts, thoughts that seemed more and more terrifying.

Downstairs, Mark was trying to make a plan, but he was just overwhelmed with scenes from his past and he had no skills to deal with the memories. The walls seemed to be closing in on him. He knew this feeling, all too well. It seemed there wasn't enough air to breathe. He remembered when he was a boy and had this same intense fear.

It was June in Bakersfield, and the air was stifling. Hands pushed against him, shoving him into the small closet; he stumbled and fell. Frantically he tried to stop the door from closing, but he was only five. The door slammed in front of him with such power that his strength was useless against it. He heard the latch turning.

Mark's world filled with darkness. A cry of absolute terror burst from his throat. He dropped to the floor, drawn to the one slim line of light that reached for him under the crack. Please, leave it on, he thought, please…but then he heard the click of the wall switch and the blackness closed around him. He screamed, pounding on the door.

"Let me out!" His voice rose in a wail of panic. "Let me out…"

He banged on the door until his fists ached, but he couldn't stop. "Ma! Ma, you come get me! Please, Ma…"

The last time his father locked him in the closet his mother had waited most of the day before she let him out.

Tears poured down his cheeks, falling to the linoleum floor. "Ma, please come…please let me out!"

What if she forgot him? Or just didn't want him anymore and left him there. What if she never came back? And the thought forced an agonizing cry that shattered the quiet.

But no one came.

Leah came down the stairs and saw Mark still lying on the sofa.

So long as he didn't have a weapon, she thought her plan would work. She couldn't force him to unlock the doors, but she might be able to outsmart him.

"Mark, we need to talk."

Mark opened his eyes, sat up, and stared at her. "About the journal?"

"That's one of the things. The other is about my leaving. I'm not going to stay here anymore."

"You can leave as soon as you tell me where the journal is. I thought you hid it but I looked everywhere…everywhere." He gestured wildly with unsteady hands.

"I don't have the journal, Mark." He got up from the sofa and moved toward her.

"You what! What do you mean you don't have it?"

"I mailed it."

"You haven't had a way to mail it, dear girl, so don't fuck with me."

His anger only emboldened her. "Hotels have mailing services, too, you know. I know this isn't what you want to hear, Mark. But I no longer have the journal and it's in safe hands." She looked at him, all her frailty gone, an actress, claiming her power. Leah had been in life-threatening situations before, but only on the stage. The script was different now, but the attitude had been well-rehearsed. She could draw on that memory.

Her voice was firm, authoritative. "Mark, I know you're angry with me, but it really is my decision to make. If you'll just stay calm, we can talk about this."

"Don't you tell me to be calm. You ruined everything!"

Leah didn't want to ask him what she had ruined.

"Where did you mail the journal?" he yelled.

He looked like someone who would do anything to have his way. He rushed toward her. His hands were fists.

Leah remembered how to invoke power and now she used it. She put her hand up in front of her. A "stop it" sign in all languages. Her voice was strong, and her calm demeanor served her well. "Sit down, Mark, and we can talk about this. The journal belongs to me, and I'm the one who can decide who reads it and who doesn't."

"Tell me who has that journal!" His face was the color of rage. He was bewildered, frail without his blustering, but he moved toward her again, a feeble sign of control.

The actress played her part. "If you want to know what I did with the journal, you just back up. Get out of my face! Don't you dare threaten me." She was shouting now.

Startled, he swallowed hard. He did stop. She hadn't been sure that he would.

His hands were shaking and his voice dropped to a slow, patronizing tone. "Okay, okay, Leah. I'm backing up. Now, tell me. Where did you put the journal?"

"I mailed it to Dr. Tabor's office. It will be safe there until he comes back from Switzerland."

His scream was that of a wounded animal. He slammed his fist on the coffee table, grabbed the large crystal sculpture, raised it over his head. Leah saw it coming and ducked out of its path. There was the high-pitched sound of glass shattering into thousands of pieces on the stone floor.

Her heart was pounding. She saw the madness in his eyes and knew that nothing she could say would talk him down.

She was no match for him in a manic state.

She couldn't run. The doors were locked.

She couldn't scream for help. No one was close enough to hear her.

Leah had to trust her instincts. It was a risk, but everything was a risk now.

She stared at him with a look of confidence that required every bit of her acting skills. Slowly she spoke to Mark, carefully choosing her words, and softly, "I don't have what you want," she said. "And you don't have anything I want. I'm not your enemy, so let's end this. It's in your interest and mine." Those were almost the same words she had spoken in a play. She drew on her memory of that power.

"My things are packed. I'll call a cab. I expect you to turn off the alarm and unlock the front door. You will deeply regret it if you try to stop me. I have skills you can't even imagine."

There were no other skills, but she hoped it sounded convincing.

Warning signs went off in her head, but she didn't waver. Leah turned and walked slowly toward the door. She hoped Mark would be intimidated by her sudden display of strength. Her hands didn't shake, and her voice was steady. She didn't hurry.

Claiming the power she didn't feel, she walked toward her suitcase that she had put near the door. She knew this was a wild choice but she couldn't imagine another option.

Suddenly there was a terrible pain in the back of her head. She was falling. The room turned black. There was silence.

Leah lay motionless on the stone floor. Mark fought against his panic. He looked down at her and checked to see if she was breathing. There was blood on the floor and he had fleeting memories of her sister. He had no feeling of regret. Now he could get the journal. That was all that mattered.

He couldn't just leave her there. Or maybe he could. Mark tried to stop his hands from shaking. He had to decide what to do about Leah. Signs of life were faint. He would take his time. She wasn't going anywhere. He could do whatever he wanted to do with her.

Mark found Paul's office keys exactly where he assumed they would be, in the top drawer of his dresser. Now he could get to the journal and find out what Nicole said about him. Then he could destroy it. Without that journal, nothing could tie him to Nicole. No one could blame him.

Mark drove Stephanie's car to Paul's office, watching carefully not to speed, not to run through yellow lights, not to rush from the car into the office.

When Mark entered the waiting room, he expected to find an abundance of mail beneath the slot in the office door. He had a moment of panic when not even one envelope was there.

He tried each key on the chain until he found the one for Paul's inner office. There he saw a stack of mail and a small package neatly placed on his desk. Of course! Paul let a young psychiatrist use his office in the evenings. Naturally he would have taken care of the mail.

There was a package just the size of Nicole's journal; it was right there along with letters, bills, and a few magazines. Mark tore the packaging apart and tossed it in the wastebasket. Now, finally, he held Nicole's worn journal in sweaty and trembling hands. It was his now. After all this time and worry and fear. This was his freedom pass, he thought. He was sure he had nothing to worry about anymore. Then he remembered Leah.

Mark opened the book to a random page and found a poem that just lay bare, without adornment. Raw emotions, filled with rage, sprawled across two sheets of paper…He had no reaction to the words.

Mark was filled with confidence now, convinced that since he had the journal, nothing could tie him to Nicole. Even if the police found their way to him, he had a strong defense. He rehearsed it, just in case.

Mark imagined he was in court. He was taking the stand. He could see his attorney defending him, the jury softening as he told them what happened.

He could almost hear his attorney asking him, "What was your relationship with Leah Vassaux?"

"We were together as sexual partners," he would say. "Everything that happened was with her consent.

"We had only known each other less than a week, but she agreed to come to the beach house and spend several nights with me in Malibu.

"Then she agreed to come with me to Montecito and we stayed in a one-bedroom suite at the Miramar Hotel. It certainly would have been easy to get away from me there, if that was her choice.

"We went to an expensive restaurant for dinner at the San Ysidro Ranch. I paid for everything. She had every opportunity to leave if she wanted to. She could have called the police from there if she thought I was forcing a relationship she didn't want.

"She liked it rough, and she taught me some techniques I hadn't tried.

"Everything we did, she initiated. She looks so young and innocent, but she is one very experienced woman. She could have left anytime. All she had to do was say the magic word: Stop.

"Doesn't it seem strange that only days after her sister's death, she wanted a sexual relationship with me? This may sound crude to some of the jury but it's not against the law. I apologize if I offended some in this courtroom, but everything we did was legal and more common than some people may realize. I should add, that if I hadn't been given so many painkillers from an irresponsible doctor, I probably wouldn't have agreed to her games."

He had rehearsed his story over and over, trying to remember what he had said. Trying to remember, then forgetting and remembering again. His carefully crafted defense was empowering. As soon as he read the journal, he would destroy it.

Leah wasn't going anywhere now, but he did have to decide what he was going to do with her.

There was also the matter of Nicole, the only detail not covered by Leah's story. Nicole was the beginning of all the problems. Fingerprints in her apartment verified that Mark had been there, but nothing proved that he pushed her down the stairs. It made him a "person of interest." Nothing more.

The journal and the poem only proved that Nicole was upset and felt abandoned. Mark regretted their relationship but breaking up with a pregnant woman was not a crime.

What if he told the detective the truth…or a portion of the truth? He would say he had been with Nicole in her bedroom, and they were arguing. She was pregnant and wanted him to get a divorce and marry her. When he refused and started to leave, she hit him. He kept walking toward the stairs. When she hit him again, he turned and put his hands up to protect himself. She lunged toward him, but she was off-balance and slipped. He tried to grab her, but she was falling. He was haunted by the memory of her hand reaching for him, the feel of her skin touching him, then falling away. Of course he tried to save her, but there was no hope. Her neck was broken. There was no pulse. He would say that he was devastated and took a coverlet from the sofa and covered her body.

He remembered someone opening the front door. He panicked and ran out through the back. He wouldn't have run if he hadn't been in shock. Once he was outside, he just kept moving toward his car. Nicole was dead and going back to explain seemed…unwise. He hadn't committed a crime. He would say he ran because he was afraid.

There was no reason a jury would doubt him. His only crime was running away.

After they heard the story from his point of view he would be cleared.

Mark was confident that even if the police found cause to arrest him, they couldn't prove that he killed Nicole. He wouldn't serve any time at all.

He still had to decide what he was going to do about Leah.

It was the pain that woke her. Leah was lying on her back, her hands tied in front of her. She tried to move and then she realized that she was pressed in a tight space with her knees bent and her feet pressed against the wall. Her ankles were tied. Her arms bound tight against her chest.

Panic was even stronger than the pain. Where was she? What was happening to her? Why couldn't she move? Her head was throbbing. She screamed for help, but no one came.

There was the smell of wool clothing, the texture of a heavy coat hanging above her, touching her cheek. The musty scent of clothes stored for another season. Leah knew she was in a closet, but what closet? Where? How long had she been there? Hours? Days?

The only thing she could see was a sliver of daylight from under the door. She didn't remember how she got there, or how she hurt her head; she couldn't remember being tied.

How long had she been there? Her memory came back like pieces of a puzzle she could twist one way, then another, then gradually, one memory at a time, the pieces slipped into place.

Was Mark going to leave her there? Her heart raced faster, and her imagination revealed the worst of all that she feared. If he wanted her dead, why didn't he just kill her after he knocked her out? What if he just left her there to die?

No matter how she tried, Leah couldn't imagine a good ending.

She knew it was important to stay calm, but that was impossible. She heard a dog barking and for a moment she imagined it was the same dog with the deep threatening voice she had heard so many times in the night. Then there was the shrill, soprano bark of a small dog. Leah remembered hearing the high-low combination that had been so irritating when she tried to sleep the first night she was at the beach house. She let herself believe they were the same dogs that had interrupted many of her dreams. She made herself believe that. If those were the neighbor's dogs, she could still be at Mark's house. Was he still here? Would anyone come to let her out? He wouldn't just leave her there forever, would he? If she could hear the dogs barking, couldn't someone hear her calls for help?

Leah tried to turn so that she could keep her face near the sliver of light under the door. She tried to get a breath of air. Why had he bound her like this? She had only wanted to leave and get on with her life. What if Mark didn't come back? What pleasure did he get from knowing that she was alone, knowing that she would die a slow, agonizing death? Leah had no sense of time. Was it hours she had been there or was it days? Her imagination turned against her. The darkest truth was that Mark might not come back.

Leah wondered what it would feel like to die. A quick death would be better than lying there until she couldn't breathe anymore. Could she invite death to come quickly? She thought of Nicole, then of their mother. She thought of death as a way to be with both of them. To be free.

The light under the door faded to a soft suggestion of sundown. Leah stared at the fading light. When she gently turned her head, she felt the blood against her cheek that flowed from the wound on the back of her head. Leah wondered how long it would take her to die. Maybe it would come soon. Her body ached and she longed for water. Leah had no sense of time, only of her progressing weakness. How stupid she felt for ignoring all the signs that led up to this moment. The light under the door grew softer, then there was none. Darkness filled the closet.

Leah had no idea how long she was there. She gave up hope and tried to remember the tenderness of Nicole's face, the comforting sound of her voice. She imagined her mother, alive in a place where there was no fear or pain.

Then there was a strong light streaming through the crack at the bottom of the closet door. So, Mark had come back for her after all! She didn't think he would. "Mark! Please Mark, let me out of here!" Leah pleaded. Her eyes closed against the strong light as the door swung open and she cried out with relief. "I'll get the journal back; I'll give it to you. I don't care what you do with it. Please, just please let me out!" She opened her eyes and saw that it wasn't Mark who stood there. It was Paul Tabor, looking bewildered and as startled to see her as she was to see him.

"Leah! My God! What happened?" Paul knelt and touched her arm. "I'll get you out of here! You're safe now. Who did this to you?" It was Mark, of course it was Mark. So many questions rushed to his mind, but answers would have to wait. Right now, he needed to find a way to get Leah out of the closet without making the situation worse. How could he pull her from the cramped space when he didn't know what bones might be broken?

Where was Mark now? Paul wondered. *On a plane to some remote country? Upstairs with a gun?*

Stephanie went straight to the phone and called the police. "Send the paramedics quickly and the police! Something terrible has happened here!"

"I need scissors," Paul said when she hung up the phone. His first move was to reassure Leah. He kept his voice soft, the cadence comforting. He held her hands. Moving her would be a slow process. How badly was she hurt? He had no idea how extensive the damage might be. Paul kept talking to Leah. The cadence of his voice was soothing, almost hypnotic.

"Mark Favre did this to me," she whispered. "I've been in that closet for days! I know he killed Nicole! I can't prove it but I know he did. He killed my sister. Now he tried to kill me." She was sobbing hysterically, tears of relief, tears of rage, tears of fear. "He was obsessed with Nicole's journal, and I refused to give it to him. I don't know why I didn't see it earlier. He pretended to want to help me but he only wanted to have that journal for himself. And the only reason was so he could destroy the evidence that he killed her."

Stephanie felt a shiver race through her. She thought Leah was in Switzerland. Why was she at their house and what had Mark done to her?

Then she saw the shattered pieces of glass, splayed across the floor like a large abstract work of art. There were large chunks with jagged edges, then smaller pieces, and oh so many tiny sparkles the size of raindrops smashed on the stone floor. It had been the favorite piece in her collection. She looked away and ran to get the knife and scissors for Paul. "How can I help?"

"It's going to be hard to get this tape off without hurting her. I'll just peel enough to get her free and leave the larger strips for later. In the meantime, she needs some water."

Paul cut the tape that bound Leah's arms, then those that bound her legs. Her face was bloody. Before he moved her, Paul checked for wounds, making sure there were no sudden movements that could be painful or harmful. Leah cried out when he touched her shoulder. He pulled back, deciding to wait for the paramedics before he lifted her. He lived by the code, "First, do no harm." It took less than ten minutes for help to come. First the paramedics came, then the police. Paul knew better than to get in their way. They moved Leah from the cramped space of the closet. She asked for help to use the bathroom. Stephanie was on one side, a paramedic on the other. Then they helped her walk into the living room and rest on the sofa. She cried out again when her shoulder touched the cushion. The paramedic said, "We'll get you to the emergency room in no time." Those were not comforting words for Leah.

"I don't want to go to the hospital," Leah said, sounding stronger than she felt. "I don't want to be by myself. I can't. Please don't let them take me," she pleaded with Paul.

Paul had already made his assessment. "I think the priority is your mental health and you need to be here for now. I think you'll feel better after you tell us what happened."

He looked at the older of the two policemen who seemed to be in charge: "I know you have questions and as soon as you finish, I'll drive her to the hospital, and they can start some tests."

"I may not even need a hospital," Leah said.

"Actually you do. But let's just take this one step at a time."

Paul spoke to the policeman, "We can let the paramedics go now, then when you've finished with your questions, we'll be on our way."

"Not a problem," the officer said.

"In the meantime, Leah, I'll get you a pill to help with the pain."

"I've seen what those pills can do. I don't want any."

"It's not that kind of pill, Leah." He saw her resistance. "Okay, I'll get out of the officer's way and if you change your mind, I'll get you something that will lessen the pain and won't make your head spin."

"And I'll get her something to eat," Stephanie said. "She must be famished."

Paul listened carefully as Leah told her story to the policemen. He was relieved that she was able to keep the facts in order. She began in short sentences, almost like a list.

"He killed my sister and told me he was her psychiatrist. He kept trying to get her journal, but I mailed it to Dr. Tabor's office. Mark wouldn't leave me alone…" Leah could tell the story in a linear way, which was a good sign that her cognitive skills were not seriously impaired.

When she finished, Stephanie called her into the kitchen, where she was heating a can of soup for Leah. It was Paul's turn to reveal what he knew to the police. He decided to leave out the parts about Leah's mother, the years Mark had lived in the attic above Leah's family home, Mark's illegal practice of medicine. It would all be explained in time.

Paul asked the officer to step outside with him for a moment. "I think you'll be interested in this." He held a leather case and said, "I just saw this by the hearth. Mark keeps his meds in it but he doesn't have many left. He must have left in a hurry and not too long ago because he never goes anywhere without his drugs. You can bet he'll be coming back here when he runs out. Which leads me to think that it was just hours ago that he forced Leah into that closet."

"Why would the girl lie about it?"

"She isn't lying, she's telling you what she experienced. She felt like she was there for days but that was sheer panic talking. If she had been in that cramped position for days, she wouldn't be able to stand alone, much less walk across the room, which she just did when Stephanie helped her to the bathroom. I don't doubt that she experienced terrible abuse and a lot of bruising. She has signs of a concussion. That could influence what she remembers.

"Also, she probably lost the ability to estimate time. If she was there for three hours or six hours, it could feel like days. She drank the water quickly but look how slowly she's eating the soup. If it had been days, she wouldn't be sipping it so slowly.

"Mark's certainly going to come back here, even if he stashed some pills somewhere else. That's his Porsche in the garage. He's not going to abandon that. He took my wife's car, probably so his wouldn't be identified and I think I heard Stephanie giving your partner the license number."

"You lookin' for my job?" the officer said with a grin.

"Sorry." Paul laughed. "Of course, you knew that already."

"Your wife told us he's driving her car. I've already put out an APB on him. There's only one way he can get from the highway to this house and my men are watching it. She also gave us your office address and that's been staked out as well. What's in the journal he's been trying so hard to get?"

"I don't know. Leah's the only one who read it. Mark must think something's in there that would connect him to the murder of her sister, Nicole Vassaux. I can't think of any other reason. Oh, by the way, Detective McKenzie has an open file regarding her sister's death," Paul said. "I'm sure he'll want to hear about what happened to Leah."

"I have a call out to him now. He'll be in touch with you."

"Let him know I'll be at the hospital with her for a while. After that, I'll check her into a hotel. I'll let you know which one. Well, I don't want any of us to be here when he comes back for his drugs and his car so Stephanie and I will stay there too."

The officer nodded and said, "We'll turn out the lights and wait for him. He doesn't know Leah's out of that closet or that we have any reason to expect him. Our job's a lot easier if he doesn't know he's in our sights."

"We won't be going anywhere but the hospital and a hotel," Paul said.

"I'll let you know if he comes back here tonight. A roadblock is set up close by. If he comes this way, we'll get him. It's just as well that you stay as far away as possible. Do you know if he has a gun?"

"I know he doesn't like guns. That doesn't mean he doesn't have one."

"Okay, do you think they'll keep Leah at the hospital overnight?"

"That depends on what they find when they do an evaluation."

"You know, I wasn't at all sure he would come back here until you found his drugs. No addict would leave those behind."

CHAPTER 23

SANTA MONICA & MALIBU

Mark sat in the back booth of The Dandy Lion restaurant, not far from Paul's office. He had just finished a steak dinner and several martinis. Then he realized that his meds were at Paul's house. He always kept extras in his car, but he was in Stephanie's BMW now. He would drive carefully and slowly, not attracting attention, not inviting a cop to give him a ticket.

Traffic was light that evening and Mark made good time as he headed back to the Tabor house. He pulled across the highway, then slowed down when he saw the roadblock. He didn't see it until it was too late to turn around. Mark thought he had nothing to worry about. He would say he was driving his mother-in-law's car, headed to her house to return it to her. No one would be looking for him. Entitled and drunk, he acted like he was the one in control.

"What's going on?" Mark asked, confident that he wasn't the target of the search.

"Please step out of the car, sir," the officer said.

"I'll get my registration," Mark said as he reached for the glove compartment.

"Stop right there! Put your hands on the wheel." The driver's door swung open and the officer grabbed Mark's left arm, near his shoulder. "Now get out! Slowly. Keep your hands where I can see them."

"Let go of me! I only had one cocktail and I wasn't speeding. So keep your fucking hands to yourself!" Mark struggled and yelled when he was pulled from the car. "You have no right to touch me! No right at all." Mark swung at the officer with his right fist and landed a hard blow on the throat of the man who held him, which made the policeman gag and cough, and as he choked, Mark broke free. He didn't see the other cop running after him, didn't know a gun was aimed right at him.

The first cop stumbled and recovered. He was running toward Mark, closing the space between them. Mark turned to face him.

"Stop or I'll shoot!"

Mark heard the words, but he kept on running.

Again, the warning came. A moment passed.

The gun was fired the instant Mark slipped on the loose gravel, struggling to right himself, plunging down the hillside. His face slamming into the jagged rock that cracked his skull. It was covered in blood before the police could catch up with him. He hadn't even had time to scream.

At St. John's Hospital, Leah took all her insurance cards and her passport from a zippered section of her purse. It took a long time to complete the paperwork and the exam. Paul thought she had a concussion, but the emergency doctor didn't find one. Her head was throbbing, but it had stopped bleeding. The doctor gave her some meds for the pain and agreed not to admit her,

Leah looked him right in the eyes. "Your word. Your honor. Okay?" She handed the journal to him.

Then she turned to the attendant. "I need a minute."

He started to protest but Paul said, "This is important. Please, she needs to do this."

The attendant stepped back. Then he left the room.

Awkwardly Detective McKenzie moved to lean against the far wall. Paul went with him. They waited, both wondering what Leah needed to say to the dead man who killed her sister.

Leah's full attention was on Mark. Her hair fell forward and shielded her expression. What message was she sending to one who was dead, who was beyond hearing?

Leah had no idea how long she had been there, no sense of others across the room. "I would have killed you, if I could," she whispered to the body. "I thought about it, plotted how I would do it. And worse, I would have enjoyed watching you die."

When Leah turned away, she didn't cover Mark's face with the sheet. She would give no sign of respect for the dead.

"Dr. Tabor, I need the phone number of that psychiatrist you want me to call. I don't want to live with the hatred I feel now. I would have killed Mark, if I could."

"Everyone in this family has work to do, Leah. Acceptance will come in time," Paul said.

Stephanie sighed, suddenly aware of how hungry and exhausted she was. "I found a pay phone in the lobby and made a hotel reservation. The only thing they had was a two-bedroom suite. That sounded perfect, so I took it."

What Stephanie wanted to say was, "I could really use a cold glass of chardonnay, a light dinner and a good bed." Instead she sent a silent message to the universe that she remembered from years earlier. *May we be strong, may we be healed, may we find peace in the midst of challenges.*

"Are we ready, Paul? Leah? Let's go."

In the hotel suite, when the wine bottle was empty and their emotions drained, Paul decided he was past ready for bed.

"I'm ready," Stephanie said as she placed a kiss on the top of Leah's head and walked across the deep shag carpet to her bedroom door.

Leah kept thinking about how close she was to dying in that closet. What if no one had come for her? She couldn't stop thinking about all that had happened in the last twenty-four hours but failed to ward off the thoughts that taunted her. When she began to relive the terror, she forced herself to create an imagined future.

In her daydream, she was on Malibu beach at the Tabor house, a blanket was spread out in the sand. Leah imagined herself sitting there with Paul and Stephanie. Feeling safe. Feeling welcomed. When Mark tried to appear in her daydream, Leah demanded that he go. This was her dream, her life, and she would shape it her own way.

Leah imagined she was surrounded by her chosen family. It was only a daydream, but it soothed her, and she felt empowered by it. She was feeling safe, feeling grateful. Finally, she drifted off to sleep, just listening to the music of the sea.

THE STORY
BEHIND
THE STORY

THE STORY BEHIND THE STORY

"Now you know, dear, they don't allow you to be a writer until you've collected many rejection slips." So said my mother, Perla Earle, when I was nine and submitted my first story for publication. When the inevitable happened, I celebrated. I had my very first rejection slip! I was on my way. My father, J. B. Earle, bought me a typewriter and lots of paper and so it began.

Many years ago, my chosen-sister-friend, Mary Christianson, MD, and I were celebrating the publication of my fourth non-fiction book. The day was warm, the chardonnay cold and her question was intriguing: "So when are you going to write your first novel?" I told her I would, just as soon as a character showed up in my imagination who was interesting enough to spend a year or two developing their story. So it was Mary, a child psychiatrist, who introduced me to my potential protagonist, a character more intriguing and psychologically complicated than anyone I had expected. I finished the first draft in about a year, which included a trip to Switzerland for research. I'm grateful to Mary for her watchful eye as the story developed. Then . . . at some point . . . the manuscript disappeared. It was written before I used a computer so there were no backup copies. Many weeks later, I stopped looking for the manuscript, dealt with my loss, and moved on. The year was 1975.

One Saturday afternoon in 2020, my son-in-law and resident genius, Jeff Rutherford, was searching through mounds of boxes in one of our storage units. He didn't find what he was looking for, but right there, in a box mis-labeled "Memorabilia" was the long lost, original manuscript for this novel. Jeff helped me transfer the text from my typewritten pages to my computer. He bailed me out every time the screen went blank, or the keys froze, or I pushed the buttons that made everything go cattywampus. And he never once told me I can be a high maintenance mother-in-law.

Now, the manuscript was in my hands. Susie Cronin, sculptor, poet, and lover of stories, read it overnight and showed up at my door the next morning to give me her thoughts. "Come on, listen to this," she said. We settled down in my tiny "Writer's Nest." Susie started reading aloud from the old manuscript. What a treat that was to hear my characters' coming alive after all this time! I could hear the cadence of each character's voice: There was Mark, with his condescending tone, Paul with his tender voice grounded in strength, Jayne with her air of entitlement. Stephanie, who's gentle, confidant manner could hold the room. And then there was Leah.

Over the years, and through various versions of the story, I have had three professional editors whose contributions kept this story on track. So many thanks to Madison Riley, Chryss Yost and Barbara Anderson.

My youngest daughter, Tamara Riley is a strong supporter of my writing and other wild adventures. She provides inspiration, critical evaluation, and always, loving support. There were dozens of dinners she cooked for me when I was "on a roll." That was no small gift for a busy designer of homes and hotels to add to her schedule. She makes me laugh at myself for obsessing over the smallest details at 3:00 AM.

While I was working on the original story in 1975, my eldest daughter Gina Somers, helped me run my corporation, Right-Brain Resources, Inc. (now put to sleep). I think she grieved the loss of the first draft of this book almost as much as I did.

There were those who chased down every misplaced comma, duplicated sentence and overused adjective. Others gave general comments about the story or a character's motivations. My chosen-brother, Zev Nathan, MD, another psychiatrist, critiqued this manuscript and his comments were always insightful.

Laurie Ashton, a Santa Barbara attorney, and I have been in the same book club for more than a decade. This is not the first manuscript of mine she has read, then sent back to me with suggestions that improved the story.

Before Margi Mainquist had her own consulting firm, she was the Director of Arts and Executive Services at the University of California, Santa Barbara. She created educational programs for the community and many times she invited me to present week-end seminars on various subjects related to the development of innovative thinking techniques. I'm grateful for her careful reading.

My thanks to Judy Cowell, and psychologist, Dr. Betsy Freed. And to Pat Aptaker, entrepreneur and Court Appointed Advocate for Foster Children. Their comments were spot on.

I'm grateful for Stanley J. Leiken, MD (yes, another psychiatrist). In addition to helpful comments on the original manuscript, he was also helpful in connecting me with experts in the field of brain research for my non-fiction book, *The Right-Brain Experience*. But that's another story.

And then there is Grace Rachow, who keeps the Santa Barbara Writers Conference running smoothly and inspires so many of us with her advice

My muse, Duma the cat, sits on my desk and loves to play on the keyboard when I'm not looking. Her favorite key is 'Delete.'

Back in the day, my literary agent was Don Congdon. He was Ray Bradbury's agent and William Styron's also; the list is long. Against all odds, he accepted me as a client when he read the first fifty pages of the first draft of this book. I can just imagine him saying, "What took you so long?"

The End

Visit **marileezdenek.com** to explore Marilee's earlier books, discover free guided imagery exercises, and enjoy Marilee's notes for readers and writers.